BURNING TRUTHS

C.M NYX

BURNING TRUTHS

Consume Me Series: Book Two

By: C.M Nyx

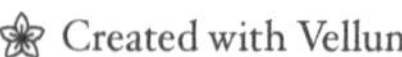 Created with Vellum

TRIGGER WARNINGS

This book is labeled 'Dark' for a reason. It has graphic depictions of themes that some may find triggering such as:
Abuse/Bully
Fire Play
Choking
Murder/death
Gun violence
Torture
Sexual abuse
Slight Degradation
Explicit sex scenes
Non Con/Dub Con
Rape(She doesn't say no- only because she's doing it to survive. I would still consider this rape)
Starvation.
Mental Manipulation.

Explicit language is written throughout the book. If you're sensitive to these types of words, DO NOT READ!

AUTHOR NOTES

These characters have called to me for a long time and while I was happy to see them grow I didn't want to let them go. Thanks to my band of baddies, my Alpha team, the panic and pains to my hades, I have decided to continue on this journey.
The world I've built inside Del Mar is still growing and I have SO MUCH left to give these wonderfully frustrating people. Kenna Kingston has learned so much about herself, but giving her more time to develop who she is, is the right thing to do. She calls to me as I hope she does to you.

DEDICATION

This is for the girls who clawed their way back from hell only to realize it's where they belong. Take a seat on your dark throne, Queen.

P.S Don't be a dick, ride one. Just not Rykers, he belongs to Danielle.

BEFORE THE FIRE

Kenna

My heart pounds in my chest, pushing my legs to pump faster, I don't see the dip in the ground until it's too late. There's only the sound of a snap before my lungs fill with air to release a scream. Heat and pain shoot through my right leg from the break. I just know it's broken. I can feel the damp ground seeping through the knee of my jeans when I hit the soft patch of grass. Tears spring to my eyes from the sharp ache, but I breath through it like Alec taught me. My second father, the man who raised me alongside my own father when my mother died.

"Kens!"

"Kens!"

The voices of my boys bounce off the brick siding of their house. My scream drawing them from their hiding place. I just know Cole will reach me first. He's the fastest. And the sweetest. The pounding of their feet vibrates through my legs. I can feel everything and nothing all at once. Yet, I still breathe through the pain. Swallowing down the tears before they reach me, not wanting him to see them, I tip my head to the sky and let them fall back where they belong. Unseen.

Cole comes into view first, his wild green eyes assessing me, West not far behind. Fear reflects back at me through their faces until they see I'm safe. Minus the ankle of course. West breaks out a carefree grin showcasing his perfect white teeth.

"Always getting yourself into trouble." He winks.

I love his winks. He's my second favorite and for good reason. I'm his princess. Not that Alec would allow any boy to claim me as theirs without going through him. They kneel on each side of me, Cole looking over my body, while West peers into my eyes. My chin wobbles slightly.

Using his finger he tips my head up, closing my mouth and stopping the shaking. "We've got you."

I can feel my cheeks grow red from his words. Eyes bore into the back of my head from the third Stone brother. He's never far away, but right now I wish he were. I'll never live this down if he sees what my clumsy two left feet caused. He's always hated the fact that I was set to be the one to take over for my father when he retires. It's my birthright. One he would love nothing more than to steal. Not because he doesn't have an empire of his own, no, it's because he can't stand to see a girl in power.

"Come on, let's get you to dad so he can take you to the doctor." Cole says, his voice soft like velvet.

He smiles a crooked smile at me and my pain melts a little more. These boys. My boys. They will always be mine.

"I'll take her."

Ryker's voice grumbles from behind me, but I keep my eyes on Cole and West. Leaning back on their heels, both brothers stand at the same time, crossing their arms. It's like they rehearsed the move. I can see the concern cloud their eyes, but when they look from me to Ryker it turns into caution.

"We can handle it." West says.

He doesn't stand up to his big brother often, unless it involves me. I seem to always be able to make the brothers fight. Though Ryker always wins, so it's not really fair. My heart pinches at the sight of my boys standing tall against their big brother. The one male in my life who doesn't drop to the knee for me. Instead he forces mine to fold to him. And I will every time because what Ryker seems to forget is he promised me forever. And I intend to collect that promise.

Without speaking I can feel Ryker inch closer to my back, his legs almost up against me, he bends down. Thick arms scoop me up in a tight hold. The move jolts my leg, making me cry out before my teeth sink into my lip to silence myself. Biting down hard enough to break the skin, my gaze drifts past the blue shirt hugging his form to peer into the brown eyes of Ryker Stone. My skin itches under his stare.

"Rye." West says, stepping forward.

Cole stands in place, his eyes on the side of my face, watching me. He's the only one who knows how I feel about his bossy brother. My secret is safe though. I'm drowning in deep brown pools unable to look away when Ryker breaks our connection first.

"I've got her." He grunts.

Holding me tighter to his chest to prevent me from bouncing around, he walks from the side of the house towards the front door, but swerves to the left at the last minute. Their house is massive. Large white column posts are positioned on each side of the whitewash wood porch. The grey stone walkway leading to the front steps curves and curls all the way to the cobblestone driveway. It's a palace for princes and a princess. I spend more time here than at my own home, but dad. My mother used to do the same before she died.

"Where are we going?" I question.

I lean forward putting more weight down, but he doesn't lose a step or slow down. Ryker has his eyes trained forward, refusing to look down at me. So, what's a girl to do? Ignoring the shooting pain traveling up my leg from my ankle, I take this moment to soak up Ryker. From his jawline to his thick soft lips, I allow my eyes to roam over his face. My fingertips twitch with the need to run them through his unruly black hair. He's a god. No teenager should look this damn good, but Ryker has never been normal or average. He's the future king and I'll make sure I'm first in line to become his queen.

"Kens." He growls.

He looks at me from the corner of his eye, so I futter my lashes innocently.

"Yes?" I smile.

"Stop fucking me with those doe eyes of yours." He snaps.

Jerking my head back in shock, I let out an awkward laugh. I've never tried to hide how I felt about him, but this is the first time he's called me on it. I guess we've reached the crossroads.

"Stop giving me something to look at and I'd be able to stop."

If I were standing I'd toss my long hair over my shoulder and storm off, but instead I'm pinned against his chest.

I am so not complaining.

We reach the small white gate to the family garden when Ryker abruptly stops to toe it open. Turning to the side, he moves us through the tight opening into the vast garden filled with different flowers, bushes, and vines. It's my favorite place to think and he knows this.

"Why are you bringing me here?" I ask.

His face is blank as he continues forward, leading us

toward the soft field that expands down a small hill. My leg has moved to a low throb, but I know it's broken and in need of medical attention. Yet Ryker keeps walking down the hill, putting more distance between us and the house. Away from Cole and West. Away from the outside world. Eventually my muscles relax into a sense of ease with his calm presence. A small dark voice whispers in the back of my head that if he cared for me at all, we'd be headed the other direction, but what did a love drunk girl know? The aroma of sweet flowers wafts through my nose, my eyes drifting closed, I allow myself to breathe in my surroundings. Flowers, summer air, and Ryker swirl around me in a heady combination that I'd wear on me for the rest of my life.

"Open your eyes." Ryker orders.

My eyes pop open when he comes to a stop. My lips tip up with a wide smile before my brain has time to catch up with my body. In the far back stretch of garden, where my reading spot is settled, sits a small stone bench that Alec had put here for me. The most beautiful array of lilies grow in patterns of orange, red, white, and my personal favorite, black. I find myself immersed here every day after school. My own personal escape from the place where all the elite prep school kids attend with their fancy cars and posh clothing.

"Why are we here?" I ask, bringing my eyes to his caramel ones.

The corner of his mouth lifts in my favorite crooked smile, one that he doesn't show often, the same one that makes my heart stutter in my chest.

"Because, Kens. You need to learn to breathe through the pain. Block it out fully until it's nothing more than a dull ache."

My brows dip at his words. "Now you're training me too?"

His arms shake slightly when he moves to lower me on the bench. Kneeling down in front of me, his gaze never leaves my face. My tongue slips out to wet my dry lips. Alec and my father have been hounding all of us lately when it comes to safety, training, and torture training. That feels overly normal to me, but Ryker forcing me to suffer through a broken ankle to see if I can block out the pain? It sets me on edge.

"Stop overthinking what's right in front of you."

His thumb and finger pinch my chin, dragging my face so close to his that the warmth of his next words fan across my lips.

"Never give in to the pain. Look to the lilies and breathe through your nose. Remember the steady sound of my voice. The feel of my hands on you. Find this place and calm your heart."

He looks at me waiting for a response. "I'll look for you in the lilies." I whisper on my next breath.

Chapter One

PRESENT DAY

Kenna

A raspy laugh bubbles out of my chest, "You seem a little tense." I snark.

My throat aches from the chemicals that I inhaled when he took me. Two- no- three days ago? Fuck. How long have I been sitting in this chair? My ass starts to go numb, as if it needs to remind me that I'm strapped down, unable to move positions. I shift my weight to one side in hopes that I can save at least one asscheek from flattening out.

I huff out a laugh with that thought, effectively bringing the bastard to a stop just to the left of me. He's been pacing for the past few hours or at least that's how long it feels. Time passes differently when your body is weak from no food. I would ask for something to curb the gnawing hunger that's rolling through my stomach, but I don't trust this shit fuck.

Find me in the lilies.

It's what Ryker taught me. Before. Before everything in

our lives got flipped on an axis and whatever burning flame we had was singed, left as a pile of ashes on the warehouse floor. But this is after and now the lilies are tainted with all the scorching lies that have consumed us the last two and a half years. .

"Oh Princessa, that smart little mouth of yours is going to feel so good wrapped around my dick."

My eyes almost widen. Almost. It takes effort I didn't know I had to keep a straight face at the remark he let slip. Knowing that the man standing in front of me has some delusional fantasy of having his way with me makes acid build in the back of my throat.

"No thanks." I chuckle.

I'm good at hiding what I don't want him to see and that's the fear of any part of him touching me.

Swinging around, his hollow empty green eyes land on me. My smile slips an inch when he starts to storm my way. My gaze moves up his dirty jeans past the worn black belt and stretched grey shirt to the salt and pepper beard. His mouth is hidden by the coarse hair on his face, but the look in his eyes has my jaw clenching shut. When he's only a foot away, his hand lashes out far too fast for me to track until the burning spreads across my flesh.

Fire creeps through my veins. Pain exploding through my head, forcing my eyes to clamp shut. *Shit.*

Breathe through the pain.

Inhaling deep through my nose, I force myself to swallow past the blood spilling from my lip into my mouth.

In and out. Rykers voice floats through my mind and suddenly I find it hard to swallow around the lump in my throat.

"You belong to me, Princessa. He was never supposed to touch your perfect skin." His thumb trails down my cheek.

"When Ryker comes for me, and he will, I'll take pleasure in watching him rip your throat out for touching what's his."

Using my tongue, I swipe up the blood from my lip and push it inside my mouth. My eyes widen in mock horror. "Although I think I'd rather him fuck me while you watch. Feeling how full he makes me while you see what he does to me. Knowing you'll never feel me wrapped around you like that."

His fist raises and suddenly I'm thrown into darkness.

———

My lips are cracked and sore when my eyes finally open, I find myself in the large space alone. Or should I say eye? I swear, if I don't get my smartass mouth under control I won't make it long enough for the boys to find me. Ryker, West, and - my train of thought stops. My chest cracks open with the image of Cole lying on the floor of the empty house. I've refused to let myself think about that day until now. What if they are so stuck in their grief that no one knows I'm gone? Would I notice if I were them? Cole was my best friend once. Family, even through the past two years of trauma.

Memories flood my vision. Images of his face smiling, the sound of him laughing when we were kids flash through my head. The pranks we would play on West, has a smile finding my face.

My chest heaves with silent sobs when my memories betray me with snapshots of that day. Each blink of my eyes brings me closer to Cole's body hanging there lifeless. My mouth falls open with a wail of all consuming heartache that shakes me to my core. A loss like this is like losing a limb, phantom pain sets in and every time you sense, and sometimes feel, them with you, the pain gets to be too much. At that point, the only thing left to do is to lose yourself in the pain, because nothing can fix a soul that's been lost.

Losing a loved one is hard, but losing a best friend? No one prepares you for that pain and then here I am shaking, and heaving through the worst pain in my life while being tied to a chair. Snot and tears pour down my face in a mess of darkness. Each tear that falls is another part of me that I lose. Kenna Kingston slowly drips away into someone I don't know, a shell of myself, empty and cold. My voice is hoarse when my cries slowly come to an end. Eventually the cries for Cole turn into whimpers for me. For the girl I could have been with three powerful men at my fingertips, before they were turned against me. For the girl who lost her dad. Her mother. I cry until both eyes are swollen and raw.

It's not until the room is shrouded in shadows that the sound of a door scraping against the floor wakes me. Licking my lips to wet them, I blink through pain while my eyes attempt to adjust to the dark room. I can hear the sound of footsteps growing closer to where I'm seated in the center of the room. Rustling, bounces off the walls with all the extra space around us, and it startles me, but I catch myself before I react.

"I brought you something to eat."

As soon as the last word leaves his lips, my stomach growls loudly.

"I'm going to untie you so you can eat, but first-" He stops mid sentence to pull something from a brown backpack over his shoulder. "Don't try anything and I won't have to use it."

My vision is still blurry from the blow to the side of my face, and the room is still cloaked in black, so I don't see it coming. Instead I can feel the chill of leather mixed with metal touch my neck. A small gasp slips through my lips before I can drink it down, but it's not until I realize what it is that bile rises up my throat.

My mouth opens and closes like a fish out of water, but I choose to keep quiet. He clasps it behind my head with a harsh yank, making the final adjustments and snapping a lock through the clasp ensuring it won't come off without a key. Bound, starving, and now collared.

Ryker, I've never needed you more than I do now.

Lifting the remote up to my face, he bends down to inch closer, his rancid breath fans over my lips, our gazes clashing.

"I promised I wouldn't hurt you again, but I will if you force me to. Be a good girl, and do what I tell you, and I'll take good care of you."

He closes the distance, pressing his mouth against mine in a harsh kiss that has my stomach rolling. The stench of his breath coats my skin, making my nose wrinkle in disgust and tears burn at the back of my eyes, yet I refuse to let them close. Keeping my stare on his face. I fight my own instincts that beg me to pull away. When he's done getting his taste, I lean to the side, letting the acid flooding my mouth spill out onto the floor.

"You stuck up little bitch. You think you're too good for me?" He grunts.

One hand yanks my head back, twisting my neck at an awkward angle while the other hand presses down on the remote, shooting electricity down my spine. My body locks into place unable to move, muscles spasming, my entire body on fire all at once. It's not until my eyes roll that I realize that I'm soaked and sitting in my own piss.

"I'll break you bitch. One way or another. Next time you'll take whatever I give you with a smile on your face." He turns and heads back to the door, the food in his bag long forgotten.

With his hand on the door knob, he looks at me over his shoulder, "Why don't you sit there in your own filth for a while and maybe you'll learn you're no better than me."

And then he's gone and I'm still here. I'm still here and Cole is dead. I'm still here and my body is cold. I'm still here and Kenna is floating away into the abyss. I'm still here.

I'm still here. I'm here. Ryker I'm still here. I'm still here.

Chapter Two

KENNA

"Open up, Princessa" A male voice breaks through the heavy blanket of fog.

I try to flex my fingers but my arms are numb from sitting in this position for so long. The pants I've been wearing for the last several days are crusted with sweat, blood, and piss. I've grown used to the stench floating around the room, but his lip curls slightly with his next breath. His long thin fingers dig into my cheeks when he starts to tip my head back, pressing a plastic bottle to my lips. Luke warm water spills down my throat easing the dry feeling in my mouth. He yanks the bottle away mid gulp causing the liquid to splash over my top drenching my chest in water.

"That's enough." He says, his voice coming out softer this time.

My eyes are almost too heavy to open, but when I manage to clear my vision his salt and pepper beard is just above my head. Clearing my throat, I open and close my mouth a few times to work my stiff jaw. Everything is stiff and sore, but I shove the pain to the back of my mind.

Looking up at him with soft eyes I try to work the words out of my throat, but it takes too long. By the time a small sound escapes he's standing above me instead of kneeling.

"Ca-can I shower?" I ask, my gaze roaming around the room trying to judge if there is a functional bathroom in this dinghy rundown place.

He steps back to look over me, the heat of his stare making my skin crawl, but he must see something in my eyes. He runs his hand over his mouth, those sinister eyes studying me.

"The collar stays on." He answers.

Nothing more, nothing less. He's barely spoken to me since he first put the collar on me. Fuck, how long ago was that? I've refused his company which is why my throat is so sore. No food or water for three days will change so much about you. No amount of training could prepare you for being starved. My energy has depleted so low that my body feels like it's floating and that has fear creeping up my spine. The worst thing I can do is lose control over my body while stuck here with this fucker.

He slowly moves behind me, the sound of his shoes the only noise in the vacant space. His calloused hands reaching out to grab mine. Tugging my arms further back, a yelp slips past my chapped lips.

He must lean down because his warm breath skates across my shoulder sending a shudder through me, "I'm sorry I hurt you, Princessa. You just made me so mad. I never wanted to hurt this perfect, beautiful, skin. Be a good girl for me and I'll make you so happy."

Each word that comes out his mouth makes it hard to hold back the tears threatening to fall. Swallowing back the bile that's crept up I nod my head in agreement. I don't plan on trying to escape right now. No, I need to build more energy, and that involves being on my best behavior so he'll decide to feed me. If I'm going to get out of here or at least make it long enough for Ryker to come for me then I'll need to control my smartass mouth.

My stomach churns when his lips press into the side of my neck, "That's a good girl. You're going to love the room I put together for us. I've been waiting so long for you." He says, his voice cheerful.

The excitement in his tone makes me nervous, but I need to get out of this chair before the muscles in my arms are permanently damaged. My eyes slide closed for a second, but snap open when the rope around my wrist falls away leaving only the burn. When he moves away from me I use the space to bring my arms around so I can see how bad the damage is. I whimper when the blood rushes into my arms shooting pin needles over my flesh. Biting my lip hard enough to draw blood I flex my fingers while twisting my wrist.

A large hand skates over my messy hair, "Let me show you our room. I designed it just for you."

My heart skips a beat when the words *our room* fall from his lips. Inhaling a deep breath I push off the metal chair to stand but my legs wobble with the weight. I'm fucking exhausted and my thighs shake with the attempt to stand without help. Turning to Shadow, I give him a soft smile letting him drink in my reluctant submission. Calling him Shadow in my head keeps the betrayal from ripping me apart.

Extending my left arm with my palm up, "Help me?" I ask.

The light that enters his eyes shines back at my dull grey ones. He clasps his fingers with mine and slowly leads me to the door. Shifting slightly I allow myself to look over the empty room with a single chair in the center. The discoloration around the bottom of the chair is the only sign that I was here. Even when I leave the stain will remain. I've tainted this room, marked it with my presence, yet I'm the one scarred with the memory. I start to raise my hand to touch the collar, but stop myself short when I spot the remote in his other hand.

"Do you want to hurt me again?" I ask.

His step falters with the question, and for a split second I tense preparing for the electricity that never comes. Tossing a look over his shoulder he ignores me, and continues through the rundown building that I don't recognize. The hope I had of leaving the room I was locked in, and suddenly knowing where I am, quickly vanishes. Nothing I see looks familiar. We make it down the hall halfway when he jerks to the left down a smaller hallway where a deep forest green door is at the end.

"I painted it your favorite color." He says, a smile in his voice.

I don't correct him when he says it, but my heart pinches when chocolate brown eyes float through my head. Green may have been my favorite color as a kid, but it hasn't been for a long time. Letting myself come to this realization almost sends me over the edge, but I straighten my back, and continue forward. Ryker needs me stronger than I am right now. Shadow's hand pauses over the door knob, twisting his head over his shoulder to look over to me. A sheepish look crosses over his face when he finally twists the metal.

Pushing the door open he moves to the side allowing me to fully take in the space. My throat constricts and the four walls surrounding me begin to close in, suffocating any hope I had of being set free. Creating a cage of nightmares right before my eyes. Everything spins, my eyes unable to focus on anything, though it's my hands that won't stop shaking. He steps in behind me, but I ignore the feel of his body against mine. I block out his hand moving my hair to the side, my mind shuts off as his lips touch my skin.

"It's perfect just like you my sweet sweet Princessa."

His mouth trails my neck, nipping, biting, and my entire being quakes with the need to escape. Self preservation kicks in and I bolt to the massive king size bed in a last ditch effort to get away from his invasive touch but it's no use. Lightning licks down my back when the force of the collar shoots power into my body. A wail forces itself free from the overpowering pain causing my knees to buckle and slam into the floor.

I let my body crumble to the floor too weak to hold myself up anymore. The lack of food and water are nothing compared to the bone shattering pain coursing through me right now. Fuck, the voltage in this collar is going to kill me.

Maybe that's for the best. The demons being held hostage will finally be set free, the chaos harboring inside me will rain down on my enemies and I can watch peacefully on the other side. Find me in the lillies.

I search for the lilies behind my eyelids. A garden with endless rows of color clouds my vision. Orange, red, white and black. My favorite stone bench taking residency in the center, awaiting my arrival with a new world to escape too. Within the paths I see him, stalking through the flowers and picking my favorite one. Our gazes clash and the mixture of brown eyes and blue skies combine with my flowers bring my breathing back down. Inhaling through my nose I repeat those words over and over until I can finally open my eyes.

Breathe through the pain, you can find me in the lilies.

I can feel him standing behind me but I don't dare move. Not when I'm vulnerable here at his feet.

"Look what you made me do. I didn't want to do that. You made me, Kenna. I had no choice!"

He's frantic and angry so I curl in on myself. The sound of his shoes slapping against the floor echoes around me. The sound of the door slamming and locking has my shoulders slumping into the wood planks I'm laying on. I don't know how long he's gone or how long I laid there in my own filth but by the time he came back to bring me a small glass of water I'd climbed in the bed and watched the door until my eyes grew heavy.

It wasn't until my fingers trailed over Rykers name carved into my skin that I finally fell asleep.

Chapter Three

KENNA

The sound of running water wakes me from a restless sleep. Rolling over in the black silk sheets, my body stretches out and I almost forget where I am. That feeling you have right before you fully wake up, not quite asleep, but your mind is drowsy. That's where I find myself forgetting where I am until the small details start to creep in. The smell of sweat and urine, the hollow sound of the room being too empty, but most importantly it's the man standing at the foot of the bed.

Hank fucking Harlow. The man our fathers went to college with. The one man that my father trusted outside of Alec, yet here I was laying in a room that he designed. All in the name of trying to break me while my father sits behind bars for a crime he committed. The pictures on the wall make my stomach ache with disgust. It's familiar in a way I wish it wasn't. A replica of a room I was in recently and it's the only reminder I have of the last time I laid with Ryker. The matching bed posts a constant reminder of the ones I held on to mere nights ago.

All four walls are plastered in photos of me, every inch of space covered in shade me. In my dorm, on campus, leaving the prison, in the cemetery. Zoomed in shots of me with Ryker in the garden on campus, but what startles me is seeing Rykers face. His entire face was removed from the picture altogether. My eyes skate across each one, avoiding the looming black hole threatening to swallow me whole. I pull myself up against the headboard, still avoiding the vacant dark eyes across the room, I take in my surroundings. Ryker's bedroom, or the exact set up of it, is blanketed in snapshots of my life over the past few years. My bottom lips tremble when I come across photos of a younger me sitting in the Stone's garden reading a book.

"How-?" I start, but my words trail off when I see it.

Wetting my lips, my gaze trails from the last photo, up to the man before me. His appearance is different today. His stubble is growing out as if he hasn't shaved. The salt and pepper coloring has shifted into a slightly darker color unnaturally. Shaking off the observation, I look away to keep from giving him the wrong idea when my eyes fall on a small stack of clothes at the end of the bed.

I stare at them for a few moments before he leans down to place the palms of his hand on the bed. The mattress dips from the weight, but I keep my focus trained on the threat ahead of me. The searing heat of his stare scorches my skin, making me want to peel it off me. Hunger and greed fight for dominance behind the mask he wears, but he doesn't wear it well. I can see right through it to the devil inside.

"I brought you some clothes to change into. The shower's waiting for you, Princessa."

He motions with his hand to the door off to the right corner of the room. The need to feel clean wars with the need to prevent being vulnerable around him. I've seen what he can do when upset, but I know that's just the surface of his capabilities. With one last look around the room I make the mental note that he isn't just obsessed with me, but Ryker as well.

"Thank you." I say, my voice raw.

The attempt at a smile must work because he steps back with a wild grin. It takes fucking effort to keep my arms steady as I crawl from the center of the bed. The only thing I find myself thankful for is his distaste for urine because that's the only reason he hasn't ripped my pants off. For fucks sake I'm almost disgusted with myself, but I shove that thought from my mind only to replace it with Ryker. Where is he? Is he too distracted with burying Cole to realize that I'm gone? Does he even care after what his brother did? If he doesn't blame me, I sure as fuck do.

Bringing my legs forward, they dangle off the side of the bed, my ass firmly placed on the edge while I try to get my bearings. My hands tremble from the lack of food, my stomach rumbles with hunger as I spot a small cream colored plate on the nightstand. Sitting in the center of the palm sized plate is a sandwich. Nothing special, nothing extra, just a single square filled with something unknown. My stomach lets out another gurgle that has my cheeks turning red.

"I brought you a little gift, but first I want you to shower and eat. Once you're done, knock on the door and I'll bring you a little surprise."

He studies me for a few moments, the heat of his stare burning into the side of my face, but I keep my gaze trained on the food. My body urges me to scarf it down as fast as possible, but something in the back of my head tingles with awareness.

"Don't worry, Princessa. I have no wish to control you with substances that will taint the way you taste." His words don't match his tone, so I take the threat for what it is.

Nodding in agreement I clear my throat, "After I clean up." I state.

Pushing to a stand, Hank hoovers off to the side to make sure I don't face plant. Or run, both options on my list. Shoving down every bit of snark that threatens to spill from my mouth I grin, which I'm sure looks more like a grimace. It takes a few minutes to fully make it to the bathroom where I take the liberty to shut the door in his face. I would rather be struck by lightning than have him see me naked.

No thank you.

Once I step under the scalding water, the fresh tears break through the wall I've kept up. I cry thinking about Cole, thinking about West and the heartbreak he's going through from losing his best friend. I cry for Ryker losing his little brother and for me. I cry for the girl I was before the fire, before I was taken. For the old me that had a group of brothers who would do anything for her and for the girl who had to find her best friend's lifeless body dangling from the ceiling. . No matter how hard I try to fight off the knowledge, I know where this is heading. He's been stalking me for years from the look of the photos. Hank seems to not only have an obsession with me, but a vendetta against the Stone family. Or Ryker himself. Either way I plan to get to the bottom of this shit.

Rinsing the last of the conditioner from my hair, I let my forehead fall to the cold tile. Darkness covers me when my eyes drift closed, allowing myself a second to succumb to the situation I'm in. All thoughts go back to my training and what the best method is for this type of torture.

"Stop!" I wail.

My legs thrash, kicking out at the man that grips both my legs, missing with each one. A thick black mask covers the man's head, but his sleeves slide up when he starts to drag me from my bed, giving me a sneak peek of a small tattoo. A hand tattoo that looks so familiar. One that I saw just this morning, so my body relaxes. The fear drains from me, leaving only annoyance and a touch of anger.

"Dad?" I ask.

He stills, his hands dropping his hold, allowing the blood to rush back under my skin. That's going to bruise tomorrow. Rolling my eyes I kick out one last time to nail him in the knee.

"Shit, hellcat. Easy on the old man."

Sitting up in the center of my bed I pull my knees into my chest wrapping my arms around them.

"What's going on dad?" I ask, a little freaked out.

I mean here it is the middle of the night and my dad is dressed like a damn maniac while attempting to drag me from my bed. What the hell is going on? Our training sessions never start like this, so I don't know what to make of it. He lets out a deep sigh before slowly lifting the mask to reveal his sweaty face. My brows dip down at the worry that flashes behind his eyes before he blinks it away.

Looking away his massive hand swipes down his face, "You need to be prepared for anything, hellcat. That's all we are trying to do with your training. You never know when someone will cross the line to get to you."

"We?" It's the only word that sticks out from his sentence.

My eyes try to adjust in the dark, looking for another figure in the shadows, when Alec walks from behind my bedroom door. Black mask in hand, his eyes assess me where I sit.

"Uncle Alec?" I murmur.

A loud bang pulls me back to the present and out of the past. One where my father is a free man and the Stone brothers' dad is still alive. If I'm going to understand why Hank has me, I'll need to uncover what happened between them. Why he would kill either of them, but more importantly why he's doing this to me. Shutting off the water, I reach for the white towel sitting on the counter of the bathroom. It's a decent sized room with a beautiful stand up shower with black tile and gold fixtures, but even that little reminder has me feeling dizzy.

Snap out of it Kenna. Stop being so weak.

Shaking my head, I continue to towel dry. The cold breeze floating through the cracked door sends a chill down my spine. Walking forward my bare feet slap against the cool tile that leads to the cream colored carpet in the bedroom. My eyes stay on the floor knowing what I'll see if my gaze lifts higher. The organ in my chest hammers faster behind my ribcage with each step closer I come to the massive king size bed. There on the bedside table is the plate still in its spot. Bypassing the food that screams for my attention, I opt to get dressed first in case he comes back in the room and that's when it hits me. The noise that jolted me back to the present was the door slamming closed and now I'm curious.

Hank has left me a tight pair of black leggings with rose lacing on the calves and an oversized grey t-shirt. No under-wear. How fucking fitting for a pig like Hank Harlow. I'm tempted to throw on my dirty ones, but then the image of the piss stain at the foot of the chair comes to mind and I decide against it. He'll pay for every action he's taken since I got here. For every death or painful thing he's caused. When I finally get my hands around his throat I'll make sure to drain the life from his eyes. For Paige. For Alec. For my father. For Cole.

The last name has my throat closing, unable to process the loss, the overwhelming feeling of it being my fault. It's too much to stomach, when I start dry heaving nothing comes up, there is nothing left inside me. Yellow foam and stomach acid bubble into my mouth, forcing its way out until I have no choice but to spit it all over the floor. The taste sours on my tongue so I reach for the glass of water beside me and chug half of it down. Swallowing down the bile, I stare down at the bread wondering if that would settle my stomach. I'm far too weak to refuse food, but I'm still weary of his plans for me.

Fuck it.

I decide to pick the bread off the top first and slowly eat that to prevent myself from getting even more sick. It only takes seconds before I'm done and wanting more, so I lift the warm meat and remaining bread up and bring it to my nose. Inhaling, I breathe in the scent of deli meat and soggy bread, but find myself satisfied with that. I start to take a decent sized bite, but end up shove the entire fucking thing in my mouth. My stomach groaning at the sudden fullness of food and liquid after being empty. I'll regret eating so fast later, but I can't bring myself to care. Drinking down the last of the water I dash into the bathroom to refill the cup and sit at the edge of the bed. Now that I have access to water, the least I can do is clear my head enough to think of a way out.

After struggling to keep my head down I finally convince myself to be the Kingston I was born to be and face my problems head on. Lifting my eyes to the madness surrounding me, I fully take in each photograph plastered to the wall. From the age fifteen all the way to last week, each stage of my life, every milestone, everything. It's all documented right here in front of me, but Ryker is gone. Scratched out and replaced. Absorbed by greed and evil. He's trying to imbed himself in my life where the Stone brothers are, but I won't let that happen. They belong to me just as much as I belong to them. Even when I've caused unforgivable damage to their family. I'll be their princess again, even if I have to carve my name on the walls of their hearts.

Ryker, I'm coming home to you. I bleed, you bleed remember?

Chapter Four

KENNA

My thumb passes over the raised ink at the dip of my hip again. Over and over. My eyes trace each line, bump, crack in the ceiling. I do everything I can to keep my mind busy without allowing myself to study the faces staring at me around the room. Hank has only been back twice over the last three days with two sandwiches and once he even brought chips. I guess he knows I have the sink for water, so at least I won't die of thirst. Not that I'd allow that to happen. I've been conditioned to drink my piss if I have to and I fucking will to get back to my family. What's left of it.

The rustling of keys pulls me from the trance I've been stuck in for fuck knows how long. I've repeated the last 10 years of my life over and over in my head to sort fact from fiction. He's slowly breaking down who I am and trying to rewrite me into the Kenna he thinks I should be. I refuse to let him. Though I give him what he wants in the end all the same, because the pain is too much to bear. Dragging in a deep breath, I force myself to sit up in the large bed that's far too familiar. Two seconds pass before the green door slowly opens to Hank Harlow carrying another small plate, yet a sandwich is missing and in its place is a small portion of macaroni and cheese. My stomach grumbles at the sight.

His smile pulls at the skin around his eyes showing the age he tries to hide. No amount of hair dye and grooming stops the age from creeping back through. I bite my tongue from telling him just that and instead give him a shallow grin of my own. Scooting to the edge of the bed, I mentally stop myself from clenching the sheets in an attempt to slow my movements, but the food urges me forward.

"Come eat, Princessa." He purrs.

If I weren't starving I'd gag from the sickening way he mewls at me. Breathing through my nose I keep my teeth clenched and that smile in place. *Bide your time Kens.* My ass meets the edge of the bed and that's when Hank makes his move to step between my thighs. I should have known when he left the shorts and tank on the bed last night that I'd regret wearing them. Not that I had a choice, after all I'm wearing a collar that knocks a few brain cells loose every time I disobey. His clammy fingers grip my chin tilting my head up to force my gaze on his.

"You've been such a good little girl." He says, voice low and hungry.

My lip twitches, but I control myself, "Thank you." I say my tone flat.

He wants to be praised. To be thanked for giving me food, a bed, a place to relieve myself. That's how he functions. After he sets the plate on the table beside me, he pulls a single rose from behind him and hands it to me. A thorn stabs my finger so I quickly plop it into my mouth to clean the crimson from my skin. Licking his lips, he moves even closer until our thighs are pressing against each other. Mine tremble with the friction, but he reads the reaction wrong.

"Mmmh. Maybe you are ready for me." His eyes trail down my frame.

Recoiling back I sneer, "Touch me like that and Ryker-"

Red hot searing pain rips through me. A scream tears from my throat, my legs giving out, and my ass slipping from the bed to the floor. My entire body shakes with the force of the after shock floating through me. Tears that I can't stop start to fall, but still I hold his stare. Dropping to his knees, he adjusts his legs to straddle me without fully giving me his weight, but that doesn't stop me from feeling the stiffness in his jeans.

"I'm Ryker now, Princessa. Say his name to me again and I'll fuck you until you're nothing but a broken mess at his feet. And then I'll kill him in front of you before I fuck you into the floor. A beautiful bleeding mess that we made together. Is that understood?"

He slaps my face hard. Once. Twice. A third. My lip splits back open. Blood invades my mouth, filling the back of my throat until I swallow down the copper liquid. Still my eyes clash with his. Pupils growing darker, his eyes wide, frantic.

"Ryker would- "

My limbs lock. Bile and blood mix together. I sling myself sideways and hurl everything I have inside me onto the floor. Hank's rage flows from him in waves. The button in his hand continuously being pressed. My brain and body war with each other until my eyes grow weak.

Breathe through the pain.

All I see are lilies and Caramel eyes. Oranges, reds. Yellows, pinks, and blacks. The smell of throw up and flowers swirl through my nose. My muscles seem to take forever to finally release, but once I'm able to open my eyes again Hank is standing at the door pacing. His hands rake through his hair, pulling at the ends, pacing back and forth. Wiping my mouth, I drag myself up against the bottom of the bed so I can fully sit up. My entire body screams in pain, but I inhale through my nose ignoring the taste in the back of my throat.

"You said you had a present for me." I rasp.

My voice, shaken and damaged from screaming. Hank stops with his back to me, both hands on the top of his head, unmoving. The way his shirt hugs his back has my mind flashing back to Ryker, but I quickly shake away that image. It's a silent few minutes before he belts out a loud laugh that has me jumping. Spinning to face me, he almost seems back at ease with my question.

"Hmmm. I did say that, didn't I." Looking back at the door before moving forward a few steps, he pulls out a napkin from his pocket.

Rubbing it between his fingers, his legs eat up the distance to me and suddenly he's crouching down at my side. Lifting my face to his, I take in his expression watching for anything, something, that will give me more. I need to know more. Why? Instead he holds my face under my jaw and uses the napkin to clean up my face from the blood and puke that's covering my lips and cheek. The whole time he does this he hums out a slow melody that pulls at something in the back of my head. It lulls me into a state that is almost impossible to escape. My limbs feel heavier.

"You'll get better, I promise. Once you see how much I love you, you'll know that this is where you belong." He coos at me.

"R-" I start, but slam my lips closed at the look that crosses his face.

Bending closer his lips graze my ear, "I'm your Ryker now. The next time you say his name it'll be when you're begging me to go deeper." He grunts the last word against the side of my face.

His wet lips press into my temple, the humming picking back up, his other hand rubbing the other side of my face. The tender flesh smarts when he touches it, but still he rubs it in small circles.

"You'll get your surprise when you learn who truly deserves you." He says.

Leaning back on the heels of his feet, he waits for any sign of fight, but I push it down. Being strong sometimes means keeping yourself safe until you're stronger. This isn't a battle I'm waiting to die for. I'll always belong to Ryker, but for right now I'll bite my tongue to stay breathing for him. Instead I ask for the one thing that will keep me sane in this moment.

"Can I just have one thing?" I ask, my words soft.

Batting my eyes I try to soften my expression, but not too hard. The sudden shift would be too obvious for a man like Hank. He's aware that his hold on me is weak, so switching up too soon would be far too easy. Looking away to break the hold he has on me, I let the tears fall, but I remind myself that it doesn't take away from the fight I have burning inside of me. Instead its fuel to the flames that stoke the fire that threatens to consume the room we reside in.

"And what do you want my beautiful Princessa?" He hums.

Looking up at him through my lashes, I smile sheepishly at him.

"Could you bring me a pack of Cigarettes? It'll help with the nerves for when I ask you to join me here." I rub my hand behind me on the bed sheets.

A lump gathers in my throat, but I swallow it down, and hold my composure. Hank Harlow assess me, watching me, reading my face. I know he knows that I don't smoke. He knows everything. Does he know it's the only way I'll be able to taste Ryker? Does he know that it's the only thing that will keep me from joining Alec and Cole? My lip quivers.

Bending forward he presses his mouth to mine, applying the softest amount of pressure, but our eyes stay wide open. He waits to see if I pull away and everything in me screams at me too, but I hold steady. My soul weeps for the truth I've yet to admit, but then he finally pulls away with a satisfied smirk.

"Ok." Is all he says.

Standing he moves towards the door before stopping and looking at me over his shoulder.

"Clean this mess up before I get back." He orders.

Once he's gone I scramble up from the floor and run towards the bathroom. Throwing myself at the toilet, barely making it in time to dry heave all the empty stomach acid I have left. Tossing my head back I wail into the vacant void around me. Flushing, I stand and step over to the sink. Turning on the hot water until it's scorching, I scoop it up and fill my mouth. Everything is on fire. My skin, my lips, my mouth, it all feels like it's drenched in flames. Yet, the real fire is in my chest, tearing a hole in my heart. A hole that used to house a family I'm not sure I'll ever get back. Will I ever deserve them again? As the question crosses my mind, I break a little more inside.

Flipping the water to cool, I splash some on my face over and over again. Scrubbing until my flesh is raw and blistered. Looking up at the woman in the mirror. No, a girl. She's a scared little girl who is struggling to find the signature Kingston fire inside her. Hank is slowly digging himself deeper and deeper in her skin. Dark circles lay underneath her eyes, broken, bloody and bruised.

My hands white knuckle the counter top as my head hangs down and my eyes pinch shut. After taking a deep breath to collect myself, I shut the water off and move away from the reflection that haunts me. Licking my lips, my body winces from the pain that shoots through me. Catching remnants of blood that remain along the cut, the taste of copper sprouts along my taste buds. Everything aches, my mind, body and soul.

Walking back into the bedroom I stare down at the mess

on the floor, but choose to leave it for another time. He never comes more than once a day. Instead, I make my way towards the bed. My ass plops on to the mattress before I gently lift the plate and spoon. With each bite comes a steady throb from filling my starved stomach, but the hunger is worse in more than one way. The smell of the room makes it unbearable to eat in until it blends in with the pain. Soon I feel nothing at all. Soon, my legs are pressed into my chest. Soon, my fingers are tracing the tattoo. Soon, my eyes are drifting closed. Soon, I'm lost to the darkness.

"What the fuck is this?"

I wake with a jolt when rough hands drag down the band of my shorts to reveal Rykers name on my skin. My eyes open to a red faced Hank who's heaving with fury. My hand jerks to cover my exposed flesh, but before I can he's pressing the remote sending my eyes to the back of my head.

"I see he has his claws deeper than I thought. Don't worry, Princessa. I'll fix this for us." He growls.

My thighs spasm around the shock. My chest falls with my next breath only to heave when I see the sinister look he gives me.

"Move and I'll slice your throat wide open." He orders.

He's gone in seconds, only the wind from his movements left to skate over me, the door slamming behind him.

Shit. Shit. Shit. Fuck!

I fell asleep. How long was I out? Sitting up, I turn to the mess on the floor and find it clean and gone. Shit. I'm losing time. The sound of footsteps storming towards the room has my heart stopping in my chest. When the door finally opens again my eyes almost roll to the back of my head. Panic sets in and I scramble to the far side of the bed.

"No! No. No. I'm sorry. I- I"

"He did this to you. To us. I'll fix it, don't worry. I'll make you whole again." His words are gargled behind his anger.

I'm climbing the walls, blocked in, stuck in a corner with nowhere to go. Hank stands at the edge of the bed with a remote in one hand and a hot iron in the other. Steam billows from the latter while his thumb hoovers over the other.

"Crawl to me." He demands.

My skin itches with the order. Something once said to me by Ryker now tainted with the voice of the devil. A demon. A succubus consuming my life. My head shakes back and forth but not in refusal. No, I'm too far gone in utter fear to deny this man anything. My body is reacting in any way it can to hold off the pain to come. One he's caused once before by the flames that licked up my leg.

"Crawl. To. Me." He grunts through clenched teeth.

I make my way to him. Crawling on my hands and feet like a fucking dog. It takes a millisecond for me to pause before he's pressing the button and grabbing my ankles at the same time. In the throws of my shakes, my legs end up wrapped around his waist. Thrashing. I'm thrashing and screaming, but no one can hear me. My wails bounce off the walls around us, my eyes meet those around the room watching us. The stares of the past watching him break me. Dropping the remote, he snatches my throat and slams me into the mattress twice to gain my attention. My vision blurs, from pain or panic I don't know, but then I feel the cool air on my bare skin. He's pulled down my shorts and my eyes blow wide.

"I'll fix this," he mutters. "I'll fix this. I'll cleanse you. I'll fix this." He repeats these words over and over again.

Lifting the branding iron, he focuses in on the letters that spell out the one man who will always have my heart. And he slowly. So fucking slowly. Brings it closer. Are we moving in slow motion? I'm watching it happen, but my entire body is cold. It's like I'm floating above us seeing it from another's point of view. Then, it happens. A sea of flames engulf my flesh.

"Stop!" I screech.

I'm screaming.

My skin bubbles and boils around the iron. The stench of burnt skin and hair fills my nose, bringing back nightmares from the past. My toes curl in from the pain, the clench of my thighs impossibly tighter, as my hands lash out.

"I told you I'd fix it." He grunts, his breathing ragged from holding me down.

My fingernails dig into his arms. Digging deeper until blood trickles to the surface, slowly dripping down to his hands.

"Please-" My words break off into a silent scream.

I can't breathe. There is no air to pull into my lungs. The lilies are on fire and my eyes burn from the image in front of me. Shivering. I'm shaking with chills so I must be going into shock. My fingers throb from the hold I have on his skin but I refuse to let go. Blinking past the tears I allow myself to take in the gruesome mess. Melted flesh rips away from the iron when he lifts it, pulling the last of the ink from my body. Yanking the last piece of Ryker from me.

Ryker, are you bleeding? I'm bleeding, are you?

Screaming. So much screaming. The inferno and embers. And then nothing. Black space consumes me. There's no more Ryker. No more Cole. No more West. Only me and Hank. Only Hank. There is no one else.

Nothing.

Chapter Five

RYKER

Blood splatters on my face, feeding the rage boiling beneath my skin, urging me forward.

Blow for blow.

Flesh on flesh.

Red liquid mixes with sweat. I ignore the ache in my arms, I push through the bone crunching under my fist. Screams and roars fade from around me until there is nothing. The pile of flesh and bone under me fades away. Smokey grey eyes stare back at me in the void. Eye's that have been vacant.

Killer.

My muscles tremble. Suddenly arms are wrapped around me, the scent of overpriced cologne filling my nose, swirling with the aftershave from the other set of hands. G and West fight for control, but my frustration and anger explode from the bottle I've shoved it into. Kenna Kingston dug her way into my bones, tattooing herself on my soul and now she's vanished in the wind. No one will sleep in Del Mar until I have her back. I'll show them what it means to touch one of us. She's always been one of us and she's fought her way back in, even when I've done everything in my power to drive her into the dirt. Turn her to ash.

Instead, she lit my world on fire. The little phoenix.

"Ryker, that's enough!"

"He's had *e-fucking-nough*!"

Both voices blend into each other. Blinking once. Twice. Again. Grey eyes fade into crimson until the mess on the mat of The Basement comes into view.

"Ryker Lee Stone!"

G and West freeze on both sides of me. The color must drain from my face because my legs wobble under me. If it weren't for the two beside me holding me, I might have dropped to my knees. That voice. My full name. My chest shutters when the crowd parts. Everyone slips to the back wall letting her through. No one lives here without knowing her face. That's why no one speaks a fucking word. The only sound heard through the buzzing of the lights above us is the click clack of her heels. Red Bottoms of course. The powerful woman wearing them bends to step between the ropes and comes to stand at the head of the man under me.

Recognition flashes in her eyes and for a moment I think I see a slight smile before her deep brown eyes meet mine. Cold. Dead. Eyes. Ever since my father, she's been a shell of herself, but that's not to be taken lightly. She's still the savage bitch she's always been, the same savage that made my family what it is, the head of the table. Most people think my father built our empire with his bare hands, but my mother, Juliana Stone, is the mastermind. She molded my father into the King he was before his death. The women of Del Mar are the head of the families. The ones who come from money. The foundation may breed billionaires, but they also marry into them. It's the whole purpose of this fucking school and it never disgusted me until Kenna Kingston was added to the list.

"Mom?"

West drops my arms to move in front of me. I know my brother and he isn't scared of what I'll do to her, but more afraid of what she might do to me. Staining her name with senseless violence? It's easy enough to cover up with the town in our pockets, but it's not the way we work, and that's enough for her.

"Move." She says, her voice like velvet ice.

Looking over his shoulder West moves to the side in one step still partially blocking me, but that does nothing to refrain her from causally moving in front of me. G tenses when her hard gaze falls to him and the disdain in them reflecting back at him. A stone settles behind my ribcage with the move of her hands knowing the itch is there. When her eyes fly back to me, her red polished fingers lash out and strike me across the face. Shoes screeching across the concrete floor signal the crowd dissipating behind us. She doesn't spare them a glance, instead tossing out a threat as if she were saying goodbye to a long lost friend.

"Speak of this and your tongues will be cut from your mouths." Her words are venom.

West spins with the threat and comes to her side with a wide toothed smile, but I see the strain. I don't have time for this shit.

"I don't know what you're doing here, but we don't need you." I state.

Moving to the edge of the ring to grab my bag, I hear her trying to follow, but West must stop her because the person stepping into my back is my size.

"G, don't. I don't want to fucking hear it. Until you have her back where she belongs, I don't want a goddamn word falling from your mouth." Slinging my bag over my shoulder I turn, "I left her to you and you lost her. Cole's- " I stop shaking my head.

I swallow past the lump in my throat. It takes monumental effort not to punch him in the face, driving his lip rings into his skin, making him hurt like I do. Clenching my fist I pull in a breath through my nose and squeeze my eyes close.

"Rye, I'll find her. I've already-" He cuts himself off.

Moving back a step, his eyes drop to the floor then move up to meet my hard stare.

"You what?"

His tongue slips out to play with the metal ring hooped through his lip.

Stepping forward I push into his chest, "Spit it the fuck out."

"I called for a little help. They'll be here tomorrow. I promised I'd find her and this is the only way I know how." He leans into me, the fight coming back into his eyes, "She's like a sister to me and I'm going to get her back. For you, for us. She's a Stone through and through, no matter what her last name is. It may have taken you way too long to see it, but I've known from the first moment."

I nod, letting his words sink in. "You've known huh?" I question, eyebrows raised.

"You can't build the loyalty that girl was born with."

He clasps my shoulder before moving past me to climb down from the ring. I follow suit and head for the stairs when West calls out to me.

"You know what today is Ryker. You can't push it away any longer. Now that mom's here, it's time."

I don't turn, "Time for what?"

Rolling my shoulder to loosen up my muscles, it's the velvet voice that answers.

"You have three hours to clean up. We'll take care of the disaster here, but son-" She pauses, waiting for me to turn, but I don't. She lets out a heavy sigh, "Don't let this mediocre shit happen again over a fling with a has been Kingston fallen princess. I've taught you better. This school has the best of the best in bloodline and you can have your pick. It's time to step into your father's shoes and I won't allow the Kingston trash to tarnish this family's name for a second time."

I don't give her the response she was pushing for, instead, I climb the stairs two at a time. It takes everything in me to hold back a retort, but I know she thrives on the bullshit, so I keep moving. G's pacing on the phone outside when I step through the front door out into the bright sun. It's barely five in the morning and the sun is out in full force. It takes a few beats for my eyes to fully adjust to the brightness, but once it does I take stock of the scene in front of me. The yard is marked with tire thread and torn up grass, the house and yard is littered with trash, and no one is in sight.

"I don't fucking care. Handle it or I'll do it for you, got it?" He snaps into the line.

Gio has never been one to refrain from speaking up and handling business. It's why he's been with us from the start. He's loyal and strong. A fucking force. One that can and has matched my own when pushed. It's the reason I hold so much respect for him. His hand runs through his black hair. He passes the SUV two more times before he stops at the hood and spins to meet me.

"No one can locate that bitch Jax. Little Savage seems to have lost her little pet and is now intent on passing the bullshit onto us so she can play detective for Kenna." He spits.

I can see the weight he's holding, the guilt eating at him, and it's my fault he's feeling it at all. Looking away, unable to look him in the face through my next words.

"This isn't on you. It's all on me. I'm the head of the family. It's Stone business and she was my one blind spot. Cole, Kenna, dad. It's all on me, brother." The words taste like acid on my tongue.

Slipping my hands in my pockets, I feel the pack of cigarettes in my left one and pull them out. I place it between my lips, but come up short on a lighter. Patting my back pockets, I look to G, but see he's already heading to me with a small metal lighter in hand. For a second, a flash of scarred skin and red blisters flash in my head.

My Killer.

Striking the flame, I puff until the end burns bright red.

"When is the funeral?" He asks, letting what I said go. He knows better than to push me too far right now.

"Three hours."

Shaking his head, he drops the lighter into my hand and walks towards his car.

"Where are you headed?"

Opening the silver car door of the Audi, "To find our girl."

I almost growl out *mine,* but he slams the door before the word can fall from my mouth. Climbing into the SUV, I head to the one place that I can feel my girl the most. I use the next three hours to prepare myself to do the hardest thing I've ever had to do. Lay my little brother to rest while my girl is out there being put through god knows what kind of nightmares. The way she disappeared into thin air and no one has reached out for ransom or leverage means one thing. They wanted her for her, not for monetary gain. If they used her to get to us, she'd be plastered all over media sites and our phones would be ringing. It's been silent. That means they took my girl to make her theirs.

The first mistake they made was underestimating the strength and fight she has running through her blood. The second is thinking I wouldn't set the world on fire to find her, even if we both die in the process. Because even after the flames fade, our souls are singed together in the ashes.

KENNA

They're coming for me.

A manic laugh slips past my lips. With each rock forward my back slams into the headboard of the bed. Each one is more harsh than the previous but the pain does little to break the stare I have on the door. Watching. Waiting.

You think they'd come for a washed up Kingston with no power?

Shut up. Shut up. Shut up! I want to scream and claw at the voice in my head warring with me. It's almost funny that I've started talking to myself but really, it's predictable. My father is a convicted killer, true or not, and my mother is buried six feet deep. I was bound to break at some point. Why not now?

Ryker and West have to be looking for me. Killer or not we're bound together by the bonds that made us.

You're bound to nothing. Not power. Not the foundation. You can't even break out of a bedroom. You're useless, who would want you?

Picking at my cuticles, the pinch of breaking the skin barely registers.

I'm trapped in this room until they come. They have to be coming. Ryker's walls have fallen, showing me how much he cares for me. West hasn't hated me for a while so even if Ryker had his doubts West wouldn't let him abandon me.

Right? My eyebrows pull together for a split second.

Right. I concede, giving myself a curt nod, my eyebrows relaxing once more.

And if he does? You have nothing. No one will come after you. Who is looking for you?

Shut up!

My breathing picks up, the inner bitch breaking away at my walls, tearing me down piece by piece. I won't let her break me. There has to be something left for them to save when they come.

Slam. Pick. Repeat.

You're losing it, Kenna. Give up, you know it's what you want. You know deep down that it's easier to know the truth than believe a lie. We've been here before. Lies and truths mixing together in a burning battle.

Wetness streams down my cheeks. My eyes strain from staring at the door but I can't stop. My body moves on it's own continuing the onslaught of torture but the mental war inside my head causes the most damage. The blood dripping down my fingers is nothing compared to the screams inside my head.

Stop. Make it stop!

You've seen the look in Rykers eyes. The disgust. The hatred. No one is coming, NO ONE.

I said shut the fuck up!

I let out a guttural scream that shakes the walls around me. My hands fly to cover my ears, as if that would silence it, but all it does is keep it trapped inside. My chest heaves from the force. Sobs wrack my body.

Pick.

Rock.

Slam.

Pick... Rock... *Slam.*

What are you going to do? Shut me out? You can't get rid of me, I am you.

My pace quickens, blood drips down onto the bed sheets as I see those deep brown eyes turning away from me. No matter how loud I scream or how hard I fight to get to him he still turns his back on me.

I told you. We're stuck in this room until our corpse rots. It's just me and you and our empty screams.

Chapter Seven

RYKER

"I feel like a fucking penguin." West grunts.

He pulls at the jacket of his suit, aggravation laced across his features. My hands run over the pants of mine, trying to calm the hammering organ in my chest, my eyes slide to my brother.

"You made the call?" I ask.

The entire town knows what today is, the past two weeks we've been fielding foundation bullshit and hunting down answers of our own. No one's batted an eye at the professor's death, hell I forgot Kenna pulled the trigger, until Addington came crawling back to town. Gio found him in a hotel at the edge of Del Mar trying to pull a meeting together a few days after Kenna was snatched. We hoped he would lead us to her, but he was just as surprised as we were. The other council members have been tight lipped about any information related to who may have taken her or how we could find her. That ends today.

"Yep." West says, popping the P at the end.

His eyes are locked on the moving scenery around us, the limo speeding down the beachside highway, heading to our family cemetery. Juliana is going to meet us there, leaving this ride the only alone time we've had since she got here, and I plan to use it.

"You know what we have to do." I state, pointedly looking at the side of his head until my stare pulls his attention. His normal playboy smile hidden behind tired and sunken eyes. It's been the longest couple weeks of our lives, but hopefully today we start to gain back the footing we've lost.

Brushing off a small piece of lint from my knee, my eyes flash back to him. "Cole would track her if he were here, but he can't, so we're going to bring Ally with us. If she tries to refuse, we cut her dad's throat in front of her." I say, my words empty, but my threat firm.

He nods once, "G said he heard some muscle rolling into town early before dawn. I think their presence is going to rattle a few cages, but maybe that's just what we need."

I rub my lips together, "Use whatever we can to draw them out. No one person could have pulled all of this off. The fire, planting Ally, the snakes in the foundation, Kenna being grabbed." I pause, my throat catching, "Cole. He told Kenna he found something on his last call."

I trail off, giving us a moment to swallow down the mess we've found ourselves in. Two men in college just becoming the kings of their family's empire. One that was snuffed out by hands from the inside. How did we find ourselves here? Kenna has to be the missing link in the circle of questions that we need answered and just thinking her name has my soul roaring to find what belongs to him.

"Once all the players are in place, I want to start the ceremony."

The limo slows, making a sharp left turn, West turns from me back to the window.

He nods, "It'll be one the town won't forget."

Tinted windows block the peering eyes lined up and down

the walkway, waiting, watching, ready to see what the Stone men have planned. There have been rumors that have circled the town, but none close enough for us to care about correcting. There's another limo up ahead with an older man standing next to the open door. His hand is stretched out, ready to help the woman wearing deep red heels from the back seat. A dainty gloved hand grasps his, hoisting herself from the leather seat to stand at the edge of the curb. My lip curls slightly at her wide smile.

"Doesn't she know she's burying her son today?" West snaps.

My fingers pop under the strain of my fist, but I ignore his comment. We all know why we're here, so it's a rhetorical question that doesn't need a response. Instead I roll my shoulders and slide on my mask, ready to put on whatever show was needed to get the point across. Our ride comes to a stop behind Julianas, but we don't wait for our door to be pulled open.

Filing out, one by one, we steadily make our way across the lawn until we're standing next to my mother., I let my gaze slide across the faces surrounding us. Some red and puffy, some masked in bravery, but the ones dipped in fear stand out the most. A sea of sheep waiting for the next orders that trickle down the pipeline. Fucking Christ. My skin itches with disgust. The urge to flee, to scour the world for Kenna. It's suffocating.

"Wipe that sour look off your face." My mother snaps. Her velvet voice laced with venom.

West walks over with a solemn look on his face and it's then that I remember that this is a funeral. Black on black, a wave of people follow us to the site where Cole is to be laid, their footsteps an echo of how empty I feel. G stands off to the left near the front row waiting for us to reach him. He ignores the icy stare from my mother and instead walks up to me and leans in.

"We've got him."

It's all he says, yet it's all I needed to know. Breathing in deep, I turn to my right and motion for my mother to take a seat before I finally take my own. Quietly, one by one, the chairs behind us fill. When the Stone's call for attendance people show up, so it's not until I look over my shoulder that I see people spanning through the isles all the way back to a small valley of graves.

Swallowing the lump in my throat, I turn to see the preacher standing next to an all black casket with gold accents. The body inside no longer my brother but a shell of a soul gone too soon. When the man dressed in all black with a white tie speaks, everyone listens. Eventually he ends his speech and all eyes fall to the box being prepared to be lowered into the pre-dug hole. Crying. So many people are crying. It almost makes me laugh at the irony of the situation. Cole hated it here. Hated the school, the students, and most people. Yet, here we were, listening to people crying over the death of one of us.

Looking over my shoulder, a quick flash of purple hair has me doing a double take. Ally. She'd been warned not to show her fucking face here, but it looks like West might need to get his little toy back on her leash. She's supposed to be taking care of something way more important, not here where people might see her. Kenna blew up the fact that she was related to Addington and since we had our guys out looking for him, we had her lay low. Gave her a job to keep her little ass busy, but it seems like our bite needs to be worse than our bark.

"Looks like your little rat doesn't follow directions." I growl under my breath.

I only speak loud enough for him to hear. Fuck, if Juliana

got her claws into Ally, we'd be cleaning the towns streets for weeks. The woman to my right eats college girls for breakfast. Ones that betrayed her sons? I pray for the day Kenna and my mother go toe to toe. If-

Don't go there.

Shoving down the foul thought that just floated through my head, I stand. My eyes connect to G's and I give him a slight nod. West moves to his feet and starts to the SUV parked on the other side of the gaping hole in the ground, the hole mirroring the one in my chest. G struts up to Juliana and grips her forearm with a rough hold. Before she can speak, I spin towards her and give her a look that brings her to a full stop. Out of fear? No. Fuck, I don't think anything scares this woman. Except one thing. Out of fear of embarrassment? Yeah, that's the only thing that's keeping her lips sealed shut.

Turning to the town, I give them a wide toothed smile, but it doesn't touch my eyes. The looks I get back prove that my mask isn't in place as well as I thought. Sweat starts to pool around eyebrows, some women lean back in their chairs, some of the men look to each other, but they have no reason to be scared. Yet.

"We all know why we called you here today. Cole Stone was killed two weeks ago." I pause for effect.

No one needs to know the truth. Not right now anyway. The people who do know the truth don't flinch with the lie.

"Not only will we celebrate his life today while we lay him to rest, but we also bring to light what he wanted us all to know."

I don't look behind me to confirm what I already know. West, dragging a man from the back of the SUV by his throat. It's not an easy task, but West is powerful and has the strength to haul a grown man a few yards. G moves my mother to the other side of the aisle to keep her out of arm's reach, but he stays on her left side so he can jump my way if needed. It's not.

"Everyone take a seat."

Several eyes gaze around attempting to find an open chair, but coming up short. My fuse shortens with impatience.

"Sit the fuck down!" I shout.

By the time West reaches me, every breathing fucker around me is either in a chair or on the ground. West drops him at my feet, my eye snapping to his in warning. Red dots play in my vision, the sinister look I'm throwing his way clearly staying I'm not in the mood for his games.

Holding his hands up, he backs away with that playboy smile showing. He steps behind me, standing just to the side so everyone can see him. Our presence is felt. Juliana looks like she's ready to skin us both alive, but I don't bat an eye. Instead, I shove my fingers through his hair, clasping it in a punishing grip before yanking his head back.

"Stand." My voice is hollow, void of all the emotions I'm harboring under lock and key. It wasn't a suggestion, but an order. One he obeys like a good little bitch.

"I think everyone wants to know your name."

His knees buckle under his weight, but my hold on his hair keeps him from falling. It doesn't stop the wince from the pain from crossing his face. I push my knee into the back of his thigh, reminding him that I'm waiting.

"Trey."

"Trey-?" I prompt. My grasp getting tighter with annoyance.

He clears his throat, "Trey Thompson." His words are shaky.

Nodding my head, I look from him to the crowd.

"Our friend Trey here works for my family. He's been one of our hands men for a year or two." I pause, scanning the faces below me, waiting. Turning back to Trey, I drag his face close to mine until I'm sure he can feel my breath on his skin.

"Trey's always been really good to us. Right?" I let out a dry laugh. "He's been so good to us in fact that he brought us a little gift. Something my brother and I have been dying to get our hands on."

West chimes in, "Hell yeah, he found exactly what we were looking for, and being such a good worker he brought us right to it."

Murmurs start to pick up, but when we both jerk our heads towards the gathering silence follows. West moves to the side and slowly begins to walk through the isles, his hands lazily placed in his pockets. Juliana watches our every move, confusion painted across her face, but when she catches me looking she swipes it clean, cooling her features in a blink of an eye.

"Trey, the people want to know what you got us. I mean, it's something that's worth sharing!" I yell in enthusiasm.

"I- um- I-." he trails off his eyes turning glassy as he continues,, "I'm sorry." His words start to spill out. Pleading. Begging. The words 'please don't', trigger something deep in my chest, knowing that Kenna could be screaming those same words. Boiling rage floods my system.

My fist slams into the side of his face, blood flies out, coating my suit, blending in with the black.

"Don't worry, Trey. We didn't take your gift without bringing our own."

I jerk my head to the side, calling G over. He releases my mother, leaving her standing there to bathe in silent rage. Coming to a stop at my side, G pulls out a long carving knife and drops it in my hand. The town audibly gasps, but no one moves a muscle. They may not want to witness what's about to happen, but they respect us enough to stay in their place. Even the cops of Del Mar keep their nose out of our business.

"West, how much do we appreciate our little gift?" I ask, my gaze focused on the man before me.

Trey slides to his knees, pleas fall from his lips, his skin glistens with fallen tears..

West has made his way to the back of the group, but I can still see the top of his head.

"You bleed, I bleed." Is all he says.

It's a reminder that you cut one, you cut all. You betray one, you betray all. What you do to one of us, you do to all of us. That's what we're instilling here today.

"You bleed, I bleed." G and I repeat at the same time.

"Trey, you bit the hand that fed you and now you owe a piece of you to us. I'm here to collect that. I'm leaving you with your life, minus a pound of flesh. Let this be a learning curve we avoid next time. Our family is not to be mistaken for weak. Our enemies may have pretty little lies, but the truth is in the crimson we spill today. In the same spot we lay our brother, a son, down to rest. Our pain is yours." I lift the knife in a show that only my brother acknowledges.

G uses both hands to hold Trey's head steady. Using my free hand, I pull the skin away and hold it tightly while I use the other to slice in one swift movement. Trey's piercing scream shoots through the open space, but no one moves. No one breathes. And then Trey's being dragged back to the SUV by G and one of his men, minus an ear.

Holding the only part left of Trey over my head, I hold the eyes of several town members. "You can't hear shit if you don't have an ear to put to the ground. Let this be a lesson on who you're betraying. Addington, or Adler as some of you know him, has been brought to the foundation for us to handle. The one and only thing anyone should be focused on is finding Kenna Kingston."

West has made it back up to me and Juliana remains in her place with wide eyes. Blood doesn't bother her, but I'm guessing the name Addington wasn't one she thought she'd hear. Which is why I made sure to use both. Turning back to the crowd, my stare catches on someone off near the tree line. Blue hair.

"I want Kenna Kingston delivered back to us in one piece by the end of the week or pieces of Del Mar will be scattered across the ocean floor." I roar.

With those last words I walk off, leaving them in shock while Juliana heads to the limo with her tail tucked between her legs.

"That was quite the show." Oakley quips.

She has a bright smile on her face. This woman loves a little torture. She's leaning against a large oak tree with a tall man on her left and a small curvy female to her right. Oakley's dressed in leathers, which is why we were warned about a little muscle rolling into town.

"Bout damn time you got here." I snap.

I've used my last bit of patience for the day. She must see the darkness behind my eyes because she moves to West.

"West Stone, player by day, big dick daddy by night." She winks.

The male beside her grumbles, dragging her into his side, but his small grin never leaves his face.

West being, well, West licks his lips and looks the guy up and down. Oakley takes the opening and introduces him as Havoc and the girl as Haven, his sister.

"If you need more skin for your collection all you have to do is ask, baby." His words are gruff, but his stare is on Havoc not Oakley. West has always been comfortable in his own skin, so it doesn't surprise me that he'd try this shit, but I don't have time to break up a fight if one breaks out. Instead, Oakley pushes off the tree and steps into West's chest, looking up at him with a sly grin.

"When you learn how to fuck me like Havoc then give me

a call, but until then, I have enough to fill any hole I want." She leans up and kisses him on the edge of his jaw.

Havoc grunts before snatching her away and stalks off. Haven has her eyes glued to West, but he just flashes her his crooked smile, a wink, and follows behind Oakley. Haven lets out a sigh that isn't meant for me to hear, so I pretend I don't and move to follow the three fuckers up ahead.

"I'm not caught up on everything, but if you want us to find your woman, I'm your girl." She sticks her hand out for me to shake and then walks with me back to the others where we load up and go back to the apartment. Ally better fucking be there or I may just let Oakley have a little fun.

Chapter Eight

COLE

15 years old

Stop!

My fist clench at my side, "We should be protecting her." I spit at my brothers.

Ryker stands motionless at the bay windows facing the wide front lawn while West leans against one of the walls scrolling on his phone. The small light shines on his face but his mask is in place. Neither of them flench at my outburst.

"This *is* us protecting her." West says, not looking up from the screen.

His words don't match the white knuckle grip he has on his phone. My shoes wear the carpet down with each pass I make through the large room. For a moment the screams stop and the silence echoes around us.

The cream colored carpet and white walls decorated in priceless artwork clash with the eerie feeling surrounding us.

As if the expensive items around the room could cover the filthy feeling of betrayal coursing through me.

"No!" A girl wails, ice searing through my veins with the single word.

We freeze. The plea sounding closer. More clear.

"They've opened the door." Ryker grunts out.

West finally looks up with darkened eyes, "They want us to hear. Dad's entire training method is barbaric, but this seems far past that. He's testing us." Caution laces his tone, eyes bouncing around the room.

I ball my fists at my side from the raw anger coursing through my veins, each step gaining speed, but I don't act on it. Not yet. I have to remind myself that there is always a point to our fathers ways. Kingston's and Stone's are bred to know pain. It's in our blood from the day we're born. What I don't understand is why Kenna is key to all of this. She's a princess in her own right, born to take over for her father as the only child to his name.

"She's being trained to become one of our wives." Ryker snaps. Answering my internal questions. "She has to learn what that means. Being at risk is the very reason for this madness." His words may agree with our fathers but the venom in his voice warns of something darker.

Reality finally snaps into place. And the meaning of what his words hold causes my next step to falter. Kenna Kingston is ours to protect, love and cherish, but she's not ours to *love*. Her blonde hair and bright gray eyes shine in my thoughts, but only in the way a brother loves his sister. Full of admiration and protectiveness, and I would tear any fucker limb by limb if they ever hurt her. Including any of our own.

"She's family." I state. It's not a question, but a reminder that she's off limits to our touch.

West pushes off the wall, pounding his feet until he's a

few paces in front of me. His brown eyes look at me with question, but it's the other Stone brother that responds.

"Kenna is off limits to the Elite Law." He snaps, shoving off the far wall near the window. The night sky spans endlessly beyond the back of the house.

Elite Law. Filthy old men and money hungry women built those long ago. Bloodlines must be carried on in wealth and social class. A Kingston and a Stone together would create a new foundation for our world.

Whimpers can be heard from beyond the bedroom door, and my patience has run thin. Fisting both my hands, I spin to face my brother.

"And yet here we are!" my arms expand at my sides, gesturing to the room, "We're standing here hearing her cries, listening to her as she wails, pleading for the torture to end and do nothing!" My voice bounces around us like a lethal bullet waiting to maim its victim.

"The law is in place for a reason." West says, his tone low, aggravation evident.

Ryker steps closer, the swift movement of his feet coming to a halt as he stands at the point of our makeshift triangle.

"Kenna Kingston has been promised to a Stone. Elite Law and the foundation can't touch her unless one of us refuses marriage." Ryker's eyes bounce between us, waiting for us to put the pieces together. Kenna can't be promised to another or married off to a sleazy fucker without one of us turning her away.

Footsteps sound in the hall, it barely registers as my stare bores into Ryker's, willing him to hear all of my thoughts. The door closing is the only thing that has me whipping my head towards the door, both of my brothers following suit. Another ear piercing screech fills the space around us, no longer muffled on the other side of the door.

Red paints my vision. Rage for Kenna, anger at our fathers, and disgust at us for standing by. So, I do what a Stone would do when one of us is on the line. I go for our girl.

Ryker's hand lashes out, gripping my arm and yanking me back. Whirling around, I slam my palms on his chest, a low growl escaping my throat.

"Get the fuck off me Rye." I bare my teeth with the warning.

His brown eyes darken, "What exactly is your plan, Cole? Run down there and rescue her? Be her knight in shining armor?" He scoffs, "Dad and Kingston are doing what's best for her!"

Jerking my arm from his hold, my hands fist his shirt dragging him closer, so close our noses touch. "She's one of us." My eyes look him over, ignoring the way his lip trembles with unbridled rage. He can fool everyone else but I see right through him.

"Cole's right." West says.

Shoving him away, I turn to leave when he reaches for my shoulder. Rolling it back to avoid his grip, I take one swing landing a hit to his jaw before storming to the door.

"Where do your loyalties lie?" I toss over my shoulder.

Jerking the door open, I'm met with two sets of tired eyes. Sunken and saddened, but firm in their rules. One reserved in the truth while the other covering hatred for his daughter. Because how can a man torture his own child, a fifteen year old, for the sake of training her to take his place? It's barbaric and out of touch with the times. Yet, there they stand before us covered in sweat and guilt, but they get no sympathy from me.

"Go take care of her, son. She needs you all." Kingston says.

Damn near sprinting from the room, I make it to the

basement door in less than a minute before I'm throwing it open, the sound of it slamming against the wall barely registers as I continue my descent down the stairs. West stops at the top of the landing behind me, but I don't slow my speed. Storming down the steps, my body jolts to a stop when I see a red faced Kenna sitting in a chair in the center of the concrete room. Only a table, water bowl, and towel in front of her. Her once long blonde hair is matted to her head, sweat and fuck knows what else staining the strands.

"Princess." I whisper. My voice almost breaks, but I swallow it down and hide the horror on my face with a smirk. "Aren't you a sight for sore eyes."

Making my way to her, it takes effort to blink away the pain across my face when I see how truly broken she feels. Her grey eyes are stormy, like a raging sea, and her hair has lost its shine. Bending at the knee until I'm eye level with her, I push strands of hair from her red cheeks and give her a tight smile.

She isn't marked or bloody in the way I expected. Waterboarding someone forces them to fight every natural instinct they have. To breathe, to lean their head forward, to fight. That mixed with being starved, locked in a basement with no lights for days, it's easy to break someone this way. And she's been broken. Kenna looks past me at the wall as if she's lost in her own thoughts. I hope they're nicer than what's right in front of her.

"Let's get you cleaned up, Kens." I whisper.

I can hear footsteps behind me, but I keep my eyes on her. Waiting for her to speak, to scream, to say she hates us. Anything other than the silence that's suffocating me in this moment. Yet, nothing comes. Her sunken eyes peer up at me with so much fight left inside them and pride suddenly fills my chest.

"Kens-" I start.

"Tell me a joke." She says, stopping my former question.

The room is so quiet, I swear I can hear the faint sound of her heart beats slow down to a steady thrum. Chuckling under my breath, I think for a moment before I blurt, "I guess getting married to a Stone comes with it's own form of torture."

Once the words leave my mouth I instantly want to take them back, but our girl lets a soft giggle slip free. A small weight lifts from my chest at the soft sound, but then my face falls. She sees it the second it happens.

"Take me to my room." She says, her voice strong. Clear. Steady.

West lets out a laugh behind me that makes me jump from the sudden sound. "There she is."

He steps around me to come kneel beside her with a wide grin on his face. Placing both hands on either side of her, West leans in, placing a soft kiss on her cheek. Pulling back, he captures her gaze for a few seconds, neither of them speaking a word, only sharing a look before he nods. That one look says more than any conversation they could have right now. He sees it too. Her strength and fight.

"Anything for you." With a wink he stands and starts to undo her bindings.

Once she's free, she rubs the red marks on her wrist with a wince, but she masks her pain well. Once she's fully untied, the sadness and guilt morph back into rage and suddenly I'm throwing the chair against the wall, letting out a feral scream. The room swims, my entire body vibrating, all I can taste is blood. West steps back to give me space, but a little pale hand lands on my chest pulling my gaze downward. Kenna stands a few inches shorter than me with the look of a fucking warrior.

"I'm ok."

I can't look at her, knowing those big round gray eyes are

staring up at me. Instead I keep my eyes trained on the wall behind her.

Pinching my chin between her fingers, she forces my head down and I let her. I can't deny her anything. But I close my eyes, not willing to let her see the demons lurking behind them. .

"Look at me, Cole."

I can't. It's not right. Everything in this room is wrong.

Digging her nails into my skin she speaks louder this time, "Look at me."

And I do. Our gaze clashes like the sea against the sand.

"I'm okay, Cole. I'm fine." She murmurs only to me.

My chest aches from the look in her eyes but I see her clearly. A fighter. A true Kingston heir. She's calming me when I should be the one calming her, and that feeds the feeling inside my chest.

Shaking my head, I grip her hand, and push it into my chest harder. "We should be protecting you, not treating you like the enemy. This should never happen!" I'm trembling under her touch.

Her chapped lips tip up in a smirk, "I'm made of steel because of the way you all care for me. I'm only as strong as the blood that runs through you. I bleed, we bleed. It's the way it's always been. We all bear the pain of the foundation."

She's so smart for someone who's still in school. We're only kids. She deserves to be in high school planning prom or cheer squad bullshit. Not in a basement being treated like a prisoner before her sixteenth birthday. She presses up on her toes to kiss the spot just under my chin before she slips her fingers into mine and pulls me towards the stairs.

West waits at the top leaning in the doorway with a look that lets us know he's proud of how she's handling this. We both are. She hesitates when she notices Ryker isn't waiting for her, causing my fingers to tighten around her in reassurance. Ryker will come in his own time.

When we reach the top, Ryker moves from the shadows to stop in front of us. With one curl of his finger and without missing a beat, Kenna drops mine, taking a step forward before running into his arms. West and I watch as he lifts her and turns to walk away. Kenna's legs wrapped around his waist, her hands tangled in his hair.

"Ryker." I call out.

He pauses, but doesn't turn, "Cole." He warns.

He's on the edge and me stopping him from caring for her will push him over. That doesn't stop me from saying what we all know.

"It'll be you in the end. Come to terms with it now or later, but she's yours to protect. It's time you stop hiding in the shadows."

He looks down at Kenna, "She's always been mine."

Walking away he leaves us standing here feeling useless.

"Is this how it's going to be from now on?" I ask.

Feeling like the little kid that had his favorite toy stolen, I swallow down the rock stuck in the back of my throat.

Slapping a hand on my back West laughs, "We're just the middle men, little brother. I wouldn't get too close to Kenna when he's like this." His laugh jostles me. "Keep your empath powers to a minimum, Cole. It'll kill you one day. There's no reason to carry the weight of the world on your shoulders."

Wise words from the playboy bullshitter himself. West takes nothing serious and is always ready for the next party. It takes effort to keep my eyes from rolling but I manage to only let a scoff escape.

With those last words he heads to his room. Most likely calling one of the many girls bound to fall at his feet when beckoned. Me? I make my way to the security wing of our house, making sure our defenses are in place. If our fathers are preparing for something, I plan to be the first one to see it coming. I may be the younger brother, Ryker may be the head of our hydra, but I'll always be one step ahead of them.

Protecting this family falls to the one who has no blind spots. If that means pushing Kenna away to keep us all safe, then it's a move I'll make to keep the princess alive.

Chapter Nine

KENNA

One Month Later

Faded grey flashes in and out of view with each blink. From field to reality. Painted blue walls surround me in an updated room. The loss of Kenna Kingston is too strong. Smearing dark burgundy lipstick over my chapped lips, I offer up a broken smile to the woman in the mirror. A thin white spring dress hangs off my form like a poorly cut sheet that's two sizes too big. A forbidden name swallowed down by compliance and fear. The thoughts in my head fighting against the cage I've shoved them into.

You're giving up.

Shaking off the accusation I suck in a deep breath.

Thirty days is like a lifetime when your stomach aches from lack of real nutrition. Four seven day periods back to back. Four weeks. 730 hours. One meal a day. I scoff out a dry laugh at the thought of sandwiches and scraps being a fucking meal. Behind my eyelids the field is slowly fading into something I don't recognize. The beating organ in my chest pinches with the realization. Rubbing my lips together, I blow her a kiss and turn to face the door that's due to open any minute. He's never late for his lessons. The ones where he teaches me how to be the prize toy he's always dreamed of. The ways of Old and Elite ones I turned away, instead choosing torture, has now become my everyday. It's a new kind of painful, but today I plan on collecting what he's promised me.

The distant sound of footsteps heading my way alerts me to his pending arrival. One second. One minute. Three minutes. The handle twists, the green painted door swings open and Hank steps over the threshold..

His once salt and pepper hair now dark as night. His beard is long gone with nothing but stubble left on his cheeks. Hank comes to stand in front of me, his hands shoved into the pockets of his jeans. Rolling his shoulders back, he stands there silently, waiting to see what my next move will be.

With a weary smile plastered on my boney face, I reach out and place my pale hand on his arm. Flashes of grey come back, but I shove them back down. Ry- my entire body locks when I start to think of his name. No. No, I can't let myself go there.

Why not? He wouldn't even recognize the person you've become. It's a good thing he's abandoned you.

My mouth fills with bile at the reminder that I'm truly alone for the first time in my life. Swallowing down the feeling of self hatred my eyes meet his.

"Hank." I say, my words are velvet soft.

He nods with approval. His empty eyes assess me with care, yet something about the way he glides over my chest has my skin itching. Can he see it? Can he see that his name almost crossed my mind? Is my smile faltering? My heart hammers in my chest with unease, the need to please the man before me unlike any other I've ever felt. My mouth dries at the realization of my situation, but still I wait for his command. Need it. Crave the freedom of the collar that's pressed against my throat. Drinking down the words I want to speak, I ask the one thing that I fear I may never get.

"I want to show you something. You deserve to know the truth." Hank says.

The hair on the back of my neck raises with the tender tone of his words. Like he's about to tell me some long lost family member died.

"Okay." I breathe out.

Pulling his phone from his pocket he slides his thumb over the screen a few times and turns it towards me. My hand trembles but I place it palm up anyway. His eyes never leave mine as he gently drops the phone inside my hand. My muscles tense when our skin touches but when no pain comes, I release a breath I didn't know I was holding.

Lifting the phone to my face I scan the photo trying to make sense of what I'm seeing. The background comes into focus first, my mind fighting the scene in front of me, showing the campgrounds at school. The wide shoulders of West is hoisting Ally over his shoulder but her face is hidden in his back yet the laugh falling from his lips shows their happiness. To the left Oakley and Ryker stand with two faces I don't know in a small circle talking. Ryker has his usual broody mask on but it's the hand on his shoulder that has ice running through my veins.

My throat closes. Small, green painted, dainty hands grip his shoulder. The unknown woman to his right looks up at him with bright eyes.

Her hand. It's all I can see. Ryker looking down at her in a heated conversation. West, Ally, Oakley. They all fade until all I can focus on is Ryker and this new woman. She's beautiful.

Her thick stature and long braided hair pulling my attention from the contact she has on him.

"Princessa, they've forgotten about you. You're place is here with me where we can build our own empire." Hank slips his hand around my wrist tugging the phone out of my face.

I lick my dry lips trying to swallow around the thickness in my throat. No words form on my tongue. My eyes drift closed, rolling back, only to spring back open. The faint smell of lilies wafting through my nose makes my eyes water but I refuse to let them fall.

Clearing my throat I look at Hank and nod.

"I'd like to be taken to my gift today." Straightening my spine, I allow my gaze to connect with his.

Two heartbeats later his mouth falls open, but then snaps back closed.

"I'll take you to him, but you need to see the others first."

More? There can't be. How long has he been following them?

Walking past and turning to face me his ass meets the edges of the bed when he flips the phone screen to face me and a photo is left face up. This one is different from the first. With shaky hands I take the device.

"When was this?" I ask myself more than Hank.

On the screen is a photo taken outside the diner I've eaten at several times. Smiling faces shine through the glass window. A booth full of people sit and smile with food, drinks, and laughs. Dark hair and dark eyes sit closest to the window with a small little thing next to him. A short girl with beautiful rosy cheeks and caramel hair, but it's the blue hair across from her that pulls me away from them. Oakley Savage sits across from him with West at the end of the table in a chair that's been pulled up to the table. My next breath catches in my throat at the face I see next to his. Faded purple hair and a wide smile captured on camera.

"They've moved on." Hank says.

I squeeze the phone to hide the way my hands shake. It's almost impossible to blink away the tears that want to fall, but I manage. Barely.

Large hands wrap around the back of my thighs to tug me forward until I'm pressed between his legs.

"I'd find you at the edge of the world. The Stone family threw you away, Princessa. You're nothing to them. A means to an end. A bargaining chip. A sold pound of flesh. Here's your proof." He speaks of the betrayal as if he's describing the weather to the blind. With astonishing beauty.

My muscles scream for me to lash out, scream, throw things. My nerve endings are on fire with the stillness that I force myself to hold. The field of lilies are gray, the tips of petals burning, changing to black. Shifting my safe haven into midnight hell. Thumbs dig into the soft flesh under the crease of my ass. Almost bruising, but then they move, shift, rubbing the bite of pain they caused. Ebbs and flows of biting pain mixed with soothing touches.

I can't stomach to see anymore. I won't.

"My beautiful Princessa, who do you think sold you to me?" One single brow raises in question, "Who allows moves to be made in Del Mar without question or punishment?" He coos.

My eyes trace every inch of his, looking for the lie. A lie that I fear won't be found. His words coat my skin in acid, the taste of hatred filling my mouth, spilling out until all I want is to rip my pound of flesh.

Is this true Ryker? Have you all played me this entire time?

"Now, let's take my beautiful girl to her gift. Maybe then you'll have something to rid yourself of this pent up rage."

My throat bobs with his acknowledgement of my repressed anger. How easy he can read the lines of my face.

"Of course." I grin.

Stepping back to allow him space to stand, the blue walls seem more dull now. The bed in the center of the room growing larger with what I know is coming. With each gift comes a price and I'm sure this one is great. Caging my face with his warm hands, he tips my head back and for once his eyes seem soft, kind, and understanding. Leaning down, his lips gently press against mine for only a moment, my eyes never closing, my lips never returning the touch, yet my soul felt everything. Hank is slowly reshaping everything I once knew and the lilies are turning into poison ivy that climbs my legs and wraps around me like a shield.

Rubbing his thumb across the bottom of my lip he says, "Let's go see if we can release some of the pain you've carried for far too long. Don't worry, Princessa. For those who betrayed you also betrayed me. Together we'll cut them down at the knees. Vengeance will be ours."

"Vengeance will be ours." I repeat. My tone is hard.

Leading me from the room that has become my home, I'm thankful for the comfort it's provided me in these last few weeks. The dim hallway houses several doors, none of which we go through. Instead we walk out into an open space with little sunlight. Two small windows to the left are open with the curtains pulled back. The room itself is empty other than two couches, a T.V, and the two windows. Hank must feel my feet hesitate at the sight of the outside world, but he allows me to lead us to the windows anyway.

He's starting to trust us.

I can't hold back the soft laugh when my fingers clutch each side of the wall. The sun breaks through the clouds just as I step up to the window and my head falls back. The feel of it on my skin is almost orgasmic. Heat. Warmth. It takes my breath away in a way I never thought something so simple would.

To be free.

"Thank you." I murmur on an exhale. "Thank you for giving this to me." Looking back over my shoulder, I give him a real smile. One that stretches the thin skin over my cheekbones in a way that's almost painful, but welcome nonetheless.

"Your gift is this way." He motions with his free hand.

I bask in the sunlight for another second before following him around a corner, through another hallway, and stop behind him at another door. The expanse of this massive building seems to continue to get bigger. My mind wanders, how many rooms, how big, the location. All these questions bombard my thoughts the longer we stand stagnate. Spinning quickly, he looks down at me with curious eyes.

Could I find a way out?

And where would you go? You have nothing left, Kenna.

The organ in my chest pinches at the truth in that thought.

"Behind this door is your salvation. Food, clothes, comfort items. All of these things will be at your fingertips as long as you please me." he finishes. His eyes roam over my face looking for something. My stomach aches at the temptation of what he's offering.

He's the only one here. No one else is coming to rescue you. Get in line or die.

"I'm ready." I state.

He huffs, tipping my chin up with two fingers, his hold pinching me. "Then lead the way." he steps to the right.

I'm hesitant. It's a battle to force myself to grab the doorknob and twist it. Slowly pushing the door open I'm instantly overwhelmed by the smell of bleach, the harsh fumes choking me, and I'm suppressing a gag. The stark white walls are blinding, the fluorescent lights making it hard for my eyes to focus on what they're showcasing. The heat radiating off Hank reaches my back, contrasting with the cool air I feel at my front. My senses are overwhelmed completely.

A long metal table sits against the wall to the far left, an array of silver instruments glistening under the light, but my mind doesn't connect with what my eyes are seeing because I'm too busy trembling from the site ahead of me. A figure is strapped to an identical table ten feet from the first. Head covered, all I can make out are tattoos.

Hank's hands run up and down my arms, warming the chilled flesh. Ignoring the hairs raised on the back of my neck, I take a step forward. My chest rises faster the closer I get to the body lying on the table. Large metal clamps strap their wrist tightly to the table, matching ones around their ankles, and neck. My fingers instinctively touch the collar around mine before dropping my hand quickly.

"What is this?" I ask, my voice small in such a large space. My words are bouncing from the walls around us.

"This is your gift. The key to everything you want. Please me, crave me, hurt for me, and I'll worship you."

His lips brush over my neck, sending a shiver down my spine. One he must take as an opening to lay another on the opposite side.

"This is your pound of flesh." Hank says.

"Kenna?" the voice rasps.

The sound is so dry, I can't place it. He must have been here for days, maybe weeks. A black cloth bag covers his face, but his chest is broad and those tattoos are familiar. My heart skips a beat when I spot one that I know all too well.

Dear God, what am I about to do?

Any and everything to survive. Just like they taught you.

Swallowing around the rock in my throat, I move to face Hank while still keeping the man on the table in my line of vision.

Placing my hand on Hank's chest, a move I've yet to try,

"And what would please you?" I ask. Hoping my words are buttery sweet I look up at him through my lashes.

The skin under the collar burns from memory alone and it's then that I know I'd do anything to not feel the lighting shooting down my back. The concave of my stomach from starving. The loss of everyone I've ever loved. Betrayal and rage course through me. Hank sees the moment I've accepted my fate and together we smile a wicked grin. My teeth like fangs in the night, ready to sink into the necks of those who sold me to the devil.

"Rip him apart." Is the only order he gives me before locking me in the room.

Alone with the man on the table, I make my way to where his head lies. Gently taking off the bag, I look into bright blue eyes with cold resolve. The field behind my eyes is dim of light. Gray spreading further and further, until all color is leached and it's nearly coated in darkness. With a single look at me, he sees his fate.

Hank just gave me the keys to my freedom.

"Jax."

And then nothing but screams.

Chapter Ten

KENNA

"You'll see. He's going to give back what they stole."

My head bobs in agreement at my own words. I don't wait for Jax to respond. Not that he can now that I've stitched his lips together.

"I'm sorry you got caught up in the middle, but Oakley should have kept her nose out of Kingston business." I mindlessly run my hand through his stiff hair. Sweat soaked and filthy.

Oakleys blue hair pops into my head, but I shove the image away quicker than it arrives. My thoughts try to betray me even now. The scalpel pressed against his thigh is cold to the touch or maybe I've finally lost feeling in my hands. Jax doesn't flinch when I press it into the junction of his hip, digging so deep I feel the tip hit a bone. Blood pours from the opening, pulling my gaze to the metal table that is now covered, dripping onto the floor.

Drip.

Drip.

Drip.

Look at the mess you've caused.

Carving into muscle, my wrist twists and twirls, slowly drawing a picture. All thoughts escape me, my mind free of everything other than the task at hand, unaware of my next move until it happens. The beautiful crimson liquid entrancing me in a world of my own making.

"Did you know that *they* promised me to him? Hmmm?". My hand grows tired, but still I continue anyway. "Yeah, they sold me like some fucking livestock." A hollow laugh slips past my lips, "I bet Oakley didn't know that. Or hell, maybe she did. She doesn't seem like the type of chick to stand by while decisions are made." I raise an eyebrow, but keep my eyes on the task at hand.

Smacking my lips I let out a dry laugh.

Hank is going to be so proud.

His blue eyes stare at the ceiling. No response. At first I would pray for him to pass out from the pain, even now my heart pinches behind the numb curtain hiding it, but I shove away those feelings.

You can't feel for those who betray you. No matter how much you wish it wasn't true.

You enjoy this, don't you Killer.

My heart skips a beat at the name running through my head.

No. Nope. I'm not going there.

Oh come on, you know it's fun painting pictures with the blood of those who are traitors.

But was he a traitor or just a pawn in Oakleys games? Slamming the walls down around my heart I block out all feelings. Refusing to let myself ache for anyone else.

Pushing away from the table in my small rolling chair to give myself room to stand, my fingers loosen their grip on the scalpel, letting it fall to the metal table with a clink. The sound bounces around the vacant room causing my eye to twitch. I take stock of my work, waiting for the picture to change into something beautiful, instead I see darkness. The once bright liquid now slowly turns into a deep thick red.

My hands feel sticky, arms heavy, my legs shaky under me. Using the table to steady myself I stand there looking down at Jax, searching for the man who was once my friend. The man who gave me beautiful artwork, creating beautiful pictures across my skin, while I ruined his.

I ruined him.

They ruined him. They did this to you. To us. To Jax.

Biting my bottom lip I give his bloody body a second glance.

Black, blue, red. A rainbow of cruelty that I've painted. Hank's promises ring in my ears, reminding me why Jax had to pay the price of my darkness. The abyss I've sank into has to be filled with the ones who claim to be loyal to me. One by one, I'll use their bodies to climb up from the depths of their betrayal. Slow movements bring me closer to the man lying across the cold metal. Leaning closer, I can see the dried tears that he once let fall.

"Shhh." I press my chapped lips to his cheek. "I'll get us out of here soon. Rest for now, I promise he'll free us when I give him what he craves."

He'll never let you go now.

No. No, shut up! He promised me. He'll set us free.

Swallowing down the lie comes easily. My tongue swipes out to wet my lips when I straighten my back. The sound of the door knob twisting has my legs locking in place. Drawing in a deep breath, I turn just in time to see Hank push open the door.

"Princessa, what a sight you are." His voice is lighter. Pleased.

My skin tingles with a mixture of pride and disgust, but I don't let him see the latter on my face. Flashing him a small smile, I take a step toward him without looking back at Jax.

See, I told you. You belong to him now.

Fuck you.

It takes far too much effort to hold back my sneer.

I am you. Kenna darling, we're not going anywhere so you better make the best of it.

"Leave him, I'll come back for more later." Hank says, pulling me out of my head.

I let my hand slide inside his and give a soft tug to pull him back toward the exit. His large fingers wrap around mine, squeezing slightly, reminding me who owns who, but he follows nonetheless.

"Let's get you cleaned up." He says, rubbing circles on the back of my hand.

My skin doesn't crawl at the feel of his touch. My eyebrows dip with the realization that I've come to find comfort in the only human interaction I have.

Just let him in.

We follow the hallway back towards *my room,* but this time he keeps his hold on me tight when I stop to look at the window. I guess the moment of freedom vanished. A stone sinks in my gut with the realization that I may never feel the sun on my skin again. What would I do to breathe in the seasalt air? Images of Jax's brutalized body flash in my head faster and faster. It's then that I know exactly what I'd do to survive.

The long hallway seems never ending when my stare falls to the door at the very end. My legs want to lock up and refuse to move forward, but the sensitive skin under the collar tingles with the threat of fighting Hank. Pushing my shoulders back, I try to stand tall.

Remember who you are.

Reaching the door, he nudges it open with the toe of his boot and steps to the side to let me in. My body freezes in the doorway, dropping my hand Hank turns to face me, waiting for what comes next. The walls have changed once more yet this time the organ in my heart jackhammers at the sight. More photos. Yet, these seem more painful. Each one calls my attention but I'm unable to look for too long.

My feet carry me closer on shaky legs.

He's showing you the truth.

Why? Brown eyes, blue hair, smiles. So many smiles. Caramel hair blowing in the sea-salt wind. My fingers hesitate for a moment when I lift my hand to touch the photo closest to me.

They've shown you who you are to them.

It's the same picture that Hank showed me on his phone. Of the diner. Where laughter and smiles shine in the window reflection. Ryker sitting too close to a small beautiful woman. West, carefree like he never was with me. Ally, the traitor, in their group as if nothing happened. As if she didn't cause it.

I stop myself before I think of the other Stone brother. I can't. Not when I'm looking at them moving on while I stay stuck in time in the same room. Day after day.

Hank is offering you redemption. Show them that the flames burn brighter with vengeance.

My jaw clenches with frustration. I want to scream, to lash out, to fight, but all I have left to give is myself. The one thing I've tried to keep from his hold. The one thing he was promised a long time ago.

Why am I fighting him when who I'm really angry at are the ones who abandoned me. They left me in the hand of a mad man.

"Go clean yourself up." he says, his voice far too close behind me.

He must see the slight way I jump when he presses his front to my back, his hand brushing my hair to the side, giving him the perfect angle to slide his lips down the column of my throat.

"I have plans for us tonight." he whispers against the base

of my shoulder. "I'll prove to you over and over that I'm not going to leave you like they left you."

Chills spread down my arms and he takes that as a sign of submission and want instead of what it is. Fear. Panic. Horror.

"I can't wait." I croak out.

He doesn't move for a moment and I fear that he could hear the reluctance in my tone, but before I can spin around to prove myself, he steps back. Clicking his tongue he snaps his fingers for me to face him. Wild eyes meet mine.

"You've made me so proud today, Princessa. I'm going to show you what happens when you're a good little girl."

The way he says those words has bile rising in my stomach, but I fight it back down. My mind and body war with themselves. Grinning at him, I step back, my foot bumping into the dresser, the palm of my hands resting on the top behind me.

"What did you have in mind?" I ask.

I decide it's best to show interest in his gifts when he's wild with reckless ideas. Hank Harlow is dangerous.

He shakes his head with a deep laugh, "Go". It's an order, but not one I fear.

He's giving me a chance to run while I can and I fucking take it. I don't take my eyes off him until I'm behind the bathroom door and it's locked. Not that I'd let myself assume that the lock on this door would keep him out if he truly wanted to follow me. Hank let me run from him while he was knee deep in need for control. He gave me a moment to soak in the sun on my skin. And in his own way he gave me Jax. Someone to talk to while I'm here.

My body screams to fight with everything I have, but my mind is a muddled mess of confusion. The Stone family sold me. Made me a piece of property. Hank merely paid for what he wanted and gave me the chance to destroy the people who did this to me. Ryker made my body betray me while turning me into nothing but his toy. Hank hasn't touched me. He intends to, but he said he wouldn't until I begged him to. Would I?

My stomach churn with the idea of his hands roaming my body, floating across my flesh, inside of me. Hank isn't mine, yet I'm his. Turning on the water, I slide out of my bloody clothes and stand there waiting for the water to warm up. I avoid the mirror, instead choosing to stare at the wall. Once steam starts to flow from behind the curtain, I slip inside only to scream out from the biting pain.

"Fuck!"

The blistering scab on my hip smarts with the heat of the water. No amount of numbness can cover the boiling skin from the iron Hank pressed into my skin. Taking away the last thing I had from him. His name on the tip of my memory, but refusing to fall. No amount of training could have prepared me for this. Hunger, pain, torture. None of it is as bad as being sold like a pig at the market to cover the debt of a family you once loved. The Stone brothers did this to me.

He's in your head.

His voice whispers in the back of my mind. The thought I refused to think.

NO.

I shout back at that voice refusing to listen. No. They are to blame. One down two to go.

Blood paints your skin.

Looking down, I watch the red water run pink until it's clear liquid going down the drain. I tip my head back and laugh so loud it vibrates against the tile walls.

"Fuck! You're talking to yourself now." I roll my eyes at the irony of it all.

The hot water rolls down my back, loosening my muscles.

Grabbing the soap, my hands scrub at the mess. Scrubbing until my skin is raw. Scrubbing until the water runs cold. Scrubbing until the bedroom door opens and closes again. Scrubbing until my hands prune, my legs shake, and my arms are heavy with exhaustion.

Stepping out of the tub, I wrap the large fluffy white towel around me and finally face the mirror.

Look for me.

I stumble back at those words.

I can't.

Look for me in the lilies.

A single tear falls down my cheek.

I can't. I can't look for you because I don't know who you'll find in the end.

Find me in the lilies.

I won't. You left me and now I belong to the monster in my nightmares.

Swiping at the lone drop, I grip the towel and turn towards the door throwing it open. Steam billows out around me masking the room, so I wait for it to clear before stepping forward. Expecting Hank to be standing near the door or sitting on the bed, I'm surprised to find the room empty. The only thing different in the room is a box.

The little red box sitting in the center of the bed sends a familiar rush through me. The color of the box morphed into something more delicate, yet the feeling of the unknown has my heart beating a little harder behind my ribs. Pulling in a lung full of air I push it past my lips on an exhale. Numbness sits in the center of my chest, but I can still feel the tingles climbing my fingertips with each step closer. My long blonde hair hangs in wet waves down my back. The slow drip of water sounds when it hits the floor.

The beautiful new box is within reach as I step closer to the edge of the bed.

Hank promised to make me feel again. Promised to take off the collar if I wanted, and god do I want to. The skin under the metal stings with the direction of my thoughts. Lifting the corner of the box with measured movements, my gaze falls on a deep green fabric that looks like the most beautiful silk. My heart hammers behind my ribs at the notion that he may take me out of this building. Hope is a monster and I've let her sink her claws into me.

Hank is slowly taking away the pain they've caused.

No. He's the one who did this to me. My fingers twitch with the urge to slap myself.

Is he? Look around you, Kenna. It's written on the walls. They've forgotten about you.

Closing my eyes for a second to gather myself, I shake off the feeling. Gently lifting the fabric from the box, I watch in awe as it unravels into a floor length dress that sweeps the ground. The thin material is so light and soft in my hold that it almost feels weightless. For only a moment I forget where I am, who I'm with, and why I have this gift in my hands. For only a moment I'm taken back to the campus where my life should be.

"It's so beautiful." I whisper into the empty space.

Letting the towel drop to the floor, I waste no time sliding the silk over my naked body, loving the way it feels on my skin. Reaching into the small drawer of the dresser to grab some underwear, I pull them up my legs. The dress falls to the floor just as the bedroom door swings open and my heart skips a beat at the close call. Hank keeps himself in check, but one opening and he'd take everything I have left.

"Turn for me, Princessa." he grunts.

He's holding himself back and I know that wild look is there just on the edge. Rubbing my hands down the dress at my side, my feet slowly move in a circle until our eyes meet. My shallow greys clash with his bright wide gaze. His mouth damn near waters at the sight in front of him and it's then that I realize he's dressed his meal up. He motions for me to twirl with his finger, so I do what I'm told.

The green dress hugs every inch of my body, the silk slipping and sliding with each move I make, the slit up my thigh showcasing my leg. It's beautiful and if I were anywhere else I'd love it. He has me turn another circle before his hand is wrapped around my arm, tugging me into him. His body presses into me, the smell of desperation and hunger pour off him, crowding me into the edge of the bed. My eyes search for something to distract him when they fall on the pack of cigarettes on the table near the bed.

"Shall we?" I ask, nodding my head to the pack.

He takes a step back, but it does nothing to calm my racing heart. He smiles at the feel of my chest pounding from his closeness.

"Of course."

I snatch up the pack and have one between my lips before his next breath. Looking up at him, I wait. He doesn't give me enough control to have my own lighter so I'm at his mercy. Hank dips his tongue out to rest between his teeth like a starved animal playing with their food. The strike of a lighter makes me jump and a smile spreads across his face. Inhaling, the tip of my cigarette burns bright red, filling my mouth with the familiar taste. One I once craved but now dread.

"You look mouth watering." Hank says, his words a groan.

His fingers trace the sides of my neck until they disappear behind my head. The tug of metal and the pinch of pain has me stilling beneath his touch. Swallowing down my cry of happiness, I keep my eyes on him. Hank watches me while he works on freeing me from the collar. His gaze never leaves mine, searching for a sign he shouldn't do this. The final click of freedom reverberates through me and I have to grasp his forearms to hold myself up.

"Thank you."

Tears build until all I can see is a watery Hank standing in front of me with a warm smile. My body and mind finally choose the same path when I jerk forward to wrap my arms around him. My throat hurts from the sudden relief, but I don't complain. Hank rubs his hands up and down my spine, letting me cry into his chest while speaking soft sweet words that don't match the look in his eyes, yet I stay in his arms anyway.

I'm going to be free.

Together we step from the room into the dimly lit hallway. My hand in his. The dress is soft against my skin with each step I take. Hank leads me towards the open room with the window and I can't help the sudden excitement that courses through me. My only thought is the feel of the sun on my skin one more time. We both step into the room together but my feet trip over each other when I see the small table next to the open window. A small white tablecloth covers it, candle lit, and food placed around it in portions.

My ribs ache from the beating of my heart but I can't seem to look away from the sliver of light shining through the glass. I can tell that the sun is starting to set so my body moves on its own forgetting the hand on mine. Before I think more of it he releases me giving me the freedom to walk away from him. Is it a trap? I don't let myself focus on that thought. Instead I pull back the curtain fully and bask in the warm glow of the setting sun.

"It's beautiful," he says from behind me. "Though it doesn't compare to your beauty."

My next breath catches in my throat. My fingers loosen

on the cloth in my hand. Turning towards him I give him the first real smile since I've been here.

"Shall we?" I wave a hand over the table of food.

He returns my smile with one of his own as he pulls my chair open for me to sit. It doesn't take me long to notice that he gave me the one with the view outside. To mess with my head? Maybe. Or could this be his way of showing me he truly does want me to trust him?

I may never have those answers but for now I let myself eat real food while staring at the cotton candy colored sky wishing for this to be a dream.

Chapter Eleven

KENNA

Two Days Later

"That's it, Killer. Spread those pretty legs for me."

His voice skates over me, sending a shiver down my spine. The way he touches me makes me feel alive again. I want him so bad my legs tremble with need.

"Please. Please touch me." I'm begging him for anything.

The way my skin burns for him has my breath catching in the back of my throat. We're like fire and rain. Climbing in height only to fade into nothing. The smell of rain and cigarettes flood my nose, making me smile. He's here with me. The weight of his body presses me into the wet ground. It's not until my eyes open that I realize they are closed. Brown eyes hover over me, corded arms surrounding me, a cobra tattoo staring me in the eyes.

"You're mine, Killer."

My lips quiver. Tears spring to my eyes. The rain falls harder. Harder. It's pouring and now all I can see is brown eyes. I can feel the weight of him over me, but the rain blocks out everything else. The smell of lilies drift through my nose before the burning smell takes over. Someone set the field on fire.

"Look for me." His words are hollow and empty.

"Please stay." I beg.

I beg.

Rain falls and soaks my skin. Fire latches onto the ground spreading over the field. My mind tugs at something but the water washes it away.

"Can you see me? Are you looking for me?" he's calling my name.

"Why are you leaving me?" I cry out.

His weight is pressing me further into the mud and dirt. The flames growing closer. Rain and smoke mix into a deadly vapor.

"Rise little phoenix. Find me in the lilies and rise."

Brown eyes inch closer and closer until a mouth presses against my lips, jerking me forward.

Sitting up in bed, my chest heaves with the remnants of fear. The weight of a body is still against me, drawing my attention to the side. My body aches from the nightmare, my eyes scanning the dark room, every inch of my body on alert. I can feel myself start to shake, so I begin to sway back and forth trying to calm my thoughts. The green dress is still on my body and a cloud of confusion hangs over my head. Hank sleeps beside me, his arm lying across my waist, the weight I must have felt coming from his hold.

In a panic my hands start to roam my body, taking in the way each inch of my skin feels. When I come up empty of wounds or soreness a sigh leaves me until my fingers reach my throat to find the metal biting into my flesh. My lungs ache to pull in air around the panic of being collared once again.

"I told you I wouldn't touch you until you begged for it." Hank says, sleep still in his voice.

"Then why?" I ask.

He doesn't question what I'm talking about because he knows. Why is the collar back around my neck? Why?

He's never going to let you go. You belong with him. He's the only one who wants you.

His thumb tugs at my bottom lip, "It wasn't planned to go that way, Princessa."

I nod as if that's an answer. "Okay."

Why can't I fight him?

You know the outcome of that. Be smart.

He shakes his head, "You don't understand. I didn't want to have you dolled up and ready for me. I wanted to." he stops, clenching his jaw. Hank pulls in a deep breath through his nose, "I planned a special night for you, but it was ruined. It's always ruined by them. They keep trying to ruin this!" he shouts.

Who?

"I don't understand." I whisper. Afraid to push him while his eyes are wild and cloaked in darkness.

Rage drips off him like acid and the wild look behind his eyes returns. Whoever ruined his plans just made it dangerous for me to move without permission. The urge to please him and take away his stress washes over me and the fear from that feeling bubbles in my veins. Once again my mind and body are at war, but the words out of my mouth has everything turning to ice.

Ask him.

No. Not yet. I'm not ready.

You crave the relief of pleasing him so do it. Ask him.

My lip trembles so I dig my teeth into my bottom lip while I swallow down the words fighting to break free.

Do it. Show them you're not weak. Hank holds everything we need.

"Touch me." I say on an exhale.

I don't know what I'm asking. I'd never beg for him to enter me. My skin burns with the image of him over me. Those blue eyes leering over my body. Yet, those two words fall from my mouth like a sin. He stills. No one breathes. Neither of us move.

Again.

"Touch me." I say again, louder.

This time there is no missing my words. He doesn't wait for me to scream no, or back out, his hands are on me and his body over me before I can blink back the tears. Bile works its way up my throat, yet I lay there and let his hands skate across my skin. My legs lock together for a second before falling open for his touch. The numbness starts at my toes and slowly works its way to my chest. With each pass of his fingers over my underwear I float higher. I'm no longer in my body. Numb and cold cloak my skin. His fingers slip under my thong. I'm hovering over the bed watching the way his wild eyes take in my flush skin.

Finally.

Lilies.

The field flashes in my mind like an old movie. The bed, Hank, his touch. Lilies, fire, smoke.

Flames engulf the field. Lilies and embers combust into ash. Hank pushes a finger inside me. I'm cold, yet hot and nothing all at once. My vision blurs. The tears are falling, but all I see is orange and grey and smoke. The smell of grass burning. Hank and the bed flash back into view. The way he feels inside me makes my skin itch. I want to claw at the flesh covering my bones. I did this. I gave him this. I set the field on fire. I'm searching for the lilies, but they're nothing but ash and embers now.

"Unravel for me, Princessa."

Let go.

Acid seeps into my mouth. Disgust cloaks my sweat covered skin. Need courses through me mixing with confusion. His fingers plunge deeper. Over and over. In and out. Curling and twisting. My legs stiffen while my body betrays everything I am. He pulls me deeper and deeper into the abyss.

I want to scream. To beg him to stop. To shove him away, but I asked for this. I gave him what was left of me. This is my doing.

You've earned this. We are the monster of their making.

His thumb presses against my clit. My knees bend pressing away from him or climbing closer. I crave the release and the way he uses my body against me and my thoughts clash together in a raging war with my heart.

Yes. Release us from our cage.

Fire and ice fill me. My vision was lost to the tears flowing from my eyes. Blue and brown eyes fight above me.

My body shakes, trembles, vibrating with the climbing flames. Hatred and fire. Numb coldness floods my veins. His breathing mixes with the roar of the fire. Until the only thing left in the field is my soul and the ash of our flowers.

I couldn't find you. I only found the ruins of who I was.

Chapter Twelve

RYKER

"I might be able to find something if you'd back the fuck up."

Oakley laughs at Haven, Havoc's little sister, from where she's seated on the couch. There's far too many people in our apartment. The crowded space makes me want to claw at my skin but they want the same thing I do. To find my girl.

"Easy, kitten. You can put the claws away, I'm just trying to help." West huffs.

He's not used to women putting him in his place or speaking to him without sounding like she's in heat. The poor bastard's been knocked down a peg. Haven sits at the desk in the corner but my gaze refuses to move from the window. The desk and laptop belonging to Cole has my chest aching.

"Can you track an I.P address? Hmm? Can you hack cameras and security codes?" she snarks.

Looking over my shoulder towards her brother, Havoc, I get a glimpse of his eyes rolling. Havoc sits in the spot next to Oakley on the couch looking out of place with the blue haired badass on his arm. The biker rolls his helmet on his knee waiting for a reason to jump to his feet and escape the bickering from behind him. The only one missing from the heard of freaks is Ally and that's because she's chosen to lay in Cole's bed all day. Fucking useless. Not that Oakley would let her forget it either. She's given that girl hell for days and the headache at the base of my skull is proof.

My hands clench, jaw so tight my teeth threaten to crack, the need to do more than stand around strong. A month. It's been a full fucking month since I've laid eyes on my Killer.

"Fuck it, come on Oak." I jerk my head to the door.

West looks over his shoulder tensing when he sees the look on my face, but Haven pulls his attention back to the screen when she groans. Oakley stands to follow when Havoc lashes out to snatch up her wrist. Bitch boy.

"Blue." His tone is stern but his gaze is soft.

I almost laugh at the fucker for being pussy whipped, but here I am tearing all of Del Mar to the ground for my own.

Halfway turning to face him, Oakley gives him a sinister grin, "Wanna come cause some chaos and havoc with me?" batting her eyes she lets his name fall from her mouth softer than the others.

Sighing he stands and pulls her to him but I spin away before I see anything else. Jealousy and hate flood my veins in a deadly mix. Storming to the door I yank it open to let it slam into the wall.

"I'll be in the car." I spit.

It's not their fault. I know that and they understand my rage. It's something we don't talk about yet it's an understanding. They are only here to help find Kenna and then they're headed back to Seattle where they belong. Running their family while I'm left here picking up the pieces our fathers left us to clean up. The parking lot is empty of people wandering around giving me a few seconds to myself so I light up and inhale a deep pull of nothing but nicotine. The taste of her has faded from my mouth, my thoughts screaming to find it, drink it, and never let it go again.

Fuck, when's the last time I touched her skin? Felt her lips on mine? Forced a scream from her throat while she burned for me? With me. Because I always felt everything. Come on, Killer. Come back to me.

Footsteps approach me from behind but when I turn it's not the two I expect. Instead it's Ally. Her eyes are red rimmed and swollen. Faded purple hair a mess. Shit, this girl looks like hell. Shaking off the sympathy I face her full on giving her a snarl.

"Hear me out." she says, her voice raw.

Holding up her hands she continues towards me. This girl is poking a fucking bear by coming to me alone because the only thing keeping me from slitting her throat is West. He's saved her even when she hasn't earned it but he has his reasons and I have mine.

Jerking my head, I urge her to continue.

"Use me." she says.

My brows dip in confusion. "What makes you think someone would trade a rat for a Kingston?"

Shaking her head she rolls her shoulders, "No, I know that. I'm nothing like Kenna."

"You're damn right. You'll never be her and you better learn that fast, rat." I snap.

Licking her lips, a nervous tick, she opens her mouth to speak when Oakley and Havoc walk up behind her holding hands like fucking high schoolers.

"She means to use her to get information from her father." Oakley says.

Her words like a knife aimed at Ally but Havoc keeps his hand in hers holding her in place. Knowing that I'm not the only one that wants to tear her apart makes me smile.

Ally looks over her shoulder then back at me, "I'll get him to talk to me. Just take me to him and I'll help find Kenna."

she looks away, her hand coming up to whip at a falling tear, "She's my best friend." her voice cracks.

"A best friend you betrayed." I spit.

Her shoulders shrug, "We all have our own sins to answer for so I'd remember that. Don't forget who marked her the deepest." she quips.

Turning back to me I can see the decisions made in her mind.

"You'd give up your own flesh and blood?" I question.

This girl knows no loyalty.

"He gave me away to the Stone family a long time ago. It's time I do the same." Ally's eyes harden.

Well, fuck. The little rat has a backbone after all.

"I'm not one to pass up a chance to take down a snake in the foundation. Let's go, but you're riding with me." I point to Ally.

Oakley winks at Havoc, "I'm driving." she says, running towards his midnight blue and chrome bike.

Tossing his head back with a groan, "Blue!" he yells chasing after her.

Climbing into the driver's seat I wait for Ally to close the door. The ride is filled with a cold chill that still sits at the base of my spin when the iron gates stare back at me from the front of our campus. Ally fidgets in the passenger's seat, her fingers digging under her nails, knee shaking the closer we come to the parking lot.

"Where is everyone?" she whispers.

I almost laugh at the way she speaks low, as if someone might hear her and come out from the shadows.

Squeezing the steering wheel I keep my head forward watching the gate swing open far too fucking slow. "Didn't you hear? The professor was found dead. Classes are canceled for the month."

I fight a prideful smile when the memory of Kenna

putting a bullet in his head plays back in my head. My girl's a fucking savage.

Turning to the left heading to the dorms I park outside the first building I see.

"Where is he?" she wonders.

If it's a question I don't answer, instead I open the door and give her one last look.

"Betray us again and they'll find your body in chunks."

My words are void of any emotion and so is my chest. Stepping from the car I hear the sound of a bike come rolling up with a blue haired demon skidding across the pavement with a wide smile. Street lights shine from the chrome of Havoc's bike but it's the one in control that looks like she owns the world. Oakley is a rare woman that sends a shrivel of fear down the back of my neck.

Tossing her leg over the machine between her thighs she jumps onto the curb to hop over to where Ally and I stand. Far too enthusiastic to shed blood. The sun set almost an hour ago leaving a new night sky lit with different shades of blue complimenting her hair. Her excitement radiates from her. Havoc storms up behind Oakley, pulling her back into his front. He drops his mouth to her ear. I don't stick around to hear what he says.

Ally's footsteps follow close behind shooting off question after question, but I don't give her a response. My thoughts on the man in the building ahead. Cutting through the courtyard I turn around the side to slip into the ally between two dorms. Ally's legs struggle to keep up with my long strides, but I keep pushing forward. Coming up to the door hidden inside a concave in the brick my hand grasps the doorknob. Looking over my shoulder to see three sets of eyes on me I shove the door open to the grounds janitor storage room. The same room I had Kenna on her knees in and I can't help the images that pop into my head with the reminder.

Oakley claps her hands with a grin, "Let's do this."

Havoc looks at her like she's the moon and stars causing my mouth to fill with acid while Ally looks like she might get sick. At least she's just as uncomfortable as I am.

"Don't fuck this up for us." I say through clenched teeth.

Oakley moves around Havoc to step into Ally's face, "I'd say I'm sorry about this, but then," she shrugs, "I'd be lying." with that she slams her fist into Ally's face.

The force of her hit jars Ally's head into the brick wall making her lose her footing. Reaching out to grip her forearm I steady her feet. Ally looks up, blood dripping from a cut caused by Oakley's knuckle, looking shocked.

"You think he'd expect you to be untouched after we found out what you did? Who you are?" I say.

I can feel the smile on Oakleys face without turning my head to see her. Rolling my eyes I tug Ally closer. So close our noses press together, "I only plan to take one life today so make sure it's not yours." I growl through gritted teeth.

Shoving her inside and slamming the door I spin to lean against the cold metal. Havoc tugs Oakley into him and smirks.

"Let's go for a ride, Blue." he winks.

She looks from the door back to her guy before clicking her tongue, "You want to drive don't you baby." she rasps.

Havoc moves back and pulls her with him, "I'd ride bitch for you any day, Blue." he kisses her temple, "But I plan to drive a whole different type of machine."

It takes far too much effort to keep my hands at my side instead of swinging at the bastard. Being around these two is far too fucking hard.

Dragging her away with a dark look on his face she follows behind him without a fight. Left to my own thoughts I let them roam back to my little killer. My head thumps against the door over and over until my eyes start to grow heavy while the sky grows darker. Stars start to shine through in patterns and swirls. I try to find her in the sky but I know she's not up there. She's in the lilies where I ache to go.

Thirty minutes later Havoc and Oakley come walking back up with a little more bounce in their step. I can't help the low laugh that slips through, but it's not enough to hide the aggravation shining through.

"Ready to party?" Oakley chimes.

"Is she always this thrilled to spill blood?" I ask Havoc.

His eyes trail her body before looking at me, "She's one of a kind my man."

Oakley hip checks me out of the way to bust through the door.

"Alright mother fuckers." she shouts into the small space.

My hand slides down the right side of the wall to find the light switch casting a bright orange glow in the room. Ally sits on the floor with her head in her hands, her shoulders shaking with silent sobs. Addington stands in the corner, cuts and bruises covering his skin, with a vile grimace on his face.

The room is small and boxed shaped with lawn equipment covering most of the space. All three of us step through the doorway letting the door close behind us. Oakley reaches down and tugs Ally up by the back of her shirt. There's no gentle touches with the move, yet Addington doesn't flinch. My eyebrows raise with surprise and he must catch that because he laughs.

"I'm not going to pretend to give a fuck with what you do with the useless failure. You'd be better off assuming I give a fuck about what your plans are for me." he barks.

Licking at the dried blood at the corner of his mouth his eyes bounce around to each of us. He can try to hide the fear he's filled with, but I can smell it pouring off his skin. One step forward. Another. Oakley pushes Ally into Havoc's chest, flashing him a look and he immediately knows what she's asking for. They read each other's faces and move like twin flames.

Ally's eyes clash with mine and I see it. She knows who has Kenna, but there's something darker in her eyes. I almost stop in my tracks to drag her out and beat the fucking truth from her mouth, but I can't let Addington continue to breathe the same air as my girl. He doesn't have the fucking right to exist in the same world as her. I've craved the bloodshed I'm about to create, but something stops me.

"Havoc, take her to my truck." I toss over my shoulder.

Tilting my head at Oakley she tries to read my thoughts.

"I think it's time to show Del Mar that I'm done fucking around with people who don't bend at the knee."

"You want to make a statement." Oakley states.

It's not a question but a confirmation for what I have planned. I nod once before wrapping my hand around his throat and pull him towards the door. Oakley steps into his back begging him to make a move so she can shove her blade into his spine. Addington clamps his mouth shut and refuses to give us even a grunt of pain. That's okay I'll get my screams from him one way or another.

Chapter Thirteen

RYKER

Oakley kneels on the leather seat behind me, knife at Addingtons throat, a dark smile on her face. This girl scares the fuck out of me. Doing what needs to be done comes easy to me, but to say I get off on cutting skin would be a lie. Oakley Savage is one of a kind because she craves the violence. It's what makes her the best person to run her father's affairs. The added muscle she's collected along the way helps but it's not needed. We were always told to keep the savage family on our good side and now that I've met the Queen herself, I know why.

Ally sits in the seat next to me picking at the skin around her nails without taking her eyes off the road ahead. Avoiding the man behind her I can see the struggle to keep her body as still as possible. A loud rev catches my attention to the side of my window, a blue bike speeds past me, cutting me off to fly down the winding road.

"Fucking dick." I bark.

Oakley laughs, her eyes meeting mine in the mirror, blue eyes shining with excitement. Rolling mine, I look back to the road to see his bike long gone. Fucker doesn't even know where I'm headed.

"Call West." I order.

I'm not speaking to anyone in particular but Ally is the first to move. Oakley was too busy poking and prodding our guest in the back but he was true to his word. His lips sealed tight without a sound. That's okay, I'll make sure he screams for us, for her. Ally moves, pulling my gaze back to her, she places her phone to her ear. She jumps when West picks up, yelling can be heard from in the background, even from where I'm sitting.

"Hello?" she says, her tone low and broken.

Sighing I snatch the phone and press it to my ear, "West."

Silence. The line goes quiet. All screaming and yelling stop at the sound of my voice.

"Call the foundation. I'm done fucking around with empty threats."

One. Two. Three seconds before he speaks.

"And where exactly do you plan to have this little meeting, brother?" he pauses for a second, "Hmm? We already had to clean up one body and now you want to add another one?"

My fist clenches the leather under my touch until my knuckles whiten.

"Do what the fuck I said. I'm the head of the family and I call the shots. If you can't do what you're told then I'll call G. We all know he'll do as he's told." I spit through my teeth.

Oakley shifts her body towards me, her eyes boring into mine through the mirror, ready for my next plan. Ally sinks lower in the seat, her skin ashen. My foot presses the gas harder shooting us faster down the road bringing me closer to my next turn. I didn't know where I was headed until I got closer. Now it's clear where we need to go. It's then that I decide to call G either way.

"I'll text you when I get there with the location. I'm

keeping my word, *Brother*" my tone lands on a snarl with the last word.

Letting my implications sit there for a moment before continuing.

"Dad would -"

"Dad is fucking dead, Ryker. Our brother-" he stops, sighing. "Rye, we've lost too much. We've broken too many. Maybe this is our penance."

My head jerks back at his words.

"She bleeds, we bleed. You forget who we are so quickly, West?"

I don't let him respond before hanging up. Yanking the wheel to the side I send us sliding to the left around a sharp corner.

"Shit!" Oakley grunts.

Ally has both hands gripped around the seat, her eyes wide and worried. Little rat.

"Take it fucking easy, Ryker. I have a goddamn knife to a man's throat back here." she growls.

"Put it to use and shed a little damn blood instead of bitching." I snap.

Kicking the back of my seat she leans forward putting the tip of the blade to my cheek.

"I'm not worried about cutting him, mother fucker. You almost made me slip up and cut myself. I don't bleed." she declares.

I snicker, "Does that mean you're a ghost? Cause I knew there was something creepy about you, *Blue*."

Using the name her boy-toys call her, I flash a smile her way before turning back to the road. After a second I grunt from the presser of the knife returning only this time she presses hard enough to break skin.

"Watch your tongue. I'm here for Kenna, the Stone family holds no interest of mine."

Slamming into the back seat she sends a fist into the side of Addingtons head. Popping her knuckles she winks at me in the mirror before going back to beating his ass. Blocking out the little freak I pull out my own cell to call G.

"Boss man." he says as he answers.

"I need a few items. Grab a runner or two we have some weight to move."

He doesn't wait for an explanation. He only ask one question and that's what the fuck I needed. Gio keeps me in line but he always does as he's told.

"Where and when?" he questions.

Licking my lips I give him the location. "Now."

With that I drop the phone in the center compartment and continue down the road. It only takes another ten minutes before we're pulling up to a small field near the edge of a cliff. Del Mar has some beautiful sights. The night sky spans out with a blanket of stars where the city lights can't reach them allowing the perfect glow of light. Putting the SUV in park I look back at Oakley with a nod waiting for her to drag her new toy out the door leaving me and Ally inside alone.

She tries to keep her stare at the open landscape out the window but we both know it's too dark to see a fucking thing. I'm a patient man when it comes to shit like this so I lean against the seat letting my head fall to the headrest behind me. Closing my eyes I see beautiful grey iris's staring back at me.

Killer.

"What do you need me to do?" Ally's' voice breaks my focus.

Peering over at her I take in how exhausted and worn she is from head to toe this girl is spent. Tossed in a world full of snakes the rat had no chance of survival so what the hell was she thrown inside for? That's the question that digs at my inner thoughts.

"Whatever I tell you to do."

It's the only answer I give her because right now I don't have a plan. All I know is her father's death is coming tonight whether at my hand or not. Letting out a deep exhale I open the door to step out without a second thought to Ally. She'll follow. They always do. It's why she knew I was going to require something of her tonight. It's the same reason she knows I'm keeping her around when the last thing I want is the little cunt sniffing around while I'm looking for Kenna.

Because she was Coles. Unspoken or un-acted on means nothing to us. His statement meant law. Ally Addington is untouchable. For now.

Leaves crunch under my shoes the sound eerie this late at night in an empty field. Oakley has managed to drag his ass three yards ahead but stops when I shout her name.

"Oak! Where the fuck are you going?" I shout.

I can feel Ally step to my side but I don't give her any more attention that she hasn't earned.

Oakley looks back at me and then to the open field ahead. She's barely spotted in the darkness save for her blue hair twisting in the wind. Turning back to face us she walks two yards while I meet her halfway through the last yard.

Shrugging her shoulders she giggles, "I thought I'd take him to the cliff and have a little fun."

Stepping into her, my arm shoves Addingting against her chest, "I don't care who you are or who you're here for, I don't need you getting knife happy."

Pursing her lips she looks me up and down before flashing a smile. "I like you. Too bad you're twisted up inside for her. I'd add you to the food chain." she moves quickly, pushing Addington between us. She presses up on her toes and smacks her lips against mine.

Before I can pull away she's dancing back with a manic laugh.

"Look at that." she breathes.

My nostrils flare. My body vibrates with irritation and now I'm the one murder happy.

Licking her lips the woman just winks and gives me her back. Addington is being pulled behind her but his eyes are on Ally the whole time.

"She's insane." Ally whispers beside me. I can hear the fear in her voice.

Nodding my head I'm lost for words and still fuming so instead of saying anything I follow behind the blue haired devil. It's not long after we reach a small area just inside the woods that I hear the distant sound of engines and muscle. Havoc's back. When the sound reaches Oakley her entire body relaxes creating even more questions about the weird dynamics of her pack of wolves. Two steps forward and I'm standing behind Addington shoving my knee into the back of his leg dropping him to the damp soil.

"Don't fucking move." I order.

By the time I turn I see four shadowed bodies heading our way. I can spot G a mile away, the shovel in his hand giving him away, a few steps ahead of the rest. Behind him West and Havoc walk to his right and Haven follows on the left a few feet further back. Her hair piled high on her head as she gets closer. I can see the way her eyes bounce around the area. When West finally approaches I step into him.

"What the fuck is with the kindergartner?" my tone is laced with venom.

He pulls back before it clicks. "Watch your mouth, brother."

One second. Two seconds. Three.

We both laugh, brushing off the tension in the air. Haven reaches us then with an annoyed look on her face.

"Are we done measuring dicks? Cause I have my money on a certain Stone." she rolls her eyes and heads over to Oakley's side.

West drags his eyes over her with a wicked grin that doesn't seem to phase the little dare devil. If she thinks she's playing an easy game she doesn't know West Stone.

"Easy brother." I chuckle, the sound so foreign it almost startles me.

The organ in my chest barely beating jumps a little with the sound.

Killer, what are you doing to me?

G drops the shovel at the feet of Addington, not giving him a second look before coming over to us to wait for what comes next.

"Where are they?" I ask.

West knows who I mean without mentioning them by name. The foundation comes when called no matter what time of night or day it is.

"I made the call. They'll be here. Until then why don't we get started? I'd hate to be here when the sun starts to come up." West says.

"You have more important plans?"

The question comes from Haven, shocking not only me but the rest of us. Oakley snickers but manages to look away for breaking out into a full on laugh. West moves forward an inch while G and Havoc just stare at the two fucking kids. I don't hear what West says. Instead I move to drag Addington to his feet, I bend to grab the shovel, and jam it into his chest. Grunting he doubles over to take the force without a fight.

"Dig."

His eyes dilate in fear. Finally.

By the time the hole is halfway done three figures begin walking towards us from the corner of the field. Even in the shadows the twins mirror each other making my skin crawl. Addington pauses his movements.

"Keep digging." I snap, forcing my foot into the back of his knee.

Eventually the hole is finished, the foundation reaches us, and my patience for this nonsense has gone.

"What did you call us here for, boy." one of the twins speaks.

"What is the meaning of this meeting?" the other twin adds.

Fully facing them I let my careful mask drop. "Remember who you speak to, thing one and two. I have no patience for games or riddles. I call, you come. That's exactly how this goes." I pull my shoulders back.

West comes to stand at my side with G two steps behind us in a show of support.

"Were done following the rules of the Foundation. The Stone family are the rightful heirs to which we claim tonight." West says.

"In light of traitors in our midst, we think it's time to remind the Foundation exactly what loyalty demands of you." I finish.

We are so in tune with our thoughts that we mimic the creepy twin sisters.

"Do you take us as fools?" Professor Jackson says.

G moves to the front. I wave him to the side, I am not concerned with the old man that has no filter.

"We don't really give a shit if you are or not. We've let you decide for us for too long and now we're putting an end to it."

"You're useless little spoiled brats who's father never taught you the value of hard work. Doing what must be-"

Addingtons words are cut off with a fist to the mouth by Oakley herself. Flexing her fingers she looks up at us.

"He was getting on my nerves." she states with a shrug.

The foundation members grow uneasy. G circling behind them forcing their footsteps forward giving them no free space to move. Havoc and Haven stand to the side, Havoc leaning on an oak tree, while Haven's eyes are locked on her phone screen. Jerking my head, I signal Oakley to pull Addington towards me.

"Ally." I call out.

Ally peeks at me through wet eyelashes from my left. Big doe eyes stare up at me with hesitant curiosity.

"You asked what I wanted from you."

She nods.

"Show me the loyalty you swear by."

West's brows furrow but ultimately he does nothing to stop me. Addington starts to laugh but Oakley lands a few more hits to shut him up. Blood flows from his nose and the corner of his mouth but still he stares at his daughter. His own flesh and blood.

"You think she has the balls to kill me?" he laughs.

Another hit.

"Who said she'd be the one killing you?" I question.

Tilting my head I extend my hand palm up. Without looking over, Oakley places a cold steel blade in my hand. It's not the same one she had earlier and I'm betting it's because that's her special knife but a blade is a blade and they all cut the same.

Ally gulps, "I'll do it."

She reaches for the knife but I snatch it out of reach. Crowding her space I tip her chin up with the tip of the steel end.

"Make one wrong move and I'll fucking cut you from stem to stern." I snarl.

Her head bobbles. Sweat building between her brows.

"We didn't come here for a power play made by children." Jackson grumbles.

Flicking a finger in G's direction he takes my signal for what it is and slams his fist into the back of his head sending him to the ground.

"Stay on your knees." G orders.

The twins watch with amusement. Freaky ass fuckers.

Holding the knife to Ally's palm I almost set it in her hand when Addington blurts out, "She knows why she's here. She'll carry out what needs to be done or she's next."

Tired of his voice I lunge forward grabbing him by the back of his neck.

"West." I bark.

West doesn't waste time waiting for directions; he knows what I want before I do. Placing both hands on each side of his head, West holds his still. With one hand I grip his bottom jaw, my fingers on the inside of his mouth, pulling his mouth open wide. With the other I hold the knife.

"G." I call out needing another hand.

G rushes over and grabs the fucking thing I plan to cut out of him.

"I told you I'm sick of your goddamn voice."

With one jagged slice his tongue is severed. Screams fill the night air scaring away any wildlife that was out here.

Blood pours from his mouth, his entire face red and purple from lack of air. His lungs empty of air from screaming.

"I told you you'd scream for me." kicking him in the chest he flies backwards.

"Ally." I shout. "I'm tired of the games. If you want to earn your place, plunge the knife into his throat."

The twins watch with amazement. Jackson has his eyes on the ground avoiding my stare. Haven doesn't look up from her phone while Havoc keeps close to his sister. Oakley bounces on her feet silently begging someone to step out of line. Grabbing the bloody knife Ally holds my stare for a few seconds. Walking over to her wailing father she presses her knee into his chest and kneels down. Her weight isn't enough to hold him so she struggles under his movements. I don't offer her help.

"Don't." I stop West with my hand on his chest.

I want to see her fight her dad for her survival. She's the reason Kenna has gone through half the shit she has. She set my girl up. She fed her to the snakes while she sat back and watched with popcorn at the ready. No one walks away from that without scars. Make no mistake once Kenna is back at my side I plan to watch her rip Ally apart but for now the hidden scars from tonight will have to do.

The two Addingtons war with each other. Pain blinds him while hesitation stalls her.

"Now." I snap.

No one moves.

One. Two. Three.

Suddenly Ally's body slams forward landing on top of her father. She doesn't move. Addingtons legs jerk.

Leaning forward, Ally looks down at her father, his lips moving but no sound reaches us. She drops her ear to his mouth. Slowly she adjusts so she's standing over him. The black handle of the knife sticks out from the side of his neck leaving a lifeless Addington lying in the dirt with blood flowing from his throat. Ally turns to meet my gaze. Shock and adrenaline mix together causing her body to vibrate with tremors. Moving towards me she stops a foot away covered in blood and sweat with a body dead behind her.

"I know who has Kenna." she says, before passing out.

Chapter Fourteen

GIO

Two Days later

"Long day?" the redhead behind the bar asks.

Her long wavy hair hangs down her side in a twisted side clip. Green eyes look me over but stops short when she spots the bloody and bruised skin around my knuckles. She doesn't flinch, her face doesn't twitch, nothing.

"Pour me another one and I might tell you." I rasp.

Rolling my shoulders to loosen the tight muscles around my neck I try to hold back the groan.

The redhead steps back over with the top shelf whiskey I've been tossing back for the past thirty minutes and tips it. The amber liquid spills into the glass until it reaches halfway up and she stops. I curl my finger signaling her to fill it to the brim. I fucking need it.

"What's your name?" I ask.

She doesn't seem interested in giving me a real name so she tosses some bullshit answer over her shoulder on the way back to the liquor cabinet.

"Mia."

I chuckle, "Ok, Mia. I'm -"

"I know exactly who you are, your Stone property." she quips.

The brat has a smart mouth and the puffy pouty lips to go with it. My dick stiffens with the low raspy laugh she lets out but still the comment fucking stings. I'm more than a damn runner. I'm their right hand. Trusted. Gripping the glass tighter than I should, I slam it back enjoying the burn as it slips down my throat. Dropping the glass on the wooden bar with a loud clunk I look up to meet her eyes.

"I'd watch that pretty little mouth of yours before it gets you in trouble." I sneer.

Rolling her eyes she comes over with a white wash rag to swipe up the drops I spilt on the counter. Bending to reach the far edge, her tits graze across the arm I have slung over the side of the bar. The black v-neck shirt she has on hugs her far too fucking tight. *Shit.* My eyes drop to the bare skin she flashes me drinking in the tattoos skin over her collarbone.

"Keep your eyes to yourself before it gets you in trouble." she shoots back at me.

Using my own damn words to pull me from eye fucking her I give her a half smirk half sneer before I stand. She must think I'm walking away because she makes her second mistake for the night by turning her back on a fucking snake. With both hands on the wood I sling myself over the side to land on the other side of the bar where she's standing. She freezes.

Pressing my front to her back I let her feel the heat of my body against hers. Slipping my arm around her I slowly slide it up her stomach, across her chest, to land around her throat. The dark ink swirling around my arm stands out against her pale skin. Tilting my head my lips graze her ear.

"I could fuck you right here and no one would stop me. Tempt me again, little tease, and I'll show you who's property you are." I snarl.

I can feel her muscles tighten, but she doesn't try to fight me off. Yet.

"Whatever you say, wannabe." she says, her voice far too fucking steady.

This girl either has no survival skills or she's too airheaded to know how dangerous I am right now. On the fucking edge pushed too far. Teetering on the cliff ready to jump. Biting into the curve of her neck I tighten my hold on her throat.

"Easy, little tease. I wouldn't push your luck."

She laughs. In a move too fast she slams her elbow into my ribs while spinning to where she faces me with a knife pressed into my throat.

Where the fuck did she get a knife?

My eyes dart over her form looking for a place she could have stored the weapon but come up empty. Her jeans hug her curves perfectly there's no way she fit it there. She smiles wide flashing me her pearly white teeth and cocks her head.

"Do you know who I am?" she questions.

She leaves it hanging there like I should know her. I don't, but fuck I'm about to or at the very least my dick is. Curling my lip I push her hand away from my throat and step back into her.

"Damn," I lick my lips letting my tongue twist my lip ring, "Don't start something you can't finish." I say, grabbing her hand.

Forcing her to trail down my leather jacket to the bulge in my jeans I press her palm over my dick.

"I can't wait to sink into your cunt." I spit.

Letting the venom in my words settle over her I shove her off me into the back glass and storm out of the bar. If I don't get away from the tease I'll fuck her right there where she stands. Opening the door I don't look back letting the door slam behind me. Pulling out my cell I check for any updates but when I come up empty I decide it's time to work off some of this steam. So I head to the one place that does exactly that. The Basement.

"Come on, G. My man." the man begs.

Fucking beggers. All of them. The closer I appear to be more to the Stone brothers the more people expect a hand out. It's a goddamn mad house in here tonight and without Ryker in here to put on a show I have to find the fun. Shaking my head I push past the young guy who has a death wish to go over to my boy Easton.

"Yo bossman!" he hollers over the loud ass screams and cheers.

Giving him one nod I step up and check in on the guys and get a breakdown of the night.

He looks to the left before his brown eyes meet mine again, "We need something to settle these fuckers. Blood thirsty ass crowd we have tonight." he grumbles.

When the crowd wants something gnarly it's almost impossible to calm them without a Stone appearance.

"Give them a show." I spread my arms wide not giving a fuck who I hit in the process.

His brows furrow, "Who the hell is going to give them what they want, when what they want is Ryker?" he questions.

"Let me worry about that." I respond.

Sliding my jacket off I start to take off my black crewneck when he smiles. Nodding with understanding he claps his hands and leans one hand behind him motioning for the mic. I continue to strip down to nothing but my boxers. Before he speaks a woman with tiny ass shorts on and a blue sports bra walks up with a pair of gym shorts.

Perfect.

"Well, well, well. Do I have a gift for you sadistic fuckers tonight." Easton shouts into the mic.

The crowd turns all eyes on our circle. My clothes on the

floor, shirt gone, and a pretty little thing wrapping my fist. Not that I need it but I'm already sporting fucked up knuckles.

"We have a special addition tonight! Our boy G has decided to give someone hell tonight." he shouts and the crowd goes insane.

Sweaty bodies close in on us but my boys spread out to shove them off giving us room. Easton steps up to me and throws an arm over my shoulder. We head to the ring in the center of the room while he continues.

"Who's the lucky son of a bitch that gets to go against one of the most powerful men in Del Mar?" he says.

Silence falls over the room. Eyes scan the room looking for someone stupid enough to climb under the ropes with me.

"Most powerful men in Del Mar?" a voice says, letting out a snark laugh.

Easton's head shoots to the right looking for the voice.

"And who gave him that position?" the voice asks.

My skin heats, the blood pumping through my veins on fire, I shrug Easton's arm off me. Waiting for this bitch boy to show his face I move around in a small circle with my arms spread wide.

"For someone who won't step up you talk mad shit." I bark out.

I don't need the mic. My voice carries through the room because there is no sound, nothing but heavy breathing and the squeak of shoes. Black hair and green eyes step through the sea of bodies, his face unfamiliar.

"This is me stepping up." he slides his hands into his pocket.

His relaxed stance and loose appearance does nothing to me. I'm slim. Not built like a gym rat but carved with muscle from everyday labor and heavy lifting. Most people underestimate me because of that but they have no idea how hard I've had to fight to get to the top. Ryker only admits it when I have him on his ass but we both know I'm his equal match.

Raising my eyebrows I give him what he wants, "Then let's get this party started."

I give him my back knowing that even if he was dumb enough to try anything Easton would put him down before he got the chance. Leaning over the rope I climb into the ring and make my way to the far side giving him plenty of time to change his mind but like a fool he doesn't. We both hype up the crowd but the only thing they cheer for is blood and gore so I don't waste my time with theatrics.

We both step to the center to shake hands but I drop mine before he touches me.

"Around here we show respect but since you seem to be new so I'll save you the trouble."

He leans back on his heels with a wicked grin.

"You'll know who I am soon," he says.

I laugh. Then I lunge forward with a right hook slamming into the side of his jaw swinging his head to the side spraying blood from his mouth. He doesn't miss a step, righting himself, he bounces on the balls of his feet. Using one hand he swipes at the blood rolling down his chin. Winking, I step back twice giving him room to make his move.

We dance back and forth until the crowd gets restless for the taste of violence. Hands smack the edge of the ring shouting and cursing at us to make our move. Using the distraction I rush him landing blow after blow to his ribs, side, and face. He lands a few hits that sting my already sore body. We match each other blow for blow until he makes his second mistake of the night. The first was to challenge me in front of the people in this room.

"It's going to be fun watching my father take what should

be ours while the Stone family falls. It's already begun." he breathes out.

His chest heaves from the force of my last blow but his words ring in my ears pushing me harder. Anger. Rage. Kenna. Cole. Madness. It all floods my vision until all I see is red. Using my left leg I hook him behind the knee taking him down to the ring floor. My hands scream in pain. My arms get heavier with the force of each blow. Both arms swing into his face until I fall forward from exhaustion. Before he can throw me off I use all my force to slam my knee into his ribs pulling a loud scream from his throat.

Sweat covers my body. Blood drips from my eyebrow into my eye. My lungs struggle to pull in air. The crowd goes crazy around me. Rolling off of him I lay on the mat looking up at the bright white ceiling. Easton's eyes meet mine when he comes to stand over me. He has two of our guys drag the fucker from the mat while he just looks down at me with a questioning gaze. Mine matches him.

Who the fuck is he? And what the hell did he mean?

Chapter Fifteen

KENNA

Pick.

Scrape.

Pick.

My skin crawls from the sound the sharp edge makes against the tile. Hot water and steam cover my skin. The tip of my knuckle drags down the edge cutting my soaked flesh. I ignore the pain, the bright red liquid gliding down my skin, I ignore it all.

Pick.

Scrape.

Pick.

The skin around my nails peels back.

Look what you're doing to yourself.

Tears mix with the water falling down my face. The combination of water and blood make beautiful swirls down the tile wall. The crack slowly growing bigger.

Stop this madness. You're getting nowhere.

I can't. I have to keep trying.

For who? Them? Ha. Have you learned nothing? It's been two months and no one has come.

Pick.

Scrape.

Pick.

Pulling my fingers away from the wall to examine them my eyes fall to the damage. My nails are chipped away revealing soft pink flesh under the nails. Blood and skin fall from the tips like ash pooling at the bottom of the tub. My chest aches from the pain, but the darkest part of my mind tries to cloud the pain. My forehead falls to the cold shower wall in defeat. My breathing turns ragged, my fingertips no longer hurting, the water hitting my back turning colder.

We are safe here. Stop trying to ruin everything!

Please. Please just shut up!

Shaking my head the motion drags my forehead across the tile rattling my thoughts. The water is colder. My skin pruning. The small triangle piece of tile in my other hand is pinched between my fingers digging into the wet skin. Fisting around the sharp edge a sudden wave of rage fuels me. Lifting my head I take my right hand and slam it into the small hole over and over.

Stabbing. Dragging the edge down the wall. Blood and water.

You're breaking.

I was always broken!

I want to scream. To slap myself. To take the pointed edge and slice through my own skin. Paint these walls with my blood like I did with Jax. I deserve to suffer for what I've done. Nothing makes sense anymore.

Pick.

Slam.

Stab.

I continue this routine until my arms are heavy and sweat mixes with blood and water. My body trembles from exhaustion. Or could it be the frozen water cascading down my body?

I wonder if I'll die from hyperthermia.

I muse to myself but the bitch in my ear just laughs.

When he comes in here to see the mess you've made, what do you think he'll do?

A small flash of fear courses through me at the reminder of the collar still in place around my throat.

You know how to get rid of the collar, Kenna.

Shaking my head I ignore the voice in my head. She may be right but I refuse to think of that.

Look at you!

NO.

Turning away from the wall of the shower I throw the broken tile into the corner and let out a loud wail. Dropping to my knees my fingers throb when I shove them into my hair. Tugging at the strands, my body moves on it's own. Rocking in a familiar motion.

Get up.

My legs start to go numb from the chill reaching my bones.

GET. UP.

I continue to rock. The images scattered across the bedroom wall flash through my thoughts. A reminder of how little I matter.

You matter to Hank. He is your Ryker now.

Bile threatens to come up. My stomach quivering with the picture of Hank merging with Ryker. Hank's salt and pepper hair drifting into dark strands and brown eyes. Blue- brown. Back and forth.

He's ours and we are his. Let him show you.

Oh god.

Footsteps approach the bathroom. Fuck, I didn't hear the bedroom door close.

Prove to him that he can trust us. He is our Ryker now.

Lifting my head I stand too fast shooting a numbness through my legs. Moving to shut the water off I slip my hands under the water to clean them. The blood has slowed but the damage is done. The doorknob turns in time for him to see me step out of the tub with a large grey towel around me. A sigh escapes past my lips when his eyes meet mine. Blue. Brown. My vision betrays me. His now dyed hair appears darker in the bright light of the bathroom.

"Princessa." he says.

His tone is flat while his gaze assesses me. I've pulled the curtain back to cover the mess but he must sense something because he takes a step forward.

Show him.

Swallowing around the lump in my throat I give him a soft smile. His steps falter when I slowly begin moving towards him. Two steps later and I'm only inches away. Lifting my hand I rest my palm on his chest looking up to meet his stare. Pulling in a deep breath I let the chains of my mind break away freeing me from the past.

Free us.

My lips part, "Ryker." I breathe.

His eyes dilate with the name. Our chests rise faster, the oxygen between us thinning, until we are only a breath away. He closes that gap bringing my chest to his.

Show him.

Pushing up on my toes I watch for any sudden movement before I lean in softly planting my mouth on his. Twisting his fingers in my hair, his hold tugs me closer, pressing me into him harder. Drinking down the taste of my lips his tongue trails the seams of my mouth begging for entrance. Humming his approval when my lips part he dips his tongue inside my mouth and starts to lap up everything I give him.

Pulling away he leans down to my ear, "There she is."

Chapter Sixteen

RYKER

"Where the fuck is he?" I shout.

Haven flinches at the sudden noise which sends West spinning around to face me.

"Easy, brother." he says, his tone a warning.

My muscles strain with the urge to do something. Continuing to sit here watching them fuck around on computers, watching camera footage, and retracing steps. It's driving me fucking crazy. Havoc leans over the back of the couch, his eyes trained on me.

"Watch your tone with my sister." he says, his jaw clenching.

Oakley giggles beside him, her hand trailing up and down his arm, I'm guessing she's trying to keep him calm. Two protective ass alpha men with their eyes trained on each other? That's a whole lot of bullshit I don't have time for. Yet, he's right. I'm taking it out on his sister who is only trying to help and here I stand demanding more of her.

"Now that I know who I'm looking for it won't be long. I've already found a trace of him in town several months ago." Haven says, her voice firm.

Haven's fingers continue to fly across the keyboard. Ally steps around the corner coming from the back bedrooms bringing the temperature in the room lower. Ice slides through my veins at the sight of her so I turn my attention back to the computer.

"Don't you play on computers?" Oakley asks.

Knowing she's talking to Ally I tune in to make sure nothing pops off. She's a violent little thing.

Ally's voice is right behind me when she responds, "Yes."

It's a simple answer. Stepping around me she looks down at the monitor that's lit up with different squares that house several screens in one. Haven has it running separate operations at once to work faster. Not that it's helping at this point. It takes effort to keep my foot from tapping with impatience.

"May I?" Ally asks Haven.

Haven looks back at me before her eyes find West. They don't speak, but something passes between them before her shoulders relax from the stiff position she sat on. Pushing away from the desk she stands to face me.

"He's been around town, but not in the last month. The main place he's been spotted on camera has been near or at the prison. Any reason he'd visit there?" Haven asks.

Haven's question triggers something in the back of my mind that has me spinning on my heels towards the door.

"Ryker." West snaps at my sudden movement.

Looking over my shoulder I see all eyes are on me. Ally jerks her attention away and takes the chair Haven was just at. Her fingers start to fly over the keyboard faster than I've ever seen and a small spark of hope flares in me. Maybe she'll be useful after all.

"Rye." West says.

Our gaze meets again. Oakley and Havoc go back to their conversation on the couch while Haven keeps her attention focused on West. These two need to fuck it out of their system before we have a problem. Shaking that thought from my head I turn from Haven towards him. I see the wary look behind his eyes and how exhausted he is from trying to hold this family together. Part of me feels guilty for putting all of this on his shoulders but I'm far too close to the edge to turn back now.

"Kingston. Hank was visiting Kingston in jail when Kenna first came back to town. That's who he's been going to see." I state.

West nods before it fully registers with him. The reminder triggers the same memory I have of our time tracking my little killer.

"Shit. Do you think he set this up to have her removed from our hands?" he asks.

It's the obvious answer yet for some reason it doesn't feel right. Kidnapping his daughter?

"I don't know but I'm about to find out." I spit.

West reaches out to grab my shoulder. His hand clamps down hard to hold me in place while his eyes bore into mine.

"What are you planning to do?" he questions.

His eyes look over me searching for something. His worry is palpable.

"I'm just going to pay him a visit, brother." I reply.

Besides, he's behind bars. What could I possibly do to him inside? West must see the ideas flashing through my eyes because his darken.

"You're taking someone with you." he orders.

My fists clench at my sides. Taking two steps forward I face off with my brother.

"You're taking someone with you." he repeats.

He doesn't back down. After a few seconds I laugh brushing off the small pissing contest.

"Fine, brother. I'll take Haven so she can take her eyes off the computer for a while." I quip.

Havoc and Oakley's heads snap towards us with suppressed grins. He wants to push me? Fine, but I'm going to have a little fun.

"Oh shit." Haven mutters beside West.

Her caramel hair is braided down her back, a fitted black outfit hugs her curvy figure, her wide eyes shining with mirth. West's arm extends blocking her way to the door when she starts to step towards me.

"It'll be fine." she says. "I've never been inside a prison before." she shrugs with a grin.

Her attempt to make a joke does nothing to the broody fucker staring me down but he drops his arm and let's her pass. When she reaches the door next to me he curls his lip.

"Don't fucking try shit while she's with you." His tone is stiff.

Havoc sinks into the couch, "Haven." he calls.

Her head whips to her brother sitting next to Oakley.

"There and back." he demands.

My skin starts to itch while Haven lets out an annoyed sigh. All of this fucking back and forth is wasting my time.

"We're losing time. Haven, go get in the car." I look at Havoc, "I've got her. Oakley, keep these bastards in check, will ya?"

Turning I ignore the two fuckers bickering behind me to follow Haven out the apartment. It's midday and visitation ends in a couple hours so we waste no time climbing in the SUV and speeding down the road. Thirty minutes into the silent drive Haven opens her mouth to speak when we turn into the parking lot. Barbed wire, grey buildings, and dull landscaping expand ahead of us.

"This place is depressing." she comments.

I almost laugh at the conviction in her voice, but I shove

it down. I've been able to cage the beast in my chest to focus on finding Kenna, but my patience is wearing thin. The way my soul yearns for her touch, the way her cherry flavored lips taste, fuck. I swore I'd kill Kingston if I ever saw him again and now he may be the only one who knows where Hank is. Hank Harlow was a college friend of our fathers. They all went to school here where my father and Kingston took this place by storm. Meeting their wives here they all learned that becoming powerful couples means status. Money. Control. Hank was left behind and long gone from the picture around the time we were in middle school.

Opening my door I go to step out when Haven stops me. From the corner of my eye I can see her hand hovering over my arm with hesitation before it falls.

"Shouldn't we leave our stuff in the car? They won't let us move through security if we don't." she says.

Once I'm standing I dip my head to look at her.

"They won't stop me." I state.

Rolling her eyes she sighs, "That may be, but they will stop me. I have no clout in this town." she grumbles.

It's not the first time one of the Wolves bitched about being in Del Mar where their name isn't a threat falling from tongues. Where our name could straighten a man's spine theirs is nothing but a cliff note. One mentioned out of curiosity instead of fear. In Del Mar the Wolves are a myth and Oakley would cut tongues if anyone so much as said that to her face.

"You're with me. Let's go."

I don't wait for her to catch up with me. My strides are long and quick. The first set of metal gates open into a long concrete walkway surrounding us by barbed wire fences. Haven follows behind me keeping up with my pace. Reaching the second gate a loud buzz sounds opening it automatically. Cameras are placed in several areas over us so I turn towards one to show my face fully and the look I convey isn't one to ignore. Rolling my hand to motion for the second gate to hurry I step through as soon as I know I can fit. Haven sticks to my side like glue but I can see the way she searches the walls looking for something interesting. She's a curious little kitty.

Once we make it past the gate there are two double doors with glass rectangle windows. Tugging on the handle the door swings open letting a gust of cold air out as we step inside. The bright white lights bounce off the grey walls damn near blinding me but my eyes adjusted with a few blinks. Haven picks up her speed to keep in step with my long strides until we reach a glass box area where you check in to see the inmates. A beast of a woman with a name tag addressing her as Hulga slides in front of us.

"Please sign in." she says, her voice matching her looks. Gruff.

She stands almost as tall as me but my build makes me wider giving me an advantage forcing her to look up at me. Something I can tell she isn't used to and I don't give a shit. Haven looks between us before popping a hand on her hip to respond.

"We're here to see Kane Kingston, so please move." she smarts.

Her tone is soft but she doesn't hide the bite in her words. Hulga looks down at her like a lion ready for a snack so I sidestep into the beast's line of sight to cut her off from Haven. The last thing I have time for is trouble with two over protective fuckers about a little brunette kitty kat.

"Ryker Stone." I hold out my hand for her to shake.

Tossing out my name she snaps her eyes to mine but still she stands there blocking the entrance. I move forward brushing my chest against hers in a challenge when a small lanky arm shoves between us pushing Hugla backwards.

"Mr. Stone." a voice says to my left.

Turning to see a short blonde haired man with large oval glasses resting on his face, my brows furrow. He looks at Hulga flashing her a lethal glare before turning his attention back to me with a grim smile. I know that look. The one behind his eyes. Pure fear. This man is pissing his pants right now but he hides it well so I respect that. Motioning with his head for her to move he waves his hand out for us to follow him.

"Well that was almost fun." Haven whispers beside me.

Shaking my head without a response we follow the man through the metal detectors where he doesn't flinch when it goes off. We continue past two large metal doors until we reach the third one on the right. The grey brick walls resemble high school walls but with less life. Depressing as fuck. Opening the door he steps back to let us pass him where we enter a large mess hall style room with over a dozen lunch tables spread around. Looking over the room I spot a few vending machines, inmates chatting with family, and guards standing throughout the space keeping an eye on things.

"I'll have Mr. Kingston brought out. Please, sit anywhere you'd like." He says, rushing off to do just that.

Snickering, Haven walks over to a table in the corner of the far back wall where we have a view of the entire room. There are three inmates at the table but she just crosses her arms and taps her foot. One of the men is covered in dark ink and swirls of black with a long ponytail down his back. You can tell he's been here a while by the way body language adjusts when we approach. Sucking his teeth he smiles at Haven with intent but when he sits up straight to speak his eyes meet mine and he pauses.

"Well if it isn't Ryker fucking Stone." he laughs.

Looking at the men around him he nods his head when he looks back at me.

"Landon." I state blankly.

Jumping up he rushes towards me and grabs my arm pulling me into him. Haven jumps back spinning towards me, but stops when Landon yanks me into a hug.

"Call me that again and I'll beat the shit out of you." he gruffs in my ear.

Pulling away I laugh, "And what the hell do I call you?" I ask.

Both hands slap his chest, "Python."

We both let out a loud laugh pulling the eyes of the other people in the room.

"Like the snake?" Haven asks beside me, reminding me of her presence.

We both look down at her but Landon is already pulling up the sleeve on his white shirt flashing her the tattoo of a ball python wrapping around his arm spreading from his wrist to the crease of his elbow.

"That's right, pretty lady. Snakes for life." he winks at her.

Moving back to me his eyes roam over my appearance before asking me why I'm here.

"I have an appointment with a certain Kingston." is all I give him.

He nods in understanding. Landon and his crew have been vital in keeping this place in line on the inside. Every once in a while I have to give Kingston a little visit to show him who still has control.

"Anything new?" Landon asks.

Rolling my tongue ring over my bottom lip I look to the ceiling, "Kenna Kingston is missing. Has been for two months. I'm tearing apart the entire west side to find her. This is just a pit stop for clues."

He doesn't ask anything else, just offers help if we need it.

Landon taking his groupies to another table giving me the one they were sitting at without a fight.

"That was unexpected." Haven laughs.

Sitting down on the bench pressed against the wall I lean back to rest on the brick. My eyes search the room when I respond.

"Like I said. Stone family name comes in handy." My tone is flat.

My muscles tense when I spot a familiar face being shoved toward us by a guard. Rolling my shoulders I wait until they reach us before I look the man charged with my father's murder in the eyes. Familiar grey eyes peer at me sending a rod of lightning through my body. My hand fists, rubbing the ache from my chest, one he notices.

"Ryker." he greets me.

His eyes are sunken and tired. His clothes are loose and hang from his body showing his weight loss. Kane Kingston looks like he's lost years from his life.

"You look like shit." I state the obvious.

He chuckles but it falls flat. Haven shifts in her seat pulling his gaze to her.

"And who do we have here?" he asks.

Haven goes to speak but I interrupt her with a hand held up.

"Don't speak to her. We have more important shit to handle than you needing to know her name."

He huffs out a laugh dropping down onto the bench across from me. Folding his hands on the table he asks the one question I hoped he wouldn't.

"Where's my daughter?" he looks around the room to check for her but comes up empty.

Fuck, I wish she was here. His gaze searches my face, the way I tense at the question, and he sees it immediately.

"Who?" he asks.

"That's why I'm here talking to you instead of out there searching for her. We got a name but it's someone more familiar to you." I accuse.

He jerks back with his brows dipped. "Who the fuck has my daughter?" he barks.

Kane Kingston may be behind bars. He may be innocent for the murder of my father but Kane Kingston shouldn't be passed off as a non threat because he's a fucking Kingston.

"You had a guest here a few months back more than once. Why was he coming here to see you and what would he want with Kenna?"

He rubs his beard with his hand, "Who?" he asks.

Irritation flares through me, "Don't play games with me. If you have her somewhere safe just to keep from me I need to know now. She's been gone for two fucking months and I need to know she's safe!" my fist slams down on the table.

He leans forward inching closer to me, "Two months? She's been out there with some fucker for two months and you haven't found her yet?" he sneers.

I can see the vein in his neck throbbing, turning his face bright red.

"Little old man, where the fuck is she?" I'm losing control of the beast.

Haven sits up but with one look she slinks back again.

"Tell me this, Kane. Why was Hank Harlow sniffing around and sneaking to come see you?" I snap.

He sits upright with an alarmed look crossing his face. "Hank?" he breathes.

His hands start to shake, sending me over the edge with worry. Kane may be the man that possibly betrayed my father but he's Kenna's dad and seeing this reaction from that name has me on high alert.

"Kane talk to me. What the fuck does this mean? Tell me

what he wants from her." I'm tossing questions at him left and right but he just sits there stuck in thought.

Slapping the table I lash out, yanking him by the shirt towards me. "Look at me, fucker. You need to start talking and I mean now."

Closing his hand over my hold he twists my wrist, forcing my hold to loosen.

"Touch me again boy and you'll remember who I am."

His threat holds weight and gets my attention. My breathing picks up putting weight on my chest. My lungs feel like they might explode.

"He doesn't want her to get to me or you. He wants *her.*" he says.

Bile lines the back of my throat at his implication. Some sick old fuck has my girl. Has had her for two months without anyone to stop whatever he has planned for her.

Kane leans in again, "You love her." he states.

It's not a question but a blatant declaration.

"What's love?" I spit. "Affection? Lust? Attraction? Love has nothing on what I feel for Kenna and I plan on making her realize that when I have her back." my lip curls.

He looks away, licking his lips, "He won't stop until he finds a way to keep her. You need to get her back before he breaks her spirit."

"Breaks her spirit? Do you even know your daughter?" I growl.

He looks me in my eyes, "Hank was a foundation member or almost one. He knows how to break even the strongest person. What do you think we were teaching you kids all those years?"

The reminder of those days sends a cold chill down my spine. Fuck, killer.

"What do you know?" I demand.

"I know that I'm only sitting here to protect my daughter.

I know that I didn't and would never set up your father. We both lost someone that day, boy."

"Call me a fucking boy one more time."

Haven snickers beside me. Two guards pass by the table with alert eyes but continue walking when I give them a feral look.

"Ryker, I damn near raised you. You are a boy to me."

"Get back to Hank. Where can we find him?" I ask.

Lowering his voice, "I suggest you look a little closer to home once you do find her. I don't know where he might take her but I do know he wouldn't make a move without permission. And that call is made from inside the family."

What he's saying isn't registering with me. Someone inside the family? Stone or Kingston?

"What-" A loud screech stops my next words.

"Visitation hours are coming to an end. Say your goodbyes and all visitors head to the exit." a shrill voice says over the intercom.

Shooting to a stand I move around the table coming to stand next to Kane. Haven follows but doesn't move from behind me.

"Find my girl, Ryker. Don't let the ties you hold keep you from doing what's needed." he says, slapping me on the back before walking away.

Haven and I head towards the SUV with more questions than answers. Hank has had two months to break Kenna and now I have to turn inward to find the snake who fed her to the monster.

Fuck.

Chapter Seventeen

KENNA

Rough hands trail up my naked spine to grip the back of my neck. Leaning back, my eyes meet his. Blue fades to brown my eye glaze over until the room is fuzzy. Steady hands guide me towards the bed, my stare never leaving his. My heart pounds in my chest at the implications of my actions but I can't seem to slow the train-wreck I'm causing. Wild and out of control he leads me downhill towards a massacre.

"Princessa." he groans against my skin.

Chills rush down my exposed flesh covering me in pebbles that ache with his touch. Blinking is the only escape from his piercing stare as my knees press against the edge of the bed. With one steady hand he pushes me back until my ass meets the cool sheets. My teeth clamp shut at the contact. All thoughts leave me when the other hand tugs the towel away leaving me bare and exposed.

Hunger and greed grow behind his eyes turning brown and blue eyes into black pools of heat. The pressure in my chest grows bigger with each touch. With each caress. Fear and want. Need and disgust. They swirl and battle in my stomach leaving me swimming with dizziness.

"Lay back." he orders.

His voice is garbled behind the fuzzy blanket covering my mind. Somewhere between a dream and nightmare I'm caught in the crosshairs of hell. My body does as he declares without a fight but the images in my head of someone else standing over me fight for dominance. My head hits the bed as the air leaves my lungs leaving me breathless and vulnerable. Pressing the inside of my thighs, the muscles in my legs clench in an attempt to preserve the final bit of life I have left, but they open wide for him anyway.

"Look how needy you've become for me," he says.

His control is slipping. I lean my neck forward to look at the man standing above me fully dressed. His gaze heats my skin and I fucking float higher. Above my body I see the woman he made. Skin and bones. Burns and branded. Kenna Kingston died and left a shell in her place. Trailing his fingers up and down the crease of my thigh he spreads me open letting the cold air hit my heated core.

"I want to hear you call my name." he grunts.

Falling to his knees, my core is mere inches from his mouth. The heat of his breath brushes over me making me clench. Human contact has become so foreign that I begin to crave anything he feeds me. And fuck does he feed me everything he has to offer. It only takes two seconds before he drops his warm mouth over me lapping at me. I float higher and higher.

Am I dying?

I want to beat against the chains that hold me here but I'm frozen under his hold. Fingers dig into my skin bruising the sensitive flesh between his hands. I'll always have these bruises to carry with me even after they fade but I open wider for him still. My body moves on instinct inviting him deeper. Closer. Giving him the opening he needed by the sound of his answering groan against my clit. It's everything and nothing all at once. Sucking at the swollen clit in his mouth, trembles take over the body left in my place. Her hair fans out over the bed in an ashen shade of blonde.

Teeth bite down on the lip of her pussy.

"Scream for me." he orders.

It's more of a demand than a plea and her mouth obeys. Dry lips fall open on a cry when he rewards her by sucking on the sore lip. Plunging his tongue inside, adding a finger and curling it. Pain and pleasure collide in a rainbow of ash and fire. Toes curling, I watch her come undone for him. Lashing out dainty hands grip the sheets on both sides of her and my eyes widen. The ceiling is so close now. Floating higher his shoulders bunch under the weight of her legs circling him.

"Ryker!" her voice cracks with a wail.

Darkness clouds the edge of my vision with her release. The power he holds over her cloaking her body like a worn beaten blanket.

"That's it, Princessa." he coo's.

Standing, he slowly unbuttons his jeans. Her lifeless legs hang empty against the edge of the bed. My gaze meets her broken stare, our souls clashing together. Her pain breaks through the numbness until all I feel is betrayal and need. The orgasm high still rings through her blood singing against the ache in her chest. Tears prick my eyes at the train-wreck below me.

"Fuck, you are soaked for me." he moans.

Stroking his cock she keeps her eyes locked on mine. I'm the one stuck watching the flames die into smoke around us. Moving over her his hot breath blows her hair from her face with a sigh. Thick fingers dive inside her pressing and probing against her. Her legs lift, bringing her knees to his side on instinct.

"I want to feel your pussy squeezing me. I've waited so long for this, Princessa." he says, against her neck.

She watches me. I watch her. He presses into her. Deeper. Harder. Her body responds with his movements slowly. Like warming up after a cold shower. Our breathing picks up mine mirroring hers until our lungs scream from the weight.

"Fuck." he growls.

Deeper. Harder. Bruising hold on her hips. Pulling her closer. His teeth sink into her neck biting until blood drips from her. My eyes water. He rises over her broken body to grip her throat. The metal collar bites into her raw flesh forcing a cry past her lips.

"Come for me." he demands.

Forceful tremors rush through her, her body obeys the demand once again. Her legs lock around his waist as he goes deeper. Dragging her into him by her throat he tosses his head back while they come together. Broken and frayed, the pieces of the woman on the bed shatter before my eyes. I'm no longer floating instead I fall. Falling fast. Our bodies collide into the train-wreck I caused.

"So good," he mumbles.

His heavy body covers ours forcing the air from our chest. Heaving, we struggle to breathe. Standing he pulls up his pants without cleaning himself off and stares into our eyes. Her eyes. Mine.

"Clean yourself up," he says.

His tone is empty and tired. My exhaustion is bone deep leaving me unable to move so I nod instead. He moves towards the door leaving me bare and dripping. Opening the door he looks back at me over his shoulder.

"You taste better than I ever imagined."

Shutting the door, I'm left alone. Turning towards the wall my knees meet my chest, my eyes falling closed. Sinking into the bed I drift into the darkness that welcomes me.

Trees blur past the windows on the way back to the apartment.

That call is made from inside the family.

Kingstons words echo in my head. Someone put Kenna in the hands of a fucking obsessed old man with intent to have her removed from my hold. Coming up on my turn I slam onto the breaks and jerk the wheel to the right.

"Goddamn, Ryker." Haven snaps from the passenger seat.

Ignoring her I step on the gas once the vehicle straightens back out sending us down the two lane road far past the speed limit. Haven's phone rings pulling both of our attention from the road. Neither of us are expecting a call but somehow the oxygen in the air is sucked into a vacuum. Her eyes flit from mine to the lit up screen before her finger slides the green button to the right answering the call. Turning back to the road I hit the breaks less than a yard away from our next turn stopping in the middle of the street without a fuck given.

"What are you doing?" She asks, looking over her shoulder out the back glass.

Tipping my head towards her phone, I wait for her to speak.

"West." She says.

My brows raise in question, but she ignores me to listen to the other end. I can't say I'm surprised that West already has the girl's number, but what does surprise me is the fact that she gave it to him. Haven's been a fucking kitty with claws when it comes to my middle brother, but that's shit for another day. Rolling my hand I press her for information but she's stuck in place waiting for West to finish talking. Her head is bobbing, by the time the voice on the other end trails off her head is whipping towards me. My foot presses the gas to the floor spinning the tires clouding the car in smoke until we take off. I can see it in her eyes. They found her.

Haven drops the phone in her lap, chewing on the inside of her lip, she shifts to the side to watch outside the window. Three minutes. Five minutes. Almost there. Another turn, blowing through the final red light, the SUV drifts into the parking garage where a small group of people are standing outside a small blue Skyline and two bikes. Three out of the five are dressed in all black so it's easy to make out the Wolves from West and Ally except there's an extra person in the center of the group.

"Out." I order once the SUV is put in park.

Haven hesitates for a moment before rolling her eyes and sliding out the car. Shutting the door she bounces over to Oakley with a *what the fuck* look on her face. All eyes shift to me but I hit the lock on the door and pick up my phone.

Ring.

Ring.

"Sup?" The voice on the other end says.

Rubbing my lips together I let the silence hang between us for a second.

"Where have you been?" I press.

I let the accusation in my tone linger in the air giving him a second to respond.

He scoffs on the other end, "Have I not earned your trust, *Brother*." He hisses the last word.

Gripping the wheel I try to grab ahold of the last semblance of control I still have but calm is far from the emotion coursing through me.

"That may be, Brother, but I had a few things to handle." He sighs.

I realize that I'm pushing his limits but I can't reign it in at this point. I've been searching for somewhere to place this anger and right now he's the perfect target. The one person that is supposed to be here and when I look around he's the one missing.

"What's more important than finding Kenna?" I snarl.

Agitation sinks in my bones, "G." I snap when he doesn't respond.

"Ryker, I'm putting out a fucking fire that you shouldn't be concerned with right now. I'm sorry but you're just going to have to trust me on this one." He says, his tone tired.

"West said you were in the ring." I say.

West steps towards the front of the SUV, a questioning gaze crossing his face but I wave him off letting him know it's handled without a word.

"Yeah, that's a story for another time boss." G says.

"Don't fucking call me that. Get your ass to the apartment now." I demand.

A pause. Rustling in the background, a groan, and then silence.

"Do I have time to wash off the cheerleader?" He laughs.

The tense feeling in the air dissipates with his smartass remark. Oakley and Havoc look towards me from the middle of a conversation giving me a view of another man. One that I've seen before a few months back at The Basement.

"No. We found a location and I need you to ride with us. Whatever the fuck you've been doing can wait."

Hanging up I open the door to arguing coming from Oakley and West. The slam of my door has all eyes snapping to me. Walking to the front of the black SUV I look to West for the information I've been waiting for.

"Ally was able to focus on Hank's patterns and found that he only takes one way in and out of town." He stops.

This is a beach town with plenty of side roads and interstates but while that's weird it doesn't really mean shit to me right now.

"His car has only been seen in two places outside of the prison in town." Pulling out an iPad he zooms in on a map.

The screen is bright but my eyes quickly adjust to the light. West points to two red dots on the screen.

"This is a gas station." He points at a dot to the top left, "and this right here is a red light right outside of town." He points at the other dot.

"Is this all we have?" I ask.

How the hell are we going to find her with such a large area to search. Ally steps forward grabbing the iPad from West. Spinning towards her, he goes to reach out for her arm, but I'm yanking him back. Ally runs her tongue over the back of her teeth turning the iPad towards her tapping on the screen a few times before facing it back towards me. This time on the screen there is a photo of a large worn down building with overgrown grass around the sides. Large vines and bushes are growing up the side of the brick covering the graffiti across the sides.

"This building was purchased a month after Kenna came back to Hawthorne. I was able to access the deed and it has her name on it. Now, why would Kenna buy a dilapidated building outside of Del Mar?" Ally questions with a raised eyebrow.

"How would he have put it in her name?" Oakley asks from behind Ally.

Ally doesn't turn, refusing to give Oakley a pass, "I never said it was Hank. There was someone else on the deed, but the name was blacked out. It had to be someone from her family or someone who had access to her family's information. I don't know how, but I do know that this warehouse is the only thing in between both locations and it happens to have Kennas name on it." She says.

Havoc and the other male tug Oakley backwards to whisper in her ear. Her eyes find mine before a smile lights up her face. Clapping her hands she squeals and jumps over towards me. Literally fucking jumping.

"Let's go hunting!" She laughs.

Oakley's blue hair bounces with each skip she does heading towards the blue Skyline. Climbing in the passenger seat two of her men climb on their bikes, the other two missing from the picture. Haven looks towards West with a hard stare before turning away to slide into the passenger seat of Oakleys car. I can't move, my feet are stuck in place on the concrete.

"Ryker." West calls.

He sticks his head around the door to the SUV about to get in but stopping to wait on me.

"Let's go, Rye. Our girl is waiting on us." He says softly.

Ally passes me on the way to the backseat, but she stops beside me putting her hand on my shoulder giving it a squeeze.

"She'll forgive us eventually." She says, walking towards the back of the SUV.

I don't care if she forgives me, she has no choice in the matter. Kenna Kingston belongs to me. She's my broken little killer and in the end I always planned to burn us to the ground. Someone may have beat me to it, but I'll put her back together if only to watch the pretty little killer take me down with her. I crave the destruction she causes. Rolling my neck I open the driver door and get in. A blue blur flashes past us heading for the exit with two bikes following close behind. Looking to West we make eye contact for a breath. Shifting the SUV into drive I peel off leaving tire marks and smoke in my wake.

It takes thirty eight minutes to get to the warehouse that was in the photo. The building looks worse in person but I'm not taking note of this run down piece of shit. The sun is starting to set, turning the sky a deep orange and midnight blue. Reaching between my seats I grab the pistol stuffed there, closing my fingers around the cold steel. West and Ally have already unbuckled and opened their doors when I make a move to exit the SUV. No one speaks. We stay as quiet as possible making sure whoever is inside doesn't hear us coming.

"You're staying right here." Havoc points to Haven.

Her mouth opens to speak but Ally steps up beside her putting a hand on her arm.

"I'll stay out here with you. The less people walking through the building the less likely they are to be found." She says.

"Oh we want to be found." Oakley giggles, twisting the tip of a blade into the edge of her finger.

This woman looks like she's about to start whistling a tune. *Psycho.*

"Keep this one under control." I wave to Havoc and the other one, "name?" I ask.

"Silas." He responds.

Oakley pushes on her toes and kisses him on the chin giving Havoc a wink.

"Stop the weird shit and focus. West, you split up with Havoc and Silas. Oakley you're with me."

Both men start to speak, but Oakley steps forward, "This is going to be fun." She rubs her hands together with the knife in the center.

"Is she always like this?" Ally whispers but Oakley hears it anyway.

"Yep." She smiles with her teeth, but it looks more like a snarl.

Ally steps back and takes Haven with her, "Well be in the SUV." She says, looking at me.

Tossing her the keys I nod giving her the one and only chance she'll get to prove we can trust her. West and the guys are talking off the side when another car's headlights slowly pull up before shutting off. We duck down trying to get a good view of the vehicle, but they park behind an old dumpster. The sound of a door opening, shoes meeting rocks, the door shutting. Footsteps come closer. Standing, I look over the hood of my car to see a face I wasn't expecting walking next to G.

"What the fuck were you thinking?" I snap.

Storming towards them G holds his hands up in surrender, "Man, do you really think I could keep him away?" He says. "We don't have time for this shit. Let's go."

Walking past them all, I'm done waiting to have my hands on her soft skin. We make our way through the brush and weeds to a door on the backside of the building. West and the others slowly head towards the front, but G sticks with me and Oakley. Reaching for the door I twist the handle slowly making sure to not make a sound.

"It's unlocked. Cocky fucker." Oakley says.

The door opens to a room shrouded in darkness with only a small light coming from a door at the end of the hallway. Pulling out my phone for a flashlight I use it to navigate the open space.

"Fuck." G grunts.

Looking over at him, my eyes follow his line of sight. Lifting my phone to shine in his direction I finally see what he does. A single chair in a large square room with only one way out down a long hallway. The doors are wide open but it's the chair in the center of the room that has my stomach churning. A thud has me and G spinning the other direction. My light hits Oakleys face with a slight blush creeping up her cheeks.

"Oops." She whispers.

Her foot bumps into a chair against the wall where a table is pressed against the window giving the appearance that someone sat here to look out the window. The curtains are pulled back letting in the last bit of remaining light outside.

"He's been breaking her." Oakley says her voice is grim.

Walking towards the open door that leads to the hallway where the light is coming from I ignore her comment.

"Ryker, you don't know what we'll find. You need to prepare yourself for her-"

Twisting around I step into her face, "Don't finish that fucking sentence or you'll lose your tongue."

Sticking her tongue out in mock she wiggles it at me, "I'd love to see you try."

Pulling in a deep breath, I continue towards the doorway at the end of the long hall. My phone light hits the door shining against the dark green paint. A few steps into the hall and a foul smell hits me making me double over. Using the front of my shirt to cover my face I look back at the others before continuing forward again.

"It's behind this door." G says.

He points to a closed door a few feet ahead where the smell is coming from. Passing the door I hold my breath and keep moving.

"Check it out. Do what you need, but I'm finding Kenna." I toss over my shoulder.

G breaks away from us pulling out a knife from his belt loop to mess with the lock on the door. Coming up to the door with the light behind it I hear a slow steady thump against a wall. The sound is eerie and on beat.

Thump.

Thump.

Thump.

Oakley pauses beside me, both of us now just outside the door. Her blue eyes shine in the darkness, the only feature I can see through the shadows. Inhaling a lung full of air I motion for her to continue. Reaching for the door she turns the knob inch by inch.

"It's unlocked." She says barely above a whisper.

One second.

Two seconds.

Three.

The door opens. The light blinds me momentarily, preventing me from seeing in front of me. An inhale.

Thump.

Thump.

My hand rests on the pistol's trigger, unable to clear my vision. Once the white spots dissipates all the air in my lungs is pushed from my chest at the sight before me.

Chapter Nineteen

KENNA

Stuck in the in between space of sleep and consciousness my legs extend to stretch. They ache bone deep, my left more than the right, the skin too tight. I can still smell the remnants of his stale breath and sweat covering my skin. The sheets hold the stench of our sins in each thread of fabric. My stomach quivers with the emptiness but the thought of filling the void makes my mouth water with acid. Get up Kenna. Wash him off. My fingers slowly scrape down my arms pulling at the skin until it burns. Have you ever wanted to pull the flesh from your bones because the deep seated filth makes you feel like dying?

What did I do?

Tiny slivers of myself break off into shards that are too jagged to fit back into place. Parts of me are missing, gone, stolen from me.

This is my fault. I did this.

My hands grip at the roots of my hair and pull. Pulling and scratching trying to escape the person lying in this bed. I need to get up. The smells around me swirl through my nose burning the memories into my brain. Swallowing back the vomit that threatens to come up I roll over to see a small blue bowl filled with fruit. The overwhelming sweet smell wafts over to me combining with the stench. My stomach gurgles bubbling with disgust for the food. Licking my lips my eyes roam around the room looking for a hint of time. Time has held no meaning in these four walls, locked inside a loop, trapped unable to move forward.

I start to pull in a deep breath but choke on his smell. Kicking the blankets off my core is sore and raw.

Hot shower.

Just roll off the bed. Get up. You can do this. We need to shower. Come on Kenna get out of the bed. I can't move. Unable to lift the weighted blanket over my body I'm caged under the flashes of last night. With each blink I'm dragged back to the feel of him inside me.

I wanted this. I gave him control.

I have no tears left to fall. Instead I'm walking on glass cutting my skin on the shattered parts of me that I willingly smashed with my bare hands. How can I blame anyone but myself?

GET. UP.

Inching closer to the edge of the bed I grab my bare leg and drag it until it slips off the edge. Stiff shaky movements force me to sit up, the pressure on my chest threatens to pull me back under, the cold floor meets my feet. Breathe. In and out. Pressing my palms into the mattress I stand on weak limbs, my eyes falling closed to steady the dizziness. The horror behind my eyelids has them popping back open before I'm ready and I sway.

Pull it together.

I want to snap at myself. To face the ghost in the mirror and scream for her to wake up but her eyes are hollow and unfocused. Shifting to look at the pale faced, dull eyed, woman in the glass. Her hands mirror mine lifting to press against the skin under her eyes. Deep blue bruised skin sits under her blank stare. Moving my gaze lower, my eyes fall on the broken skin on her neck where large teeth marks are carved into her.

I'm his forever now.

Her collar bone juts out of her like a knife waiting to cut the hands that try to touch her. Biting the inside of my cheek I turn away from her probing gaze. Looking towards the door to the bathroom I take one small step at a time. Once I've made it inside I lean over to twist the water on wincing from the pain shooting down my legs. Between my thighs burns and my eyes water with the response to the pang. Steam starts to float from the shower so I turn and shut the door blocking it inside. Not waiting for the water to cool I step under the spray of hot water letting the heat sting my skin.

Maybe the hot water can boil the stained part of me that I want to cut away with a blade. Dropping my head to the damp tile wall my shoulders tense when the direction of my thoughts head to darker places. Trailing my fingers over the wall I find the broken piece of tile pulling the small triangle shard from its place. Twisting and turning the fragment between my fingers my thoughts start to fade to other places. Darker places where the numbness starts to crawl up my legs to my spine creeping into my chest gradually drowning me.

Jabbing the shard into the wall over and over dust starts to chip away with the force. Teeth dig into my bottom lip breaking the skin but I don't feel it. I no longer smell him yet I can still feel the way his fingers pressed into my skin so deep that the blood flowing through me rushes to the surface. My chest feels like it's going to explode with the way my heart is hammering behind my ribcage. My knuckles are sore from picking at the wall and I'm so fucking tired.

They did it. They finally did it and I gave them the key.

My fist slams into the wall, my mouth falls open with an

eerie hollow scream, my chest rattling through it. Snatching the soap from the side of the tub I pour a large amount into my palm and start to scrub. Arms, legs, neck, stomach, between my thighs. I scrub so long and so hard that my entire body feels raw. Red and sore I shut the water off letting the cold air hit me. Sucking in deep breaths my eyes start to grow fuzzy. It's a battle to get my mind to move but I manage to get myself moving to grab the towel sitting on the bathroom sink. Wrapping it around my body I let my soaked hair hang down my back not giving a fuck that water is still dripping everywhere. One foot after the other I step out of the tub and onto the floor.

My stomach bubbles again, my mouth filling with saliva, pushing bile up my throat. Heaving I rush for the toilet crashing into the floor on my knees I barely get my head over the toilet when yellow foam spills from my mouth. Empty stomach contents pour from my throat with each heave the pain almost too much. Rubbing my mouth on the back of my hand I steady myself with both palms on the toilet attempting to stand. My nose and eyes burn from the tears that try to spill but I have nothing left to give to this place. These four walls have taken everything I have leaving me empty and alone.

Ignoring the splintered woman in the mirror I pass her heading to the door without giving her a second thought. Pulling the handle steam rushes past me filling the next room. Stepping up to the dresser I search for a sports bra and shorts pulling out a small black top and short green gym shorts. My eyes catch on the tattoo between my breastbone sucking me out of the fog and shoving me into the memory of when I got it. Why I got it. The birds spread wings are covered in bright orange and red flames burning away the phoenix past. Her colorful head is tilted up taking flight, rising from the ashes, growing stronger.

Still staring at the ink etched into my skin I hear soft footsteps coming down the hallway. My hands start to shake causing my heart to beat faster. The handle jiggles. Pulling in a deep breath through my nose my eyes close waiting for him to open the door. The handle twists and the door is slowly pushed open. Two sets of eyes land on me but I don't move. Sky blue and brown eyes widen when they meet mine, the air in the room suffocating.

They don't move for five painstakingly long seconds.

"Dear fuck." She whispers.

My gaze moves from her to him trying to piece together what I'm seeing but his gaze drags me under water.

"Kenna." He steps forward.

Chapter Twenty

RYKER

"Kenna." I call her name.

Her hazel eyes and blonde hair match the woman that left me that day but the person standing before me is a ghost. My eyes take in every inch of her that's changed. Sunken eyes, pale skin, and her weight. She's lost so much weight her collar bones are standing out even from across the room. The black sports bar is loose on her and the gym shorts hang slightly off her hip bones. Oakley tenses next to me, our shock keeping us from making a move. Dim eyes flick between us but what I see behind them is something I didn't, couldn't, predict.

Anger and fear. When my eyes finally zero in on her face after drinking in every single change I start to put more pieces together. Blood boils in my veins when I see the teeth imprinted into her flesh on the side of her neck, my hands fist at my sides, gaze falling to the metal clamped around her throat. A goddamn collar is locked around her like a fucking mutt off the streets and the skin around the edges is raw and swollen.

"Ryker." Oakley whispers, her stare never leaving Kenna.

She's telling me to tread carefully, I can hear it in her tone, because my little killer is broken. Holding my hands up I step forward to move closer when I hear several footsteps rushing towards us. Oakley swings around with her knife in hand but I keep my gaze on Kenna. She hasn't moved since we stepped into the room like a scared cat cornered. She's frozen in place.

"Dear God." West breathes behind me. "Hey Princess."

She flinches at the name, finally moving for the first time. West steps up beside me so I look over my shoulder to see Havoc and Silas. My brows dip in confusion.

"What the fuck is he wearing?" I say under my breath trying to keep from scaring Kenna.

Beside Havoc stands Silas but covering his face is a mask with the face of a snarling wolf. Ignoring the weird shit I tend to see around this group turning to West.

"Where is he?" I ask.

West looks to me from the corner of his eyes then back to her. "He didn't want to freak her out." He responds.

Blowing out a gust of air I waive off Havoc and Silas, "Go find G I think he may have something else to handle."

After they walk off West and Oakley step back giving Kenna space. Her eyes are wide, her lips cracked and bleeding, her teeth currently biting into her bottom one. Moving another foot forward I hold my hands up so she can see my palms are weapon free, showing her that I'm not a threat. Everything inside me fucking burns with the need to snatch her up and drag her into my chest but I hold myself back. It takes maximum fucking effort to hold my mask in place to hide my rage. She starts to pick at her nails walking backwards until she bumps into the dresser.

"Easy, killer." I murmur.

That name does something to her because her entire body starts to tremble. Oakley warns me from behind my back but

I ignore her. Another foot forward. Dainty hands fly up to her head pulling at the strands.

"Stay away from me!" She wails.

West goes to move forward but I hold up my hand stopping him. My heart beats faster behind my ribs, it hurts to pull in oxygen, the pain of seeing her like this is too much. Memories of the scars I caused along the way flicker through my thoughts showing me the small fingerprints I've left along the way. Have they built up so much that I've caused too much damage for us? Was my affection the source of her pain? The look in her eyes when I move towards her is earth shattering.

"Killer, it's okay. We've got you." I try.

Shaking her head she starts to sway side to side in a manic-like episode so I do the only thing I can think of and I reach out to touch her.

"Ryker." Oakley snaps when my hands make contact.

Kenna freezes in my hold for a split second before she starts to scratch, claw, and kick at me. Her touch soothes something deep inside me so I welcome the sting of her nails clawing down my arms.

"If you force her out of here without her consent you'll break any trust she may have left for you." Oakley snaps, her irritation spilling out.

"I'll break every line of trust if I have to but I'm not leaving her here." Looking into shallow hazel eyes, "Baby, I'll burn everything we have to the ground as long as you're breathing because without you there is nothing left for me."

She blinks.

"We have company." Someone shouts from across the building.

Shit. West moves to head towards the front when Havoc and Silas are heard shuffling around with someone between them. I can barely see through the dark hallway so I turn back to Kenna to see her starting to shake with her fingers pulling at the collar around her neck.

"This is your fault." She says, but I can't tell if it's for me or herself.

She's so focused on what her hands are doing that she doesn't see the moment Oakley lunges forward out the room heading to meet Hank head on.

"No!" I yell after her.

Havoc and Silas come back into view now that they are closer to the bright bedroom light. Hank, who looks different than the last time that I saw him, is bleeding from his nose. A small amount of blood also drips from his lips when he smiles and it takes me a second too long to realize that he's smiling at her. Pushing her behind me, my hand slides against the cold metal of the gun, pulling it from the loop I placed it in. Oakley slams her fist into his stomach forcing him to double over from the hit. Havoc and Silas grumble from his weight but they keep their hold on him. Havoc eyes Kenna and I can see the shock in his stare when he notices the condition she's currently in.

"I see you found my little doll." Hank grins.

West pulls out his phone looking at the lit up screen a dark look crosses his face before masking it. He jerks his head to the doorway and then he's gone slipping down the hallway and through the door to the left that G went into. What the fuck is in that room? Kenna pulls against my hold trying to step around me so I shift to the right allowing her to move on her own hoping she decides she can trust us.

Oakley turns towards Kenna, "Kens." She says.

"You did this to him." Kenna says, her voice raspy.

Oakley looks to Hank and then back to my girl with a confused look, but a laugh spills from his lips.

"She isn't yours anymore. I carved her into the perfect toy." He says.

"I'll break you." I spit.

Looking at Kenna he licks his lips, "You'll never get her back now. I'll always own a piece of her."

Leaning back I slam forward, throwing my forehead into his nose crushing the bone and shooting blood across my face. Pulling back I let the blood spill down my face smiling wide showing him how wild and volatile I am. Driving him backwards his back hits the wall and I pause the air in my lungs rushing out on an exhale. Photos are plastered across the walls showcasing the past few months. In some of them my face is carved out of them leaving only my body and the background. How did I not see this when we walked in? I was too focused on Kenna and the way her body has been beaten and bruised that I failed to look at our surroundings.

"You sick mother fucker." I grit.

Striking out with my right hand I hit him again this time at the edge of his eye socket most likely fracturing the bone there. Another hit. I'm lost to the blinding rage that's built up inside me since he took her. She's no longer my killer instead she's lost, broken, a shell of who she was. The fire and fight she had behind her eyes has been extinguished into smoke.

"Stop!" A soft voice screams.

She pierces through the fog pulling me back into the room where Hank is now slumped against the wall covered in blood. Heaving I straighten allowing myself to catch my breath before I turn to look into those broken eyes. She's pulling against Oakley who is actively whispering in her ear saying God only knows. The way she's looking at me right now makes me want to cut my own heart out and hand it to her because she owns it. It only beats for her.

"Stop." She cries. Her entire body shaking with the sobs wracking her chest. Scratching at her skin she repeats the same word over and over.

Turning away from her I lift Hank to his feet and drag him towards the door knowing I'll have to pass her. Havoc and Silas who have been silent through this mess shift behind me staying back in case they're needed. They're not.

"Let her go." I call to Oakley.

Giving me a nod she releases Kenna, who steps in front of me, blocking the doorway. I'm not sure what I thought I'd find when I got here but her crying over the man who's tortured her for months cracks something inside me. Oakley tried to warn me that he may have dug his claws in too deep. Kenna places her hands on each side of Hank's face, lifting his slumped head up so his eyes meet hers.

"Ryker." She whispers.

My name falls from her lips and fuck I almost hit my knees right from the sound.

"Killer."

She keeps her eyes on Hank, "I won't let them break us, Ryker. I promise." She says, her words broken on a sob.

Ice spreads through my veins when I finally realize that she's talking to him calling him my name. Anguish floods through my chest tearing apart the organ beating for the woman in front of me. My fist tighten on Hank hauling him into me with one hand while reaching behind me with the other. Silas doesn't move.

"Silas." I snap.

Metal meets my fingers. Pressing the gun to his head I let my gaze meet hers once again but this time I'm begging her to see me. A hand lands on my arm, Oakley. Kenna looks from the hand back to me and I can see it then he's gotten so deep in her head that she thinks she can't trust any of us.

"You'll come back to me even if I have cut away everything that we were." I rasp.

Kneeing Hank in the back of the legs I drop him and step towards Kenna ignoring the way she tries to escape. Pulling her into me I press our faces close enough that our noses touch.

"Come back to me, Killer." I breathe inches away from her lips.

She stares blankly back at me unmoving. Releasing her I step away from her to move back behind Hank who is still kneeling on the floor. Lifting the gun my anger takes over and I'm done listening to this sick bastard. Pulling back the hammer my finger curls around the trigger. Hank doesn't make a sound, his eyes on the side of her face, he doesn't even beg. Ready to pull the trigger I smile at the mother fucker.

"No!" A wail comes from beside me. A blur of blonde hair rushes past me covering his body with hers.

A booming laugh, "Good girl." He coo's.

Oakley jumps into action shoving Kenna off him forcing her to the side but she trips and everything slows down. Falling to the side Kenna slams her head into the bedpost at the foot of the bed. Silence. The room is blanketed with an eerie quiet right before chaos breaks out. Oakley drops to her knees beside Kenna lifting her still body onto her lap but when she pulls her hand away from her covered in blood my body freezes. Havoc and Silas drag Hank from the room rushing to the front of the building to get the car.

"Hurry!" Oakley screams.

Her carefree attitude long fucking gone now covered in my girls blood the crimson liquid soaks her jeans. Falling to the floor beside Oakley I try to pull her into my arms but Oakley tightens her hold.

"Let her fucking go!" I seethe.

Shaking her head she keeps her hand behind her head, "I'm holding pressure." Her words are strained.

Grey eyes blink up at me, dark eyelashes fanning across ashen skin.

"Killer, baby, stay with me." I whisper.

Leaning down my lips press against the soft skin behind her ear, "Don't you fucking dare leave me, Killer."

Tears roll down her cheeks wetting her face. My thumb swipes at the drops, smearing them into her skin.

"This blood filled beating organ in my chest has your name stitched into the walls so keep yours beating for me, baby, so I can return the favor."

Chapter Twenty-One

KENNA

"Come back to me, Killer." The voice says, sounding shattered. Begging me.

Behind the fog brown eyes peer into mine searching for something I can't give him. Faces around the room start to blend together painting a dark masterpiece. Blue hair moves in my peripheral pulling my attention away from the brown eyed God standing above me. Familiar heat skates over my skin with his touch, but the following burn forces me to jerk in his hold. Voices surround me shoving me back into the dazed fog I'm stuck in.

"Ryker move." One voice says.

Cold hands travel over me probing and searching. My head throbs when fingers press into the center of my head. Black dots appear at the edge of my vision when the throbbing grows.

"Oak!" A voice shouts from far away.

"Shit, here carry her to the SUV." Warm hands replace the soft cold ones.

Words start to blur together and time stills. I want to call out to him and beg him to forgive me for what they did so he doesn't turn his back on me too but my mouth is dry.

"Open your eyes for me baby." That voice says.

My eyes are open, I think to myself. Aren't they? Clawing through the fog my eyes blink open to bright lights that force a whine from the back of my throat.

"Where is he?"

"The fucking trunk." A new voice.

"He's hers to deal with. She'll want that control when it's time."

Pain radiates through my bones. I'm so exhausted I just want to sleep. A light tap jolts my eyes open.

"Keep your eyes open for me."

Sounds start to warp and change words swirling with footsteps and doors closing. My vision tunnels. Please be quiet. I want to scream but nothing comes out when my lips part.

"Ryker, you need to see this." Another voice.

How many voices are there? Why can't I force myself to move?

"Take her to the SUV now."

More hands. My body jostles, making me cry out.

"Get that fucking thing off of her!"

Hands slide behind my neck tugging and pulling, putting pressure on the sore skin around the metal collar. Tears continue to leak from my eyes soaking my face. A click sounds and my heart stops for a second waiting for the lightning to shoot down my spine but nothing follows. Warm fingers gently open the clasp and peel it away from my neck, the pain blinding, sending me back into darkness. My head rolls to the side meeting a warm chest. Strong arms lift me pulling me in and suddenly I'm no longer on the ground.

Fading in and out I force my eyes open connecting with green eyes.

"We need you, Princess. Come back to us." His gruff gravelly broken voice rasps.

The pounding in my chest falters. The air in my lungs rushing out with whoosh. Bloody fingers reach out to touch his face. Green eyes water above me. Carrying me towards the door my head rolls to the side watching the way the entire building grows darker with each step as if I was the only thing providing it light. Passing over the threshold a strong smell smacks me in the face. My stomach bubbles and bile tries to force its way up my throat but I choke it down.

"Eyes on me, Princess." The low gruff voice says.

A light shines through a doorway to my left pulling my attention. Each step closer the smell grows worse and worse, stinging my nose and making my eyes water. He said eyes on him but I can't pull my stare away from the open doorway. My breathing picks up speed the closer we get. My eyes grow heavier trying to pull me into the darkness but I need to see. Dropping my head to the side I scan the room until I see what everyone is crowded around. A body lies stiff on a metal table naked and torn apart. The sight mixed with the smell sends me over the edge and the shadows finally claim me.

Chapter Twenty-Two

OAKLEY

Mud squelches under shoes outside the old building, making the only sound in the dark night. Licking the back of my teeth, I scrape my brain for the last memory I have of speaking to Jax. Shit. Coming up empty, resignation slowly settles into my bones, guilt that I sent him here completely blind, consumes me. Sighing, I blink my eyes trying to force them to adjust to the pitch black night.

"The smell." Havoc grunts under the weight of a bloated body.

Groaning from the sudden shift, Silas stumbles, almost dropping the dead body. "Goddamnit, Vic. Steady hands man, the last thing we need is a bloated body popping."

"Do we need help girls?" I laugh.

Skipping around the two, I try not to think about the person they are getting ready to dump in a shallow grave. The way his body is carved into pieces infuriates me. The sooner we get Kenna out of here, the quicker we can get some answers. Starting with what the hell happened in this building. A door closing behind us has me spinning on my heels. Headlights beam directly in my face, coming straight towards where I'm standing at the back of the building. Silas and Havoc have started digging in the soft dirt a yard or two away. Moving away from the red brick building, my hands find my hips and I tip my head looking directly into the blinding headlights. Swerving the car just to the right, barely missing my leg, the driver slams on the breaks and rolls down the tinted windows.

"Stone Manor. Meet us there when you're done dealing with this mess. Ryker has the family doctor coming to take a look at her." Gio says from the driver seat.

My eyes move from him to the man in the passenger seat. He doesn't speak, only assesses the scene around him, so I look back to Gio.

"Hank?" I ask, twisting my lips to the side.

Looking to the ceiling of the dark car, he shakes his head, "He's in the trunk. Don't worry, we'll let you have a playdate before Ryker has a talk with him." Gio huffs out a shallow laugh.

Leaning my arms on the window, I'm brought closer to green eyes and scarred skin. Tapping my nails on the metal window frame, I blow them both kisses flashing my red painted lips.

"Don't worry boys, I'll save some of the fun for you." Pushing off the car I head over to my men.

The car's engine revs a few times before the tires squeal, leaving a cloud of dirt and mud splattered over the pavement. Fucking boys.

"I'm not leaving the damn room." Ryker spits.

"We need to examine her." The doctor states. His tone is anything but pleasant, but he knows who he works for, so he steps back with his words.

The party has moved back to a mansion in the center of Del Mar which I'm positive is the Stone residence. West is leaning against the wall with both hands in his pocket while Ryker is going toe to toe with the good ole doctor. Fucking menaces, all of them. Rolling my eyes I stand from the small white chair beside Kenna stopping at the foot of her bed.

"Doc, he's not going anywhere. I'm guessing you knew that already, so do us all a favor and get to fucking work." Turning to West, "You aren't needed." I wave my hand to shoo him out the room. "Go make yourself useful."

Brown eyes darken his gaze, lighting a fire on my skin, "Careful what you wish for, Blue." He rumbles.

There's a threat layered underneath his words and it shoots excitement down my spine.

"You have no idea what you're asking for." I wink.

I'd eat him alive and enjoy each second of watching my men savor every single taste from my tongue.

"You too." I say, pointing to Ryker.

Ryker turns on me spewing venom, "Watch who the fuck your talking to. You're in my house, in my town, running my streets." His jaw ticks.

"Maybe it'd be best for the patient if she had some privacy due to her condition." The doc says. His white lab coat is unnecessary on a house call, yet here we are. In a fucking reality T.V. show filled with personal doctors, mansions, and filthy money. Ryker shoulders past me grabbing the doc by his jacket, shoving him against the pale blue wall.

"Keep in mind who lines your fucking pockets and looks the other way when certain parts show up on the market." He seethes.

"Let the man go so he can do his fucking job." I exhale. "Stupid, pushy, bossy bastards. All of em." I mumble under my breath.

A small moan pulls my attention back from the darker

parts of my mind. Spinning on my heels, hazel eyes meet mine. Kenna Kingston. My father promised to keep an eye on her if anything happened to the Kingston family, so here I stand keeping his promise. My phone vibrates in my back pocket, reminding me how much I have on hold back in Seattle while I've been here playing detective. I force a smile from my face when I think of all the fun I'm about to have.

"Ms. Kingston, my name is Dr. Munford." The doc moves around a red faced Ryker to slip beside Kenna.

Her eyes leave mine to look at the tall sturdy male beside her. She goes to jerk back, but lets out a groan from the pain. She hit her head pretty fucking hard. Luckily head wounds bleed a lot, and it doesn't always mean disaster. I'm still positive she has a concussion though. Making my way back to the chair on the opposite side of Dr. Munford, I make sure to keep my movements slow and obvious. Having experience with trauma comes in handy with situations like these. It's why I don't think Ryker needs to be in the room. I'd remove him myself if I knew it wouldn't freak the little princess out over here. I'd enjoy finally getting in the ring with the hot head and putting him in his place. A smirk creeps up my face and I squish it back before anyone notices.

"It's okay. You're safe here. No one is going to hurt you, I just need to take a look at you." He lowers his voice into a calm tone. Far from the deep one he held for Ryker.

Her gaze flits from him to Ryker and her eyes widen. When her breathing picks up and her fingers start to pick at the skin around her nails, reopening the cuts there, I turn to look at him.

"You need to go." I snap.

Pausing his pacing, he starts to storm towards me when Kenna shrinks against the bed. Hand on my blade, I quirk an eyebrow, daring the little fucker to make another move towards me. Del Mar doesn't want the attention of the wolves on them and he knows it. Looking back to Kenna, I rest my arms on my knees, showing her I'm not a threat.

"The doc here is going to check you out. You hit your head pretty hard and might have a concussion. You're also dehydrated and-" Looking her over, I hesitate on the right words. "You've lost a lot of weight. We want to make sure you are okay and have medical treatment. We will give you privacy-" I pause again looking back over my shoulder at Ryker who is pacing again. "We will *both* give you privacy with the doc so he can examine you. If you need anything, call for me and I'm here."

Tears form at the edge of her eyes, but she lays there silent. Looking away, her gaze floats to the ceiling, ignoring me completely. Whatever this shitfuck did to her, she doesn't think she can trust any of us anymore.

Standing, I push the chair to the wall and walk to the door. "I want her neck and head assessed first. If she says no to any treatment at all and you don't stop, I'll cut your fucking hands off an ship them to your family. Understand?"

The doc looks from me, to Ryker, to Kenna before nodding. Pulling Ryker out of the room by his shirt, I shove him against the wall outside the room.

"Swallow down that alpha bullshit you have flowing off of you like a damn river. She's been kept captive for months with no other human contact than the asshole who's been hurting her. You saw the room, the photos, the collar. She trusts me and you about as much as she trusts the damn devil." My finger digs into his chest.

Pressing into my touch, he walks me backwards until I'm the one pinned. Caramel brown eyes peer into mine, the pain behind them fighting for dominance with the absolute rage he has caged.

"Don't touch me again, Oak." He snaps.

Smiling, I shove my knee into his thigh forcing space

between us, "You only had me pinned because I let you." I laugh dancing out of his reach. "I'm going to go pay my boys a visit." Blowing him a kiss, I bound down the hall ready for a different kind of fun. "Pace the halls if you need to, but give her time, Ryker." I shout behind me, my voice reverberating off the walls.

The hallway is long and opulently decorated with expensive art pieces and dusty hanging pendant style lights. You can tell the home hasn't been lived in because fuck, have they ever heard of a housekeeper? Rich people problems I guess. Passing a few closed doors, I follow the hallway down until it opens into a massive great room with smokey grey tile and black furniture. The lack of a T.V. is a little boring, but I guess when you have everything you ever wanted watching lesser people on a square box is boring. I giggle to myself.

Voices float from a space off the great room towards the right, so I follow the sound. Passing a long marble table with black Esther Wingback chairs lined up along both sides for dining, my finger trails along them as I continue past them. Expensive taste for sure. The walls are painted a dark brown almost black. Only a few shades lighter than the ebony furniture scattered across the room. Stepping through another doorway getting closer to the voices, I can hear Havoc and Silas arguing about something, making me smile.

A white door on the left side is cracked, leading to a bedroom where Havoc, Gio, Silas, and Haven are all spread around the room. Pushing it open with my toe, I lean against the trim watching them go back and forth about fuck knows what.

"Where is he?" I ask no one in particular.

"Basement." Gio answers looking up from his phone. The tension rolling off this one clouds the room.

Licking my lips, I quirk a brow, "A certain pussycat getting under your skin?" I joke.

It's a call out that only he would understand and the moment his eyes meet mine, I can see how right I am. I hope I'm around to see the disaster this is bound to be. Silas jumps off the arm of the couch and stalks towards me with hooded eyes. Reaching me, his warm breath fans over my neck, leaving a trail of goosebumps.

"Blue." He rasps.

Tisking, I lean away, "It's not fun unless someone's covered in blood." Pressing forward on my toes, I kiss the edge of his mouth. "I want to get a little dirty first, Si." I whisper against his lips.

Groaning, he pulls me against him, giving me an idea of how bad he wants to see me lose control. Havoc can feel the change in the air because he's headed towards us rubbing his hands together with a dark grin.

"For fucks sake." Haven groans, plopping backwards on the couch.

Ignoring her snark, I move out of Sila's arms and step towards Gio, giving him a serious look. "We need to have a little chat about what you saw soon. For now, I'm going to pay a visit to our new friend." Turning to Haven, I level her with a look, "I need you to go bat your eyes for a certain playboy." I wiggle my brows with a smile.

Havoc jerks his head, looking at me like I've lost my mind, "His bark is worse than his bite." I reassure him. Rubbing my hands together I snicker, "Let's go spark up some chaos."

Chapter Twenty-Three

KENNA

Knees pulled tight to my chest I allow myself to look around the empty room. The doctor walked out a few minutes ago leaving me with the voices echoing off the walls outside. My thoughts are clouded leaving me grappling for ways to put together a string of words, or thoughts, or fuck. Anything. A dull ache rattles at the base of my skull radiating from the stitches where I hit my head on the edge of the footboard. Trying to piece last night together has done nothing but make my head hurt worse. Instead I use this time to look for any way out of here so I can get as far away from the Stone family as possible.

The walls are bright but the room is sparse with very little actual furniture outside of the obvious bed and dresser. Pulling the thick black comforter closer to my body my eyes continue to roam until they land on the window across the room. Flexing my fingers I survey my muscles making sure I have the physical energy to run now or if it's better to wait. Tossing off the blanket I roll my ankles and stretch taking a better count of what hurts. My stomach gurgles, reminding me of one very important thing.. Hunger.

You'll starve either way.

Fucking hell. Here we go again. Huffing out a deep breath I throw my legs over the side of the bed letting my bare feet touch the cold floor. A chill climbs from my toes to my spine with the new sensation. Pulling my shoulders back I let my head tip up, my eyes landing on the popcorn ceiling, running through my options.

It's not like you have anywhere else to go.

The dorms are too far for me to walk in the condition I'm in and I have no clue where my phone is.

You have no one left to trust.

Biting the inside of my lip until I draw blood my heart starts to pound behind my ribcage. Panic grows in the pit of my stomach leaving me with an uneasy feeling that takes over my entire body. I have no one left to trust. No one I can call to get me out of here. Hank was my last hope.

Maybe you can get to him.

He needs me as much as I need him. I'm not chained to a bed or strapped down. If I can get to him we can think of a way to get out of here. My eyes close pulling images of a plan from thin air when the sound of someone coming down the hall floats to my ears. Sliding back on the bed I drag the covers back over me using them as a shield. The doorknob turns. A second passes. Another. The door slowly opens revealing brown eyes.

Swallowing the stone in my throat my body automatically sinks against the headboard when he steps through the doorway. His eyes skate over me searching for something, I'm not sure he finds it, but he pauses to close the door, shutting us in the room together. His jaw is clamped shut giving his jawline more of an angle reflecting the struggle he appears to be having. Those deep brown eyes darken, taking a whole new shape under the shadows of his eyes. Fear bubbles in my veins putting me on alert but my heart skips a beat when his expression pinches.

Taking a step towards the bed my hands grip the blanket between my fingers trying to press it so close it's almost like it's stitched to my skin.

"Kenna, baby." His deep voice rolls over my body.

My stare is probing looking for any weakness so I can get past him and run for Hank. He's the only one who can help me. Licking my dry lips, the action pulls his attention to my mouth, and the look that follows has my blood running cold.

"Stay the fuck away from me." I snap.

Looking around the room frantically hoping to find something to use if I need to fight him off but I come up empty. He holds his hands up trying to calm me. The irony.

"You-" I choke. "You did this. TO ME." I yell, my voice cracking on the last words.

My breathing picks up and my hands start to shake. I'm trapped and my skin starts to itch. Stretching over my bones too tight to allow air through my lungs. Everything is too close to me. Throwing off the blanket my legs kick at it until it's out of reach. My fingers start to pull and claw at the collar of my shirt. I need it off my skin.

"Calm down. Easy baby." He says. His voice growing further away.

Black spots start to fill my vision shooting dark stars across the room blocking my view of the monster of a man standing in front of me.

"Stop, Kenna." He orders.

My eyes try to focus on where he is but the tunnel is growing longer. My chest aches with the effort my lungs make to pull in oxygen.

"This is your fault. This is your fault." My words spill from my lips.

Something wet drips on the back of my hand pulling my attention from the figure at the edge of the bed. Looking down, a small drop of water sits on my pale flesh. Smearing it away I look above me for the source but a soft sigh distracts me.

"Don't cry, Killer. Please, let me help you."

The tips of my fingers drag down my cheek bringing with it the tears that continue to fall. I'm crying. Thrashing my head back and forth trying to shake the pain away I can feel the darkness creeping forward.

"Why? Why did you do this?" I chant.

The words sit out in the open for seconds. Minutes. The door opens and closes. And now I'm alone in the empty room filled with pain and shadows.

See how easy it was for him to abandon you again?

A bone deep exhaustion pulls at my body begging for relief. Sliding down the headboard until my head lays flat I count the marks on the ceiling until eventually I drift off to sleep.

———

A soft touch trails down the side of my face pulling me from a deep sleep. Rough fingers drag along my temple slowly drawing circles into my skin.

"Open your eyes, Kenna." A low scratchy voice says.

The voice is wrong. All wrong. The undertone is familiar, tugging at memories, but it's warped or damaged. My lashes flutter, opening my eyes I turn towards the voice, meeting soft emerald green ones. The air catches in my lungs forcing a cough from me. Twisting away from the man sitting in a grey chair pulled up at the side of the bed my mouth falls open. No words form on my tongue, shock and confusion taking root, I snap my mouth shut.

"It's just me." He says, his words gruff.

His palms in the air, a worried stare meets mine, his face the same as the day he died. My gaze takes him in, traveling from his perfect hair down to his neck, stopping on the jagged scar across his throat. A small gasp slips from my lips.

"How?" I murmur, speaking more to myself than the ghost in front of me.

Sitting up against the wooden headboard I pull my knees to my chest giving me a shield to hide behind. Resting my chin on my knees I watch as he looks me over. Bright eyes shift through several emotions before settling on something I can't pinpoint.

"I'm so sorry, Princess." He whispers.

Leaning forward he starts to reach out but snatches his hand back when I flinch away from his touch. A dark flicker passes through his expression and I'm reminded why I can't trust the Stones and anger takes over replacing the fear.

Shaking my head, "You died. I watched you die." I shout. "How? Was it all a trick? Is that how Hank knew where to grab me?" My voice bounces off the bare walls. Pure rage takes over and now I'm leaning over my knees yelling, "You sold me to him like a fucking cow to the slaughter house. All of you!"

The sting of pain tells me my fingernails broke skin yet I continue. Unable to hold back the overwhelming feelings I've been trapped with.

"Why? I begged you to breathe, Cole! I was the one who found you. To walk into that room and see you hanging there." My voice breaks. "Just tell me why Hank? Is this to get back at my father?" I'm speaking so fast I'm not sure he can understand a word I'm saying.

The organ in my chest pangs at the anguish in my tone. Shattered at the lies, the fucking betrayal, watching the burning truth looking me in the face. Cole Stone faked his death and let me watch him die. Green eyes look away, unable to hold my stare any longer. Using the back of my hand I swipe at my cheeks fighting the tears that still fall. Frustration, heartbreak, and exhaustion war inside me.

Shifting in the chair, Cole rests his forearms on his legs. "I did die, Princess." He says. His words are deep and hollow but a lie.

Shaking my head I refuse to believe any more lies from this family.

Placing his hands on the edge of the bed he drags the chair closer with his foot. With his knees pressed against the bottom of the bed he leans closer letting me see past the mask they wear so well.

Licking his bottom lip, "I'm only here because of sheer fucking luck. Anything outside of that and I'd be in that grave marked with my name. There is a lot you've missed." He says. Clearing his throat a free hand rubs at the scar there. "Our scars match, Princess." Reaching out, his fingers hover over my fresh scar.

He gently strokes my throat, eyes cast down at the ragged mark across my tender flesh, he hesitates. "It took me a while to speak and when I did your name was the first to fall from my lips. You bleed, we bleed."

I suck in a gasp at his words. Our words. What we live and die by.

But they sold you.

"Then why?" I ask.

His head shakes swaying his blonde hair, "You were gone for a while, Kenna. We have no idea what he put you through or what he has you believing, but you're safe now." He states.

The light outside is slowly growing darker with each passing second. A shadow cast across the room bringing a chill with it. Pulling his hand away Cole shifts in his spot.

"If I'm safe, why am I locked in this room?" I ask. Looking for an opening to get the hell out of here. Chewing on the inside of my cheek I remind myself that they still have Hank.

"Have you tried the door?" His eyebrow raises with the question. Like he already knows the answer to that he laughs, the sound haunting, "You're not a prisoner here, Princess." Waving a hand at the door in a show of freedom he pushes away from the bed and stands.

Stretching out his arms he rolls his neck popping it in the process. Bright eyes peer down at me, "Where you go is up to you. As long as we have Hank you're safe I promise."

Walking towards the door he doesn't look back until his hand is on the knob. Dipping his brows, his lips twitch, "Remember who we are and you'll figure out who to trust."

Stepping through the doorway he lets the door swing shut once again leaving me in the room alone. Only this time it's unlocked and I have no plan of sticking around to see who's next to visit.

Chapter Twenty-Four

KENNA

Rummaging through the first drawer of the tall mahogany dresser I pull out two mixed matched socks. Sniffling through the tears that slip past my lashes I make an effort to swallow down my feelings. Breathe in through my nose and out my mouth. Repeating that in my head I'm able to focus on slipping the socks over my cold feet that also prevents the sound of my steps. Gently shutting the drawer my eyes cast down to take in my outfit. Somewhere along the way I've gained a large baggy shirt that I know it's mine yet the same gym shorts hang on my hips. Squeezing my eyes shut to block out the image of my bones poking out it takes me several seconds to flush out the shame.

Pulling open the bottom drawer a sigh leaves me when I come up empty. Who the fuck has only socks in a dresser? Psycho that's who. Licking the back of my teeth my nails dig into the paint with my frustration. Angry tears take the place of the ones that fell before it and now adrenaline is coursing through my veins.

"I need to get the fuck out of here." I whisper to myself.

Turning towards the door my teeth bite into the skin of

my bottom lip pulling and picking at the raw meat there. Long tangled blond hair hangs in messy waves down my back and I'm reminded once again of how dirty I am. How dirty I feel. That feeling returns, my skin itching and stretching over my bones. Pulling too tight around my skeleton.

Stop being weak.

The usually snarky bitch in my head actually has a point this time. Where did Kenna Kingston go? Is she dead? Were the Stone brothers able to break me so easily?

Get out of the house and then we can come up with a better plan.

Nodding my head to myself, my slow steady steps carry me to the bedroom door. My hand rises to grasp the knob, twisting it an inch at a time to prevent any noise. Dragging in a large gulp of air I pull the door open, almost shocked that it worked. The hallway expands in two directions and only someone who has never been in the Stone mansion wouldn't know where to go, but their mistake is bringing me to a place where I grew up. Looking left and then right to make sure the hallway is clear my gaze runs over the subtle grey walls framed by glossy white trim. Large beautiful otherworldly paintings hang every few feet on each side of the walkway.

The Stone family love their art pieces and each one has its own certificate of ownership. Another way for the rich to flaunt their money, yeah I know, I'm rich too. Licking my lips to wet them I take soft steps walking as fast as possible down the hall to the left where it leads into a large conservatory. Passing by empty rooms I take my time, making sure no one is around, and listening for anyone coming to check on me. Memories of myself and the boys playing games through this massive home slam into me like a freight train unable to stop before demolishing the car in the middle of its tracks.

Hide and seek, tag, nerf wars, it was all we could do to keep ourselves busy as kids. Choking down the intrusive thoughts I keep moving forward past the bedrooms, past the stairwell, past the kitchen. Finally, an enormous doorway comes into view up ahead but my feet jerk to a stop when my eyes catch sight of a familiar door to my right. I'm just past the kitchen that looks to be recently repainted and designed with all new solid black appliances to replace the stainless steel ones that used to be in their place. The tall white door seems to grow larger, hovering over me like a distant reminder, a familiar demon that calls my name.

Biting into the tip of my tongue the pinch of pain manages to clear some of the fog caused by the monster from the past. Making my way closer to the door I drag my fingertip over the chipped paint and a memory I've suppressed flashes through my thoughts. Pictures play like an old style movie showing me Cole's face as he climbs down the basement stairs to see me soaking wet and crying. Another of West coming to kneel in front of me to make me smile but the final image makes me jerk away from the door taking the image with it. Burying the sight of him storming towards me calling me to him like a siren into the deep waters. And what tears my heart from my chest is I went willingly into his arms allowing him to carry me away to where I felt safe.

Covering my face with both hands, my chest aches and all I want is to claw out those memories. Those lies. Spinning on my heels my stare falls on the open doors and I run. My feet pound against the tile. I'm in nothing but shorts and a baggy shirt with no shoes on my feet but I run. My muscles scream at me but my fight or flight kicks in and I burst through the final door skidding to a stop when I see the front door. Shaky hands grip the handles and shove once. Swinging open the darkness greets me yet it feels like home. Dropping my head back my eyes fall closed taking in the open air that kisses my cheeks.

"GAHHHHH" I scream until my lungs are out of oxygen.

Ignoring the pain bouncing around my ribs with each

shattering breath I run down the driveway not looking back at the house that I used to love. Escaping to the open street it only takes me a short time to find my way to the edge of the neighborhood. Every inch of my body needs rest but I keep walking. My stomach burns from nothing but acid filling it but I keep walking. I walk until holes are worn through the bottom of the socks from the asphalt. I walk until my eyes droop lower and my knees shake. I walk until I reach the dorms. And when my hand finally meets the cold metal of my dorm room my legs give out and my body slides against the wall until my ass hits the floor.

My head thuds against the wall when I realize that I have no way to open the door because my keys are gone. Leaning back I let my eyes drift closed allowing myself to rest until the dorm's open and I can get a spare key. Promising myself that I'll only rest for an hour, I drift off into a deep sleep right there in the hallway of the Hawthorne dorms.

———

Something digs into my ribs pulling me from a dreamless sleep. The pain fades when the pressure is removed and my eyes start to drift again when it returns. That's when I hear a voice above me.

"Kenna?" It says.

My brain tries to catch up but I'm too weak to move from my spot. My hand stretches out rubbing something rough and scratchy.

"What?" I murmur.

Blinking, my palms rub at my eyes until the sight in front of me changes from blurry to clear. Brown eyes and thick brown hair frame a face I haven't seen in months.

"Romero?" I rasp.

Leaning back on his heels he looks me over and I can see

the moment he pieces it together. The way my cheekbones stand out against the pale color of my skin. Horror flashes across his face before a mask slams down and a smile takes its place. Dropping down to balance on his heels his milky chocolate eyes roam over my face taking me in. His baby face has small changes that I'd point out but I can't find it in me to give a fuck. A laugh slips from my lips startling the man in front of me.

"Where have you been?" He questions.

Reaching over his large hand clasps my elbow pulling me from the floor and I don't fight the help he gives me. When I'm eye level with him he finally sees me fully and his eyes widen. Looking away to avoid the pity behind his eyes.

"I lost the key to my dorm. Can you help me get one from the desk?" I question. It falls from my tongue like a plea and somehow he knows it's what I need.

Nodding he motions for me to stay here, turning, he takes off down the hall. Returning a few minutes later he steps around me to unlock the door and open it for me. The lights are already on lighting up the empty living room and a sigh leaves me. I didn't know if Ally would be here or not but fuck am I happy she isn't. Stepping inside I turn to close the door but Romero follows me inside. Leading me to the couch he sits me down and starts to pace.

"Kenna, you look like hell. You've been missing for over two months and you show up on campus looking like a fucking hostage victim. The Stone family has been searching for you day and night yet when you're found they're nowhere to be found?" His hands comb through his hair.

Sinking into the soft couch I pull my knees up to my chest to give me that shield I need to keep myself safe.

"Are you asking me a question?" I say, my voice raw.

Stopping in his tracks he drops forward bringing himself eye to eye with me. His hands rest on his knees.

"They found you." He breathes,

Shaking my head frantically my heart starts to pound.

"No. No, they did this."

His brows pinch in surprise. "Kenna you don't." He pauses, pulling in a deep breath. "I don't know where you've been and by the look of you I'd say it's been a fucking nightmare so I'm behind you no matter what but, Kenna." He stops again, "They've been looking for you nonstop. People are dead. Some people are missing. Ry-"

My hands fly to my ears at the name that drips from his mouth like venom.

"Stop." I cry out.

Standing he holds his hands out in surrender. "I'm sorry, Kens." He breathes out.

My eyes burn from the lack of tears due to dehydration.

"Tell me what you need." Romero says.

Looking around the room my gaze lands on the kitchen.

"I need a shower and food." I nod to myself in agreement.

"Ok." Is all he says before leaving me to head into the kitchen.

While he starts pulling stuff from the cabinets and fridge I force myself to go take a shower. An hour later my stomach is far too full and sleep threatens to take over again. Romero stands from the chair across from the couch I'm laying on to grab a blanket from the blanket ladder in the corner of the room. Opening the large grey quilt, he tosses it over me, and drops to his knee.

"If you need a place to hide, you know where to find me. I don't know what's going on at Hawthorne, but things are shifting, and people can feel it. It started with Cole's death, but when you went missing Ry." He stops and clears his throat. "His eyes went dark and nothing, but death and anger followed in his path. If you think they did this then I believe you, but you need to know that he forced Allie to kill her father because he was connected to your disappearance."

Romero must see the confusion painted across my expression because he nods.

"It's all people have been talking about." He blows out a deep breath, "Listen, Kenna. I know we had our thing at the beginning of the year and I blew you off out of fear. I'm sorry for that and I would be bullshitting if I claimed I wasn't still worried about what they might do to me but I'm betting they'd want you to have someone on your side."

Pushing off the edge of the couch he stands over me with a soft smile. "I'll keep this to myself, but you can't hide here forever." Walking away he leaves me alone to my thoughts.

With food in my stomach and fresh clothes on my body I let myself slide into a deep sleep.

Chapter Twenty-Five

KENNA

Wiping the steam from the mirror, smokey eyes peer at me through the glass. Soaked blonde hair drips down my bare skin sending a chill through my bones. Her cheekbones are prominent and sharper than I remember. The blue and black circles under her eyes seem to be fading which could be from the ten hours of sleep.

You just left him there with the snakes.

The voice in the back of my head reminds me that I'm alone. Reminding me that I abandoned the only hope I have of getting real answers.

Where is your father?

She's fucking taunting me. Perched on her high horse looking down at the broken little princess she sneers as she ridicules me.

I'm you. So, really who's to blame here?

If I can prove my father's innocence.... I trail off because how can I do that when I can't even figure out who to trust.

Nothing but a scared little girl.

"Enough!" I scream, my fist smashes into the mirror shattering the glass into ragged cracks.

Blood rolls down a shard of glass, my eyes follow the stream, watching it drip from the wooden frame. The bright crimson stream distracts me from the sudden sharp pain radiating from my knuckles shooting its way down my arm. Anger takes the place of the ache fueling my movements. Jerking my hand away from the broken mirror my grey eyes take in my reflection. Cracks and jagged lines shoot in different directions distorting the image in front of me. Nodding my head at the broken woman in the glass my throat bobs when I swallow down my emotions.

Running my fingers through my wet hair they thread three sections together making one long braid that I leave hanging over my shoulder the tip of the braid resting against my bare ribcage. Looking away from the smokey grey eyes, I storm through into the hall shoving my door open. Blowing out a breath through my nose, I don't let myself look around the messy room instead I walk straight to my closet and shove the door into the wall. There's a subtle tremble in my hands that I decide to ignore choosing to snatch a black tank top from a hanger and a sports bra from the hook on the back side of the closet door. Pulling on both, I manage to get fully dressed in seconds, adding skin tight leggings with lace ends where they meet my ankle. The shirt hangs loose on me but it works and that's all that matters.

Blood falls onto the carpet from my still open wound.

"Shit." I groan when I realize there's nothing here to wrap it.

An idea pops into my head and suddenly I'm dropping to my knees, reaching under the bed, my fingers feel for a pair of all white Nike shoes. My gaze drifts to the small red circle on the cream carpet watching as each fiber of the carpet drinks in my blood. Pushing off the floor with one hand I use the other to pull up my shoes. Propping my ass against the bed my legs shake slightly as I balance against the bed to slide my shoes on. Heading towards the door I head to the only place I can think of where no one would look for me.

The fucking man has to live on the top floor. Rolling my eyes, my chest rises and falls faster, my calves burning from the workout. Listing off the names in my head I drill them into my memory so I don't forget who I can't trust. Starting with the brothers and ending with Ally. Each person on my ever growing list makes my heart twist with the knowledge that for most of my life I've been a fucking pawn. What doesn't make sense is why my father is sitting in prison for something he didn't do if he knows more than he claims. Why would he allow himself to be held in that hellhole unless he had his own reasons? Then another thought hit me. Why would the Stone brothers sell me to Hank for cash when they have more money than God?

Climbing the last flight of stairs my mind is all over the place by the time I reach his door. Lifting my hand to knock, I drop it to my side. Turning away, I hesitate for a second. Rolling my neck I pace back and forth trying to run through my options before deciding this is the best I've got. Using my foot I kick his door and slip my hands behind my back. A voice calls out to tell me to hold on, the sound of footsteps follow, and finally the door swings open.

Those milky eyes lighten at the sight of me at his door and I can't help the annoyed grin that wants to follow. Lifting my hand from behind my back I let out a shaky laugh flashing him the split flesh across my knuckles.

"I figured you'd have something to wrap my hand." I state.

He is on the football team after all. They get hurt all the time and let's not pretend that I haven't seen him with a busted lip a time or two from the Basement. Yeah, even the preps and jocks go to let off some steam by getting their pound of flesh. A wide tooth smile breaks out and a warm feeling sneaks into my veins.

Shoving it away I step forward and lift my head, "You said if I needed anything." I remind him.

Leaning back he steps to the side and holds out his arm in welcome, "Come in, Kens." He says.

Romero's dorm is simple. It's an open concept like mine but instead of making it full with things that fill a home his is bare of anything other than the essential. Typical man cave with video games, sports gear, and junk food wrappers on the table. It's cleaner than I thought it would be and that takes me by surprise that I would even notice something as trivial as a clean house. A low laugh slips from me when I realize that I'm thinking about sports and junk food instead of the fact that I was sold and.. Stopping that next thought, my steps pause at the back of his dark brown leather couch.

"Go ahead and have a seat. I'll be right back with what we need." Romero says.

Doing as he says my ass sinks into the soft cushion pulling a sigh from my lips. I don't have long to look around before he's walking around the corner with several things in his arms. Dropping them on the coffee table he sits beside me. He reaches out to grab my wrist making me jerk my hand away. The reaction is sudden and unexpected, taking us both by surprise.

"Easy." He says, lifting his hands. "You wanted me to clean you up and that's all I'm doing." He reassures me. "I promise." His words are soft this time.

Nodding my head I slide my hand into his and let him get to work. Using this time to my advantage I decide to get as much information as I can from someone who isn't involved.

"Romero." His name rolls off my tongue.

He hums in response,

"I need to know what's happened in the last few weeks." I probe.

His soft eyes peer up at me from what he's doing, "I don't know where to begin." He huffs out a dry laugh.

Biting my bottom lip I search for the right question, "Where isAlly?" I ask. I saw the photos so I feel like this answer is obvious but I need to know if Hank was right.

His head tilts but he goes back to cleaning the cuts, "She's been locked away at the Stones apartment the last time I heard. Not for a lack of trying to get the hell out of there from the look plastered across her face every time she's at school." He snips. His tone is almost protective.

So Ally has been living with them but she's not happy like the photos showed. A face pops into my head and I fucking hate myself for even bringing it up but the question pours from my mouth anyway. "And the woman with Oakley?" I ask.

Sure, I avoided what I really wanted to know. Avoided saying the name that brings nothing but horror into my bones.

His thick brows dip over his eyes, "That's the blue haired girl, right?"

I nod.

"Look, I don't know much about them other than the blue one is a little off her rocker if you know what I mean." He lets out a chuckle. "The others don't come around much. Hell the brothers haven't been in classes since everything went down."

"What have they been doing?" I rush out.

He finishes wrapping the white ace band clipping it to my palm once he's done. Tapping my knee he motions for me to flex my fingers making sure it's not too tight.

"I'm not in their circle. I don't run those types of scenes, Kens. You know they don't trust anyone and now I see why. This shit has been crazy for everyone. The school board is on edge because West has completely dropped from the team. Cole is fucking dead and yet they seem to continue on as if he never lived. Now they have G and his boys scouring the streets for any sign of you. They even-" He pauses.

"They what?" I urge.

Looking up at me his eyes meet mine, "They brought in outsiders. Word has it they dragged one of the founders and Ally into the woods and forced her to kill him. Del Mar has been under the thumb of Ry-" He skips over his name, "his thumb. At his mercy and Kens," he squeezes my knee, "He has shown no mercy when it came to finding you."

I can hear his words but none of them connect. Confusion and smoky illusions collide in a bloodbath we were bound to be. Panic creeps into my blood turning it into ice. Warm hands cup my cheeks.

"Breathe Kenna." He begs.

He begged me not to leave them. He begged me to live for them. Green eyes held me and cried for me to stay with them.

"Kenna." Harsh hands shake me.

Fingers snap in front of my face bringing me back into Romeros dorm room. Worried chocolate eyes assess me before leaning back.

"I think I should call one of the brothers." He says under his breath.

"No!" I shout. Jumping to a stand my leg bumps into his, knocking me off balance.

Standing, Romero's chest is only inches from me and the short distance sets my skin on fire. The need to run away from his contact looms over me. He can see the shift in my stance and he backs away.

"Kenna." He begs.

Shaking my head frantically, words start to spill from my lips. "No! If it'll make you feel better there is someone you can call for me."

Raising his eyebrows he waits for me to give him the

name and number. Pulling out his phone he hands it over and I dial the only person I feel like I can depend on even if all I get is more questions. Handing the phone back to Romero he hits the button to start the call and presses the cell to his ear. Walking to the door I look over my shoulder when Romero goes to stop me.

"I need you to give him a message for me." I say over my shoulder. "Tell him to meet me in the garden. Oh, and ask him to bring me two things."

After he has my demands I walk out of his room turning my back on an unlikely ally. With my hand wrapped I head to the one place that will clear my head. Romero left me with more questions and mixed feelings than answers. Shutting the door behind me I leave the dorms and walk across campus ignoring the wide eyed looks I get along the way. Will they call and rat me out? Of course. I expect nothing less. Will I run and hide? Not again. I'm a fucking Kingston and it's about time I reminded myself of that.

Chapter Twenty-Six

RYKER

"I told you he was Kenna's to do with as she pleases." I snap at Oakley.

Taking her time wiping the drying blood from her hands, she looks over at me with a dark smile, sucking the air from the room. Sinister ass women.

"He'll still be in one piece when she decides to make her move." Shrugging her shoulders she drops the towel on the table and walks out of the room.

Thing one and two follow her out like little puppies that can't be away from their master. West slides past them on his way into the living room with Haven following close behind.

"Where are they headed?" He asks, hooking his thumb over his shoulder.

Cole speaks from the couch, "Do you really want to know?"

His voice is still damaged and the doctor doesn't think he'll ever sound the same. The rope caused major damage to his esophagus altering his voice completely. It's one of the reasons he's been quiet lately. Sitting on the arm of a chair across from him I look at my brothers. We're alive. We have our own reasons to keep him out of sight and one of those reasons will be walking in soon. Gio shifts his legs looking restless leaning against the wall keeping his eyes on the outside of the property.

"Has anyone seen her?" I ask.

Cole gave her the damn idea to run and she took it like a fucking lifejacket stranded in the middle of the Atlantic. Is she a prisoner? No, but to have her out of my sight after everything? My palms tingle with the need to punish her.

She was kidnapped, dick.

The reminder jars me from the dark thoughts I was having about laying her across my knees. *Shit*. Shaking my head to rattle out the bullshit thoughts I tune in to what G is saying.

"She was spotted on campus leaving her dorm hall." G confirms.

Turning to face us I can see how torn he is on what he needs to do next. We have to go against everything we believe in and spill blood on one of our own. It's not something we want to do no matter how necessary it may be. Cracking his knuckles I can see the moment he drifts to some other place.

"What is it?" I question. Rubbing my knee, I wait for him to look at me, a shrouded look crosses his face.

West and Cole both turn to give G their full attention. Light from the window shines into the expansive space reflecting off the glass tables and steel accents. Being back in this house after so long feels like returning to a war I can't win. The dark memories cover all the good until there is nothing left but resentment.

Rubbing the stubble that's started to take over his face he finally speaks. "I had a little run in with the Jackson's." His jaw clenches at the name. "Let's just say they think they'll have a chance to slip into power with everything falling apart for the Stone name."

West and Cole look at me and from the corner of my eyes I can see the questions in theirs. Keeping my gaze trained on the one person I'd ever trust with our legacy, "G." I call.

Obsidian eyes peer into mine already knowing what only I'd ask of him.

"I'm handling it." Is all he says.

Clapping my hands, "Well, I guess that takes care of that issue."

Cole and West look from me to G but decide to drop the topic when Gio's phone rings. He steps away from the wall and begins pacing, speaking softly into the phone. Ignoring his conversation I lean back against the chair.

"Where is Ally?" I look at Cole.

He tried to hide the way his lip curls at her name but I see the slight lift of his mouth. A low laugh leaves West and Cole swings his arm out connecting with West's stomach.

"Fuck, man." He coughs. "Lighten up."

"The way you lighten up around a certain hacker? Or would you rather I talk about how she shot you down like a little bitch on the playground?" Cole rasps.

West snaps his mouth shut with a sour expression crossing his face. G slides his phone in his back pocket and storms towards the door. Calling out to him he pauses for a second in the entrance dropping his mask letting his worry be known.

"She called you." It's not a question but a realization that she needs someone who isn't us.

G drops his head back looking up at the ceiling. "She needs to do something before she can face you, Rye. She needs to burn away the images that she thinks betray her." With those words he rolls his head to face me. The way his stare peers into mine I can see the underlying message he wants me to grasp without saying it.

"She made you promise?" The words leave my mouth in a rushed breath.

He doesn't answer, instead he walks out, pulling a pack of cigarettes from his pocket on the way outside. Hank did a number on her, fuck he collared her pretty little neck, filling her head with lies.

"Does she know?" I spin to Cole who looks lost.

Shaking his head, "No. Hank told her we sold her to him. Her wires are crossed and tangled leaving her confused on who she can trust. It's the reason I let her leave. If she can't trust us she won't understand why we haven't slit the throat of who is responsible."

West punches his thigh in frustration, "Are you sure you're right?"

His question is directed to Cole, the man who hung himself to cover the truth, a reason we didn't understand until the day he woke up.

Cole's nostrils flare, "Why don't we ask her ourselves?" He remarks.

The sound of heels clacking against tile comes closer.

"Speaking of the devil, here comes one now." I spit.

We all look to the door when the footsteps come to a stop at the opening.

"Mother." We all say in unison.

Her short caramel colored hair bounces with her movements. She's dressed in a long sleeve grey pinstripe dress with black heels. She could be on vacation and she'd still dress like she's made of money. Fuck, we all are.

Her heels click across the floor as she passes us for the bar at the back of the room that hasn't been used in years. The maids keep it stocked but there's no need. Who wants to be in an empty home where their dead father used to live? Opening the top cabinet she grabs a bottle of amber liquid along with a crystal glass. Setting the bottle on the granite counter she curls her finger calling us forward. One by one we stand not giving her a reason to suspect anything going on. Even for a mother her intuition sucks. Leaning down she opens the small freezer and scoops up some ice and sets the glass next to the bottle.

"You missed the meeting." She mentions it like she's talking about a football game on T.V.

Without missing a beat West props his elbows on the counter and flashes a wide grin. "We had a little party of our own to attend. I'm sure we didn't miss anything important that we can be caught up on."

Tossing back the drink she swallows it down before slamming the glass into the sink shattering it. Lashing out she pinches West's cheeks in between her polished fingers. "That playboy act doesn't work on me, boy. Make our family look like fools again and I'll do more than make a mess of this house."

Shoving his face away she storms to the door with the Whiskey bottle in her grasp. Hesitating at the exit, her short hair sways when she turns to look at me. "I saw a little mouse today making her way into the school. Looked like she was ready to set it on fire. I wonder if she'll find herself trapped in the middle of her own mess.'"

The threat hangs in the air long after she's gone.

Chapter Twenty-Seven

KENNA

Stepping from the dark hallway the bright array of colors shine against the cobblestone path. Lilies line the walkway blooming perfectly under the wide open sky. It burns to breathe in the smell I've searched for, for the past two months, suffocating me with flashes of a distant memory. My bottom lip quivers when the path curves revealing the stone bench that held me open for him. Exposed to the monster who drank me up like a cure to all the nightmares come to life. If only I could fix the damage in our wake.

"Hey there, pretty." A familiar voice says behind me.

Spinning, the sun bounces off dark sunglasses, his tongue flipping the ring through his lip. A smile fights its way onto my face but it slips just as fast. Looking from his mouth, my eyes travel over him, taking in the man before me. He's either stopped shaving or something's been keeping him from the task. Biting the inside of my cheek I allow myself to comb over his chest, wide and cut with muscle, he wears a tight Henley grey shirt, forming to the way his lean body curves. My gaze moves down to his tight black skinny jeans with a single chain hooked through the belt loop disappearing into his pocket. Steel toed boots are planted firm on the stone path.

"Eyes up here." He chuckles.

The warm sound washes over me bringing a comfort I haven't felt in so long. The walls I've tried to keep held high vibrate with the force of his gaze. He can see the slight panic start to slide away so he makes a move to step closer to me. The smell of hair gel and mens soap float through my nose bringing with it a wave of calm.

"Gio." I sigh.

My eyes start to water when he cocks his head to the side with a crooked grin.

"I brought you something." He says, "And I'm thinking it wasn't the best idea but anything for you."

Shaking my head I make a move to grab the can from his hold but he pulls it back placing it behind him.

"Not so fast, pretty. Tell me you have a plan." He raises a brow.

The way his piercing eyes probe me feels like a therapist watching their patient for signs of crazy. Rolling my eyes I hold my hand out, "I need to do this."

Looking away, G flicks that ring once again, doing what he does when he's deep in thought. He's worried I can't put out the fire I'm starting so I give in and ask him for what he needs.

"Fine. You can stay and help but this is mine."

Rolling his tongue over the back of his teeth he laughs, tossing his head back, before closing the gap between us. The can is pressed against my stomach, leaning forward his lips come close to my ear, he whispers.

"He knows."

Of course he does.

"It's nothing personal?" I quip, my eyebrow raised.

A breeze flows through the garden brushing his hair away from his eyes. I'll give it to the man he's a fucking wet dream walking in bullshit and bravery.

"Nothing personal." Reaching in his back pocket he takes out a smoke and a black lighter with a skull on the front. Placing one between his lips his thumb flicks the lighter putting the flame to the end he pulls in a drag.

He watches the way my eyes track the cigarette. "Yeah?" He holds out the package seeing if I take one. My fingers twitch, unsteady, I grab one and place it against my lips.

Reaching out he holds the flame to the end and I suck in bringing his taste into my mouth. A single tear drifts down the side of my face with the combination of the reality I'm stuck in and the dream I'm fighting to get back to in my head. Mahogany eyes flash in my head when the smoke leaves my lips.

"You smoke to remind you." G, says.

It's the way he says it so softly that has my chest cracking wide open.

"Always the observant one." I snicker past the tears threatening to fall.

Twisting, G sets the can on the stone bench, turning back to me with a stern stare. Watching me, waiting for me to bolt, his movements are slow when he reaches out with a soft touch. Pulling me into his chest, G wraps his arms around me, holding me in a cage of warmth and smoke. Several seconds pass by before my body moves on its own and my arms end up pulling him closer.

"They bleed for you, pretty. Let them show you the truth." He murmurs against my ear.

Stepping back he flashes me a wink, picking up my braid, he tugs on it. A smile breaks through the ache in my chest.

"I don't-" My voice breaks. "I don't know what's real anymore." My bottom lip trembles.

A low chuckle falls from his mouth, shaking his head, he tips my chin up with his finger.

"If you need to fight your way back then just say so, but you need to remember the name you wear." He says. "You're Kingston. A beautiful disaster that holds those men together. A group of college kids run an entire town, pretty. Nothing is real. You're looking for what's real instead of remembering what's always been true."

My chest rises faster. Fighting against the feeling of running away, my fingers close around the hand lifting my chin. G allows me to dig my fingernails into the flesh around his wrist.

"And what's always been true?" I whisper into the open.

His eyes darken, "They bleed for you." His words are so sure.

Moving around him, his hand drops to his side, I snatch the can from the bench and walk out into the circle. Opening the cap the smell of gasoline smacks me in the face. Walking up and down the cobblestone I douse every single lily with fuel. The aroma chokes me, forcing a cough out. Twisting the cap back on I toss the can to his feet and hold out my hand. A look flickers over his expression before he quickly hides it. Bending down, G grabs the now empty can, and heads towards me. Before he passes he drops the black lighter in my palm but doesn't look at me.

"I'll go get the fucking fire station ready." He snarks.

His feelings are a little hurt but he gives me the space and control I need and for that I'm thankful.

"Thank you." I say. I don't yell it and I'm not sure he heard but the small hesitation in his steps gives me hope that he knows how much his coming means to me.

With the realization that I'm fully alone I let my walls

fall, crumbling, bringing with them all the flashbacks of the time I've spent here.

Licking up my neck, he stops at the base below my ear, "What a shame it would be to taint the lilies with your blood. Then again, spill yours and I'll spill mine. I just know we'd make the perfect color to paint the garden the deepest red."

His touch against my skin scorches the image in my brain.

Growling at my words he dives in like a man starved. Both hands landing on my thighs gripping so hard I cry out in pain, and fuck, pleasure too. I'm falling. Falling over the edge of pure ecstasy, and all I see when I close my eyes are lilies and Ryker.

Another memory slams into me rattling my ribs with the force.

"That's it, baby. It'll only be me. No one can fuck you this good with their mouth. Even hate can't keep our demons from each other."

My thighs close around his head dragging him closer. My hips lift, rubbing my pussy over his face, riding him harder and harder.

"I bleed, you bleed." I whisper.

Him kneeling between my thighs sends heat down my spine.

Each vision evokes memories of the way I felt with him under my hold. A scream builds at the back of my throat, unable to escape the flickers of his face behind my eyes, my mouth falls open. Releasing a hollow empty wail the anguish floods from my pores tainting the air around me. Sucking in a deep breath I can almost taste the bitterness in the breeze. Straightening, my hands fist at my side, in one the lighter sits. Holding my head high I let the tears fall freely accepting the fact that I'm slowly breaking.

Walking on the path my shoes pound across the hard stone plucking lilies along the way. Choosing a section close to the exit I spin facing the open area of colors. Each flower is different in its own way. The beauty of a blooming lily is insignificant in this moment. The hairs on the back of my neck stand when a shadow is cast across the garden from behind me. The heat from a body moving closer to where I am cloaks me in warmth. My breathing picks up in speed, the uneasy feeling in the pit of my stomach grows, but I don't turn. I can't stop what I'm doing.

"Killer."

Chapter Twenty-Eight

RYKER

I stand at the edge of the garden watching the way her fingers tighten around the lighter. The sun is shining over her as if it's giving a blessing to the destruction she's about to call upon. She has her hair hanging down her back in a long braid the length longer than the last time I saw her.

"Killer." I whisper.

It's not meant to stop her, instead I hold steady at her back, waiting for her to need me.

She doesn't.

Dropping the burning lighter she takes one step back to watch her creation. My hands twitch with the need to yank her away from the growing fire, but I anchor myself. She's a fucking force of nature. The garden ignites and within seconds it grows higher. The sheer force of the heat smacks me in the face bringing hot air with it. Gradually turning towards me, faded grey eyes meet mine, reflecting the same bone deep ache that mirrors mine.

"Don't." She holds her hand up, her voice cracking.

The control I have fractures, a possessive hunger bubbles in my stomach, unable to stay away any longer. Long strides bring me closer to my killer. Her beautiful grey eyes widen and fear crosses her face. A shiver travels down her body, shaking, her teeth start to rattle like a child stranded in the cold. Given the heat of Del Mar surrounds us I know it's the raw anxiety finding a release. Not deterred, my steps speed up, finally opening the cage to the fucking beast.

Small hands slash at the air warning me to stop. Frantically, she looks around in a panic.

"Oh, baby. The flames wouldn't stop me from taking what's mine." My voice is raw and rough.

The closer I get sweat starts to pool around my brows rolling down my neck into my shirt. G should be here soon but the wild stormy look in her eyes means she won't go easily.

"No." She says that one word is enough to make me hesitate.

My fiery, strong, stubborn girl steps towards the burning garden.

"We loved this garden. Now, all I see is darkness." She quivers.

The look on her face pierces through my chest. She takes another step towards the fire.

"I don't know if I'll rise from the ashes this time. I'm so tired." A soft sob leaves her throat.

I move a step forward, "Killer." I warn.

The air is thick with loss, torment, and sorrow. Her face is wrinkled with despair, wide eyes shining with wetness. I'm only a foot away, so close I can smell the way her scent mixes with the gas, almost like a drug making me dizzy. She's in reach and yet I can't bring myself to touch the dream in front of me.

"Rye!" G's voice yells from behind me.

I keep my eyes on the phoenix in front of me afraid she'll disappear again if I look away. I don't have to see him to know what he's saying. It's growing taller and hotter. The school is too close and soon it'll spread.

"Come on, Killer." I urge. My hand open for her to grab.

Rosy cheeks are streaked with tears. "We're too far gone."

Stepping into her chest my eyes lower to her pink lips. "Oh, baby no. I'll follow you into the fire. If you go I go." My voice lowers. "My soul is branded with your name, Killer. Destroy us." My words are gruff. "Set us on fire, because to have you for just a fraction of my life would shatter any meaning to living."

My hands cup her wet cheeks, my thumbs swiping at the drop rolling down her face, big broken eyes peer into mine.

She sobs, "I have nothing."

She moves back until the heel of her shoe is off the edge of the stone. The fire is eating up the space around us. The back of my shirt is drenched in sweat, but it doesn't stop me from following her into the flames.

Risking everything my hands grip her forearms and drag her into me. Using one hand I pinch her chin tilting her head to mine forcing her to look into my eyes. She's shaking like a leaf under my hold.

"Eyes on me, Killer. *Fuck*, I could say I love you and pray that it glues us back together, but it's not enough." My forehead falls to hers. "How could I pray to fix us if the only God I worship is you? Do you need me to fall to my knees and praise the fucking ground you walk on?" I groan.

Her sobs quicken, making it harder for her to pull in air, she sways on her feet. Letting me hold up her weight she continues to cry.

"Ryker!" A distant voice yells over the roaring fire.

Pulling away, my hand slides to the back of her neck, squeezing. "Air isn't worth breathing without you. Your love made my soul crawl from the shadows, baby, and my heart won't beat without you." Our lips are almost touching.

Hovering my mouth over hers I whisper against her, "Breathe life back into me, Killer." Dropping my lips to hers, she doesn't move.

My tongue traces the seam of her lips and at the same time heat licks up the back of my leg. Even with my eyes closed the orange glow seeps through. Her body locks up under my touch, warring with the demons inside her head.

"I need you." I murmur against her lips.

A soft groan falls from her mouth and I drink it down. She opens for me, dropping her head back, giving me more access. My fingers dig into the back of her neck forcing her into me deeper. My free hand wraps around her waist hauling her into my chest and we both ignore the burning.

Am I a monster for cornering the wounded prey? Maybe so, but heaven and hell collide when we touch.

"Remind me what it's like." She says against my mouth. Her tears soak my face, pulling back smokey eyes meet mine, "Remind me of what it feels like to breathe again."

Running my thumb down her face, I smear the wetness over her, pressing another kiss to the corner of her mouth.

"You are my heart, my one and only thought, the light shining into my dark soul. If you need a reminder of who we are then I'll show you. Because," I lean into her ear, "Whatever our souls are made of, they're formed of the same twisted shadows."

Indecision flickers over her but the sound of voices running this way pulls us from the burning bubble that surrounds us. Firemen and water flood the garden soaking the lilies that held us here.

"Life grows from ash, Killer." I rasp. "Did you find me in the lilies?" I ask, closing my eyes, I wait for the answer.

"Yes." She vows.

Pulling her with me I drag her to the exit where G is

standing with a wild look in his eyes. Stepping into us his eyes move from me to her frantically.

"Holy fuck." He huffs.

Turning to the side he lets us pass, "I'll stick around and make sure this is handled." He waves his hand towards the smoke and embers.

Shifting from under my hold, she pulls away, her gaze clashing with mine. Fighting with herself I can see the battle play out over her face so I try to give her an out.

"What do you need?" I ask.

Licking her lips she presses her fingers to her mouth, "Home."

It's the only word she says, but it holds so much meaning. Walking away from the school grounds where fire trucks and students surround the back parking lot I walk Kenna to her dorm.

Chapter Twenty-Nine

RYKER

The door to her dorm is locked so I pull the keys from my pocket remembering the copy I had made. The overwhelming stench of smoke and fire wafts from us like a campfire freshly burning. Kenna's long hair is braided and laying flat against her rigid back. Once the flames faded into ash and smoke her body locked up slamming her wall back into place. The thin strand of patience I have left hanging between us tightens when she shifts her shoulder away from my touch. Stepping around her I unlock the door and swing it open moving to the side to let her pass. She hesitates a moment before making her way through the threshold with her eyes locked on my every move.

A single light is on in the living room giving the empty space an eerie feel that almost closes the normally open space.

"Killer." The word leaves my lips on a whisper.

The low sound bounces around us echoing into the space she creates with each step she takes. Her hands fist pulling my attention to the bandage around her knuckles. Anxious and greedy for her touch I close the space between us ignoring every fucking sign that she needs space and swallowing the air around us with eager hunger. Twisting her around she's forced to face me and that's when I let her see every shattered, broken, piece of the man at her feet.

"You want me to show you who we are?" I seethe.

The caged rage that I've buried under worry, fear, and pain is bubbling to the top and there's no stopping the madness. Both hands are now grasping her shoulders holding her in place and for a moment the sudden look of terror in her eyes has me pulling back but then she sucks in a breath and I'm gone.

"You left me." She mumbles.

Her voice is so low. So broken. The woman standing before me is a tattered, beaten, mess that's on the edge of falling. Stepping into her chest we both suck in a lung full of air with the closeness. Her stormy grey eyes widen and I try to remind myself that I have no idea what she's been through but she's in my hold now.

"Oh baby, you have it all wrong."

My words are garbled and fragmented, cutting us both in the process. I can see her start to pull away with the declaration. He's twisted so many things inside her head that she can't see how wrong she is. How far has she fallen from my hold? Walking her backward past the couch my steps guide her to her bedroom where the door is closed. Her tongue peeks out to wet her lips, smokey eyes gazing at me with an array of emotion, she nods her head once.

Kicking the door open I wait for both of us to make it through the doorway before using my heel to swing it closed behind us. The lights are off but I don't need to see to know she's already trembling.

"No one can take you from me, Killer. We're etched into each other's bones."

I toe off my shoes, our breathing ragged and loud in the

silence, only the soft movement of my feet break through the quiet.

"Did you-" She pauses. The shape of her body shifting to the side letting light shine through the window casting a shadow across the room.

I run my fingers down her arms sending a shiver through her, "Did I what?" I push.

Anger pulses wild and hot like a fucking inferno knowing what she's about to ask but I give her what he didn't. The freedom to do what she needs to put the pieces together. Waiting for her to continue I use one hand to pull my shirt from my body. The fabric falls to the floor.

Swallowing, she turns back to me, only the blonde of her hair fully visible in the dark.

"Did your family sell me to him? Did-" She sucks in a deep breath, her hands moving in the darkness. "Did you know what he was going to do to me?" She says, defeated.

My muscles tighten, a murderous ache for his blood on my hands has me clenching my fingers. Walking forward, Kenna moves back with each step I take, her knees meeting the bed stopping her from moving. Caging her in she starts to quiver but I'm too far gone to stop. Pressing my hand into the center of her chest I force her down on the bed until she's laying flat against the sheet. Kneeing her legs open I use my other hand to hold myself above her.

The moon lights up the space around me in a low grey hue that matches the scene around me. Grey eyes and wet cheeks glisten in the moonlight looking up at me with confusion and fear all wrapped into a pretty little bow. The beautiful fucking mess beneath me settles something deep in my dark heart that beats around sharp glass ripping us both into a bloody mess. My free hand moves to her throat, my thumb rubbing at her pulse point, before sliding up to her face. Pressing my fingers into her cheeks I ally enough hold to cause a bite of pain.

"No amount of money could ever buy your sweet pussy, baby." I seeth. "I'll kill him for you if you don't want to get your hands dirty, but he will fucking die by our hands." Leaning down, my lips hover over her mouth. "You're not for sale, Killer. I'll never be able to carve away his touch but I can make sure all you ever feel again is the way we bleed together."

Dropping the rest of the distance our mouths clash in a mess of teeth and tongue. She doesn't move, her body is frozen from the assault, but I take every inch of her that she offers. Pulling back I can see the war she's fighting with herself so I push further. Standing, my hands reach in my back pocket pulling out the small blade I knew I'd find. Oakley's starting to wear off on me. Lifting the bottom of her shirt, my finger flips the blade open, and slices up towards her throat.

Fuck, my dick twitches at the image of her skin under my knife, but I tuck that away for another time. Her muscles lock in place when her chest is laid bare beneath the bra and shirt now cut and laying beside her.

"You wanted me to show you who we were?" I say.

Her head bobs with unease, her chest lifting faster with each breath, but she drinks down her fear.

"This is who we are, Killer. Dangerous. Spiteful." I pull her pants down past her waist. "Messy. Wild." I fall to my knees between her thighs. "Dark. Twisted." I drag her pants to her ankles pulling them the rest of the way to the floor. Her thighs lock around me but not in an attempt to pull me closer, no. Her head thrashes from side to side on the bed, fingers pulling at the skin around her nails, she panics.

Both hands start at her ankles and slowly I drag them up

her legs. "You're mine to worship, Killer." My lips fall to her pale skin.

My eyes close when my tongue slips to slide against her flesh. I can feel her shivering beneath me but still I continue.

"I can't." She cries out.

Her shattered tone pushes me over the edge and I plunge into darkness. I'm so gone in my thirst for her that I ignore all pleas that fall from her lips. Using two fingers I shove her thong to the side and take in the sight before me. Even in the low light I can see how wet she is for me, scared, scarred, and broken yet she still craves my touch.

"I'll never be able to take away what he did." My mouth falls to her center pressing a kiss above her clit. "I can only blanket his pain with our own." My teeth sink into her clit, sucking and nipping at the same time.

She lets out a low cry and followed by a raspy moan. Drinking her down, my tongue plunges deeper, pushing inside her, I taste my favorite fucking flavor. Her legs open and close around my head fighting a war inside her own. Coaxing her free from those thoughts with each thrust inside her. Using my thumb to apply pressure my eyes roll back at the overwhelming feeling of having my mouth on her.

"That's it, baby." I say against her wet skin.

Gripping both of her hips with my hands I press her harder into the bed holding her down while I fuck her with my mouth. Biting her clit she lets out another scream this time louder and goddamn if I don't damn near bust in my jeans.

"Scream for me, Killer." I growl against her.

Gliding my hand up her bare stomach, my fingers spread between her breasts, holding her down while my other hand joins my mouth. She claws at my arm but the pain is nothing compared to the ecstasy of her on my tongue. Pressing my thumb over her clit, rubbing circles over the swollen bud, my teeth clamp into her, while my tongue thrust inside. She shatters, spilling down my throat, I drink from her until she's a crying mess. Leaning back my gaze meets hers and for a moment my heart beats harder behind my ribs with the way she looks. Her blonde hair is wild, the brain almost completely ruined, and her red cheeks soaked with tears.

Licking my lips, I press my fingers into my mouth, cleaning the mess she made while her glassy eyes watch.

"You taste like a wicked dream and I never want to wake up." My voice is low. Guttural.

She squirms beneath me, trying to climb the bed, and the look that crosses her face has me pausing. "Don't worry, Killer. I don't plan on fucking you tonight. The pain I force on you will never be more than pleasure."

Leaning up on her forearms she lets her eyes trail over me. Looking away her teeth sink into her bottom lip. Her beauty rips open my chest with the need to fill her fractured pieces. We take each other in, her flushed skin, the way she sucks in a breath every time our eyes meet, and fuck me, when her lips part at the sight of my new ink.

"When?" She whispers into the air between us.

My fingers absently rub across the fresh tattoo over my heart.

"You stole something from me when you were taken." I say, my words low, "Part of my soul left me that day and fuck, Killer. I couldn't fucking breathe without you. Darkness engulfed me until all I saw was you." Tracing the stem of the lily I move to the words below that.

You bleed, I bleed.

A tear slips down her cheek, "I don't-" She breaks off letting out a sob. "Nothing makes sense anymore." Sitting up she pulls her knees to her chest and wraps her arms around herself.

Climbing on the bed I pull her into me forcing her legs

around my waist she lets her head fall to my chest. Ignoring the way her body feels against mine I let her lay on me until the tears run dry. She stays even when her cries slow. We lay there long after the moon rises high into the night. It's not until a soft, sleepy, voice speaks that I realize she's awake.

"I've always belonged to you." She speaks softly.

My breathing slows. I've paused from rubbing her back and now there's nothing but silence. It may be minutes or hours later but once my thoughts are finally still and quiet I speak into the darkness shrouding us.

"My heart beats in your chest, Killer. Our jaded fractured pieces were made for each other." Kissing the top of her head my eyes close, "I love you, Kenna Kingston."

Chapter Thirty

KENNA

A soft tapping on my bedroom door has me rolling over to face the direction the sound is coming from. Looking down, my gaze skates over my body, making sure I'm fully covered before responding.

"Come in." I call out. The awareness of not knowing who it is is lost in the half asleep fog of my mind.

The numbness wrapping around my bones vibrates through me, shoving the cold from my limbs. Waking up to an empty bed after the memory of us drifting to sleep together last night leaves a bitter taste lining my mouth. The pit of my stomach twists with the reminder that I let him touch me. The skin around my nails ache with the proof of my betrayal. The door swings open and G stands in the opening leaning his arm across the door with a smirk painted across his face. His tongue slips out to flick at his lip ring with a brow raised. Rolling my eyes I pull myself into a sitting position dragging my knees into my chest. If he notices the way my muscles shake with his presence he ignores it.

"Let's go, Princess." He orders.

His gaze doesn't travel further than my face and it

provides me a comfort I didn't realize I needed. When I don't make a move to follow his lead his arms cross over his broad chest flexing the tattoos that cover them. The dark grey shirt he's wearing damn near screams with the way his form pulls at the fabric and I can't help but let out a small soft laugh. There's just something about him that will always give me the reassurance of being in a safe space. I think I've always known that Gio is family even when the Stone brothers were handing him orders to follow me. When my thoughts travel back to the brothers my muscles lock up and my expression must change because he makes a move to step into my room.

Pulling in a deep breath, my legs stretch across the bed, scooting to the foot of the bed I let them slide to the floor. My eyes fall to my feet, head hanging low, my chest pinches when his low voice rolls over me.

"Get dressed. You don't need to think or do anything other than follow directions. Come on, it'll be fun to spend the day with me." He jokes.

Tossing an outfit on the bed the fabric lands on my head and lap making us both laugh, softening the mood in the room. Sucking my teeth I nod yanking the black, what seems to be a sports bra, off my head and slapping it against the bed.

"I'll be out in a minute." I breathe.

It takes a few seconds, him peering at me for most of them, before he decides he's okay with what he sees leaving me alone to change. I have no idea why he felt the need to dress me but from the looks of the outfit there are only a few options for what he has planned. Either we're going on a run or he's taking me to the fucking Basement. Part of me hopes it's the latter so I can disappear into the crowd to get away.

And where are you going?

Biting the inside of my cheek, frustration sparks in my belly, that fucking voice in my head is back again. I have no idea what to believe at this point yet all I know is something isn't right. Even now I can't pull his name forward to let it roll off my tongue but I still want him near. Flashes of the wall spread with photos of their betrayal flickering in the back of my head and even still I fight against the lies mixed in with the truth. Shoving down everything I continue to change, pulling out a pair of shoes, my palms wipe down the workout shorts G tossed me.

The black on black workout gear hugs my form and holds everything into place. My hair is a mess from the braid yesterday and a faint smell of smoke still lingers in the strands but I don't have time for a shower so I opt to twist it up into a messy bun on top of my head. Rubbing my hands down my face, a small part of me just wants to crawl back in bed, picking my fingers I sigh and turn towards the door. Stepping out of my room, the hallway is empty, so I head to the bathroom yelling out over my shoulder.

"Be right out." My voice lacks emotion, even I can tell it's flat.

Flipping on the bathroom light my gaze clashes with the splintered glass that still hangs over the sink in shards. My reflection is broken, a reflection of how I feel on the inside, dried blood still present. Swallowing past the lump in my throat I go through the motions of brushing my teeth and washing my hands after I go to the bathroom. I've zoned out when tapping once again pulls me back to the present. Toeing the door open G's wandering gaze meets mine assessing me. The warm scent of power and wood wafts through my nose.

"Looks like someone got a little angry." He quips, grinning at me.

Twisting my lips to the side, I rub my knuckles, "Something like that." I huff.

He steps towards me until my hip is digging into the edge of the sink. Once again his tongue is licking at that damn ring drawing my eyes to the action. Gio is a handsome fucker that's for damn sure, but he's family. The only thing we lack is DNA but that doesn't define us. He brings his hand to my face, pinching my chin with two fingers. Lifting my head, warm brown eyes meeting mine, his lips part.

"Step away from what you think is right and just feel. We're all fighting the same battle with different scars. The only difference between your fight and theirs is they are fighting for you. Who are you fighting for?" His brow raises in question. Shifting his hold, his palm cups my cheek, a soft smile taking over his face. "Kingston. Stone. They're just the names we're born into, but what we do with those names is for us to choose." His words are so firm and strong they coat my skin in false bravery.

"I don't know if I can face him once he finds out-" I break off, turning away from his prying eyes.

He doesn't have to guess what I mean, it's written all over my face, shame. G yanks me into his chest, harsh and quick, pushing the air from my chest. Cradling my head into him he drops his mouth to my hair.

"Don't you ever let me or him hear you fucking say that." He snarls.

Rage spills from him in waves, but he keeps his hold on me steady. Sinking into his hug I let myself fall into the warmth he provides for a moment. The picture he paints is so strong my heart starts to beat harder with the hope that I might be able to breathe again. Plopping a kiss on the top of my head he pulls back with a wicked grin.

"Let's go." He says.

Releasing me, he spins on his heels, and heads towards the front of the dorm. I follow behind him a distracted partici-pant to his scheme. Gio leads me out of the dorm building into a twin SUV of the brothers and off we go to the Basement.

Hoots and hollers bounce off the walls coming from down the stairs to the basement. Where the underground fighting ring got its name. The Basement is a place where the Stone brothers started to have fights planned out for people who needed a release, or a lesson to learn. You could come here on your own for a little fun or you could end up here when there was a price to pay to the brothers. Black and white memories start to play in the back of my head the closer we get to the staircase, but I shove them down knowing they'll do me no good right now.

My legs shake a little with each step, the feeling of being too full still heavy, I make an effort to keep my feet on the ground. G opens the door and the sound grows louder making my eye squint with the onslaught of noise. When we cross the threshold onto the first step voices lower and we don't need to hear their thoughts to know they're all looking at me.

Look how skinny she is.
Where has she been?
What did they do to her?
Is she the one that made Cole kill himself?

That last one has G pulling me into his side when my knees buckle at the accusation. They don't know Cole is alive... Wetting my lips, my fingers dig into my thighs, but I keep my face blank. We take the steps slowly allowing everyone in the open space to get a good look because they won't get another any time soon. Once we reach the bottom G looks to the back left corner and calls someone over, but I can't make out who. Faces and bodies blur into each other with so many people in such a tight area. The Basement has large bright lights hanging every few feet across the ceiling casting a blinding glow around us.

The ring is now empty with a younger looking boy standing in the middle with a swollen eye and bleeding lip. Using his thumb he wipes away the crimson liquid and flashes his teeth.

"Parties over!" He shouts across the room. When no one moves he walks to the ropes and stands on the bottom one lifting himself higher over the boisterous onlookers. "Get the fuck out assholes!" He bellows. Everyone turns at once to look at G, and whatever they see on his face puts them in action. Feet shuffle to the exit not wasting any time getting out of the way. G's made a name for himself around here. People respect the man at my side.

A familiar face walks through a group of men flashing me a smile. I can't help the returning grin that lights up my face when I see him coming towards me. Romero's name falls from my mouth, and I can feel the heat of G's glare on the side of my face. Romero pauses, barely a foot away, lifting my hand that's wrapped from the broken glass in my dorm, he looks between me and G.

He speaks, his tone uneasy, G making him nervous, and of course he would.

"Kenna." He acknowledges me.

The Stone brothers warned him to stay away from me, but him taking a chance now has pride bubbling in my stomach for the jock, who usually minds his place. I've come to like Romero, not in the way I thought I did months ago, but I have a new respect for him now. Taking in G's stance, the domineering look on his face, knowing that Romero wouldn't stand a chance against him in the ring, and yet he still not only walked up to me and spoke, but is now cradling my hand. Inspecting the damage and checking to make sure I'm okay.

"How are you, Kenna?" He asks, looking up from my

knuckles, his eyes flipping between me and the brute beside me.

My cheeks turn pink with embarrassment because I know that everyone's watching this interaction and confusion has to be taking over. One minute I'm with a Stone, the next I'm with G, and now Romero is holding my hand delicately. I remind myself to not give a fuck what these pricks think right now not when everything is starting to come back together. My memories and thoughts are starting to be less clouded.

"You look like you're about to kick some ass." He nods to my outfit with a crooked grin. "Have fun but be careful." He says before backing away, making a move to go around us. Pausing, he gives G a dark look, "Take care of her." His tone is low and hard.

G's jaw ticks, clenching tight, I can feel the agitation rolling from his skin heating the space between us. A soft laugh leaves me and his head jerks to the side, our eyes clashing. The broody bastard doesn't like the threat that he feels Romero just left him with, but really it was a request to make sure I'm taken care of, so I take it with ease. I reach out to grab his large hand squeezing tightly, giving him a half smile, and jerking my head towards the ring signaling him that I'm ready.

"Hey, Kingston." A voice calls out drawing my attention to a male and a woman standing between a lingering group of people.

The others are forcing their way through the crowds towards the door but something made these two pause. G's arm whips around my waist with a tight grip pulling me close to his side, but my stare is set on the man staring back at me. Around his throat is a haunting tattoo giving the illusion of the dead pulling him down to hell. The skeleton hand wrapped around his throat tattooed there like a stamp or branding claiming him. My eyes drift from the ink to his dark eyes then to the woman standing beside him. Her stare is harsh and her lips curl into a snarl, but neither of them look familiar. She has long red hair down to her waist with tattoos covering every inch of her arms. They look like a fierce pair side by side. She's every bit as beautiful as she is feral.

Green eyes float from mine down to where G's arm connects with my bare skin and they darken. Her painted red lips twitch before she jerks her eyes away looking towards the exit.

"I'll be seeing you." She quips but it's not me she's looking at anymore. It's the man with his hand resting on my hip.

G flashes her a wide grin, "Keep your eyes to yourself, little tease." His words spark something behind her eyes.

The man finally pulls his gaze from me and tugs at her arm with a look crossing his face that says he's pissed. At me or her? Rolling my shoulder I try to shove that question away for another day. The room is almost empty. By now the soft whispers and murmurs lingering die down but I ignore them. Stepping up to the ring, G nudges me forward, making me break my focus on the weird standoff we're in. The man finally turns away and follows the woman out of the Basement. G pulls back the rope to the ring letting me step through and a memory slams into me sucking the air from my lungs. The flashes bring an array of colorful feelings, one of shock and fear, but more than that a feeling of power and seduction. At the forefront of those memories is the man in question himself. Ryker fucking Stone. He holds every facet of my memories for as long as I can remember.

Ryker Stone.

The faint phantom buzz against my throat conjures the familiar feeling of pain, but it never comes. The strike of lightning never follows.

Chapter Thirty-One

KENNA

"Fuck." I let out an exasperated huff.

My palms hit my knees, my entire body trembling from the overuse of weak muscles. G props his elbows behind him on the top rope leaning back with a crooked grin. Not a drop of sweat can be found on him.

"Getting tired already, Kens?" He jokes.

My breathing starts to slow, but I'm still short of breath when I respond.

"Fuck you." I snap.

Irritation courses through me when he peers at me with his smug ass attitude. My calves scream at me from the workout but G looks far from done.

"What are we doing here?" I push.

It's not the first time I've asked and if he bounces around the question it won't be the last. Either he's a shitty liar, which I know isn't true, or he's busy trying to keep me away from something. Pushing up my back straightens my stare and darkens, quaking a brow in response to his silence. The Basement is still empty but I can hear noise upstairs so I'm guessing a party is going to be starting soon.

Looking towards the door, his jaw clenches, "You're here to clear your head." Rolling his head back, his eyes fall to the ceiling. "You need to let go of everything you think is true and follow what you already know. You can't do that until you push past the pain."

Dropping my gaze to the mat the air rushes from my lungs. A deeper part of me screams out into the void for help that I know only I can give myself. No one can drag me from the darkness in my mind but me. G's here right now trying and yet all I want to do is crawl into a ball ignoring everything around me. That empty feeling behind my ribs twinges with a bone deep ache, a harsh reminder that even the numbness wears off eventually. Gio bounces backward making his body spring forward coming at me fast.

The sudden change of pace has me backing away on instinct.

"Fight back." He snaps.

His joking tone and smooth swagger is gone, replaced with a wild eyed fighter thirsty for trouble. His abs are cut and hard shining with fresh sweat tempting me to look lower. Twisting his hips, the distraction of his bare chest gives him the opening to hook his leg behind mine, shoving me backwards. The floor comes at me fast, my back slamming into the mat, G hovers over me with a hard look.

"Get me off you."

His body lowers, putting more weight on me and my chest caves. Unable to pull in another gulp of air my ribs rattle bringing panic with it. He's not completely on me but the close proximity shoves me head first into panic preventing my brain from understanding the space wedged between us. Instantly my palms slam forward striking him below his chest bone. He doesn't move a fucking inch and I spiral. Tears threaten to spill, my skin tingling, a cold sweat breaks out over my body.

"Stop." My words are weak.

G drops his mouth closer hovering just over my parted lips a scream on the tip of my tongue. Brown eyes shift into blue plunging me into a living nightmare. Pulling in air is impossible. My vision starts to blur around the edges mixing his form with another. Pounding my fist into his sides I take any shot I have that could free me but my knuckles smart from the onslaught. One of his large hands pins me down by my wrist. Eyes blown wide I can feel myself start to faint when his voice fills my ears.

"Shove it down and fight back. Open your eyes and fight back." He orders me.

His words hold power behind them that I reach for begging for a lifejacket in the sea I'm drowning in. He's the asshole that threw me overboard yet here he is forcing me to float in the deep waters. I don't realize that my eyes are closed until he tells me to open them and I do. Blinking back the tears and sweat that roll over my face, my stare meets his mocha colored glare. Releasing my wrist he grips my face, pinching my cheeks like a child, he pulls me forward.

"Fight." He snarls.

My teeth sink into my bottom lip biting down until the pain is all I can focus on. Feeding on that feeling I pull forward every single memory of pain, hurt, sorrow, and anger that I can muster until my bones hum with the overwhelming feelings. My tongue swipes over my lips I snake my arm around his back and snatch a handful of his thick hair yanking back. Exposing his throat I jerk forward biting into his throat before he breaks free from my grip. He's strong but I'm fast and angry. Breaking skin the taste of copper fills my mouth but I don't let go of my hold. With my other hand I punch G's jaw ripping his flesh from between my teeth spraying my face with crimson liquid.

"Fuck, Kens!" He yelps, grabbing for his throat.

Blood slowly rolls down the column of his neck painting his tan skin red. Looking down at me with a clouded expression his mouth opens but nothing comes out. Using his shock against him my knee jolts forward plowing into his ass and sending him over my head. His lower half lands over me but I rush to roll from under him and jump to my feet. Once I'm standing the adrenaline starts to slow bringing another wave of exhaustion.

Turning to the side I spit out a mouthful of his fucking blood like a rabid dog but at least now I can pull in a lungful of air.

"Don't ever do that again." I spit at the bastard.

G's holding pressure to his throat when he turns around with a look that's a mix of pride and something else plastered across his face. Walking to the edge of the ring he bends over snatching up his shirt and pressing it to the bite.

"Now you know you can get me off of you if you need to." He says, shrugging his shoulders.

"Let's not pretend like you didn't know what you were doing. Pushing me like that." I snarl. "Forcing me down on my back. Laying over me." My lip curls in raw rage. I can feel my face getting redder the more I speak.

Pulling the shirt away from his wound G tilts his head to the side, "I don't think you have a problem stopping someone." He states. "You just had to find the fight you think you lost."

Spinning away from him I move to the edge of the ring when he speaks again, "You can't run from what he did to you but you can take back control."

"Yeah, and who would that be? Because as far as I can tell two people took something from me." I toss over my shoulder.

I can hear him coming closer but I don't flinch. I don't

move. I allow him to step into my back knowing that I'm no longer cornered on the mat.

"That's for you to decide but don't forget that your mind and body often speak different words. Close your eyes and tell me which monster you see and who you're afraid of."

His words settle over me giving me something to think about when the basement door swings open bringing with it voices that float down to us. Familiar ones. We both look towards the group making their way down the wooden steps, most of the faces familiar and a couple that I've only seen in photos. Hanks pictures from the room flash in behind my eyes reminding me of the woman with the wide smile sitting beside Ryker.

"What the hell happened to you, my boy." West says, snickering at G.

Looking over my shoulder I twist my lips to the side waiting for his response when Oakley cuts in bouncing up to the ropes.

"My turn." She dances on her toes.

Jumping over the top rope, unlike the rest of us, she ignores the stares and instead comes to stand next to me.

"Have at it." I raise my hands attempting to back away from the fiery woman with blue hair and crazy eyes.

Rolling her eyes, she props a hand on her hip, "no, no." A finger is now in my face, "I meant me and you." She says. Hooking a thumb over her shoulder, "I already had my turn with G man and trust me it was fun but I think we have some stuff to work out." She winks.

This nut just winked at me after letting a sly threat fall from her mouth. Does she think I'm stupid? Shaking my head, "No, I'm good."

Lifting the rope I'm halfway through when she grabs my forearm and jerks me back into the ring sending me to my ass. Pain shoots up my tailbone into my throat cutting off the words on my tongue.

"Oak." West warns his tone hard.

"Aht aht." She waves a finger.

She's insane. Actually fucking crazy, coo-coo house, insane.

"We have something to work out. Don't y'all have some shit to discuss." She flicks her hand between West, G, and another guy who's playing with a pocket knife. My eyes roam over the man who likes to press the sharp end of a blade into the palm of his hand. Sandy blonde hair piles on top of his head but it's the pink scar down the side of his face that hold my gaze.

"Eyes to yourself." Oakley sings, dancing around the ring flexing her fingers and rotating her wrist.

"I'm not fighting you." I say.

My nose scrunches when she shrugs, confusing me further.

Looking down at her black polished nails she casually tosses out another threat, "do, don't. That's up to you whether you fight me or not, but I never said I wasn't." Smacking her lips she looks over at her boy and blows him a kiss.

Shaking his head, a smirk tips his lip, drawing more attention to the jagged line on his face. West pounces on the stage hauling himself forward to hang over the top rope.

"Oakley, I'd hate to cause problems with my guy Havoc here but you're pushing your luck." He lets the comment fall from his mouth in an easy way but the acid behind the words burns just the same.

Crossing his arms over his chest Havoc peers between West and Oakley before settling on the girl at his side.

"Come on Haven let's go see what they have upstairs." He draws out in a low raspy voice.

Oakley claps her hands letting out a giggle that rivals the creepiest witch laugh. West looks between us before nodding at me in encouragement.

"Come on, Princess. Kingstons don't back down." He reassures me.

My arms hang at my side worn out from the work out G put me through and my legs spasm from the overuse. Swallowing past the lump in my throat I claw through the pain and soreness searching for just a sliver of strength.

"G." West calls jumping down from the ring.

Behind me I can hear footsteps climbing up and then the door opening and closing. The beautiful, curvy, brunette is long gone with blade boy leaving only the four of us down here. G and West step over to a small area in the back corner where a small bar top with stools around it taking a seat. They lower their voices and no matter how hard I focus on their words I can't hear a thing. A small arm drapes over my shoulder pulling my ear to her mouth.

"I don't bite, little sheep." Oakley whispers a tinkling laugh following.

"The fuck did you call me?" I snap, jerking out of her hold.

Sucking the back of her teeth, sky blue eyes shine up at me, her smile all wrong. Flipping her hand over she chuckles before turning around and giving me space.

"It's nothing. Now, let's have a little chat." She's back to dancing but this time she doesn't move instead she shifts on her heels.

Rubbing my hands, my knuckles sting from the earlier hits, another reminder that I'm spent from today. My stomach adds a growl into the mix letting us both know how empty it is.

"What do you want from me?" I ask, moving away when she steps towards me on her right foot.

Oakley's dressed in jean shorts and a dark grey tank showing off her ink but it's far from the outfit I have on. The fringe of her cutoff shorts sway with her movements each time she pushes onto her other foot.

Tapping her finger against her chin she looks to the ceiling, "I want to know what you did to Jax."

Stumbling backward she smiles, dark and wide, at my reaction to his name. Dim blue eyes float through my vision plowing into me. Using the opening she springs forward on her toes swinging wide landing a punch to my hip. Pain radiates down my leg into my foot, almost knocking me off balance. Backing away I turn in a wide circle keeping my eyes on her next move. She slides back dragging the bottom of her shoe across the mat not looking away once.

"You remember Jax, yeah?" She edges, "The one who gave you that pretty little snake of yours." Her painted nail points to the cold blooded reptile slithering up my leg.

Scraping my teeth across my bottom lip I want to look away from her harsh glare but I'd be risking too much. Curling her fingers she eggs me on taunting me with a sneer.

"Come on don't tell me you forgot about his baby blues." She sings in a light voice that defies everything she eludes right this moment. She's anything but sweet and sugary. This woman in a venus fly trap waiting to snatch up its next prey. Deadly, yet beautiful.

My eyes burn from the threat of more tears leaving me wondering how much one person can cry in a twenty-four hour period. My throat feels like it's closing in on me when she continues to say his name. I risk a look to the left trying to spot West or G but they are deep in a conversation I can no longer hear. A hit slams into the top of my shoulder just below my collarbone, the force almost putting me on my ass. Sucking in a large gulp of air my right foot steps forward looking for an opening but coming up short. Oakley dances away when she spots my forward motion knowing just how to escape me.

"I was the one to bury him." She states calmly.

The way she speaks it's almost like we're chatting about the weather but with each word she paints a gruesome picture.

Swinging her leg around she nails me in the top of my thigh dropping me to the floor before dancing away.

"Do you remember what his smile looked like?" She asks.

Glassy sea blue eyes peer at me anticipating my next move. My entire body shakes when my palms push against the flooring bringing me back to my feet. Wiping at the sweat building over my brows, my mouth opens and closes.

Tisking, she looks off to the side, "It was a beautiful one. He was a lucky one until you decided to stitch his mouth shut." She seethes.

Tears roll down my cheeks, images and memories crash into me.

"Pretty girl."

The name he used to call me slips from my lips under my breath but she still heard. Sticking her tongue between her teeth she nods once. Lunging at me Oakley pounds hit after hit into my sides. Knocking the air from my chest my knees buckle making me drop to the floor. Using my arms I cover my head in the fetal position trying to protect myself from her assault. Punch after punch. My back, my sides, the back of my neck.

"Enough!" a loud voice bellows.

His voice bounces off the walls yet the hits keep coming. My heartbeat pounds in my ears and blood rushes through my veins. When the hits start to slow I take an opening and drop to my stomach rolling away from her reach. Using my left leg I strike out at the back of her knee bringing her down to me. It's almost impossible to breathe through the pain but

I push past it and focus on the psycho in front of me. I can hear footsteps rushing our way, but my vision blurs red covering the entire room in a haze of rage and hurt.

Crawling to her I shove off the floor throwing my entire body weight into her giving myself an advantage. Once I'm over her, I bring my elbow down on her throat, a cough spilling from her at the pressure. The hand that's wrapped has thick padding on it so I use it to take the punches to the side of her face and ribs. She tries to buck me off but I've faded into nothing but raw energy.

"Kenna!" A voice screams from behind me but I don't let go of the shattered control I still cling to.

Blood drips onto white teeth with the following punch dragging a hollow laugh from her chest. The blue in her eyes dim with each punch but she eats them like a fucking champ.

"Okay, Kenna. Back off." I make out G's voice standing over me.

Thick corded arms lift me from the mat pulling me away from a bloody Oakley. Her wide smile splattered in red she lets her head back back against the floor, her chest heaving.

"I knew she was in there somewhere." She groans.

Licking the blood from her lips she smacks them putting on a show of admiring the flavor. Sinking into the chest behind me my legs give out leaving him with my entire weight across his arms. His warm breath fans over my sweaty skin when he leans in to speak to only me.

"That's my girl." West says, pressing a kiss into the side of my head.

Oakley stands, peering at me with a chilling expression, she wipes off her hands on her thighs.

"You're a bad bitch." She chuckles holding out her fist.

Eyeing her up and down for a second my fist raises to meet her in a fist bump.

"And you're a freak of nature." I quip.

Busting out in a loud laugh, bending at the knee, she holds her side. "Damn, little sheep. I like that one." She shakes a finger at me before heading to the ropes and jumping down from the mat.

Once it's just me and West left in the ring I spin in his hold and look up into milky brown eyes. His lighthearted smile pulling out one of my own to reflect his. Lifting a hand to push back the hair stuck to my face his inquisitive gaze skates over me sending a chill down my spine. Leaning my cheek into his palm, seeking comfort, he doesn't move away instead he drags me into him for a deep hug. Breathing in his scent the organ in my chest starts to stitch itself back together with the glue his hold provides.

Tilting away from me his thumb wipes away a drop of blood from my face. "You bleed, we bleed." His tone is low and promising.

Chapter Thirty-Two

KENNA

West places his palm against my lower back to steady me on my way up the old wooden stairs of the Basement. Oakley and Haven's voices travel up from behind me with their conversations about the party above us. I'm guessing they plan on hanging around for a little after the beating party and the image of Oakley below me bleeding brings a smirk to my face.

"Easy, Princess. You're cocky is showing." West whispers against my ear.

His warm body heats up my chilled one sending a shiver down my spine. When we reach the top of the landing a full blown party is in motion with flashing lights, alcohol, and music. Rubbing my hands up and down my arms to pull in some heat G steps up beside me holding out a black hoodie. Raising an eyebrow my busted and bruised knuckles gladly take the offering slipping the large fabric over my head.

"He wanted me to be prepared." He winks, walking towards the kitchen.

Biting my bottom lip, West takes his place at my side, nudging me with his broad shoulder.

"We'll always take care of you, Princess. You have to let us." His deep brown eyes peer into mine, searing me with the meaning to his comment.

"You want a trust I don't know if I have anymore." I murmur.

The music is loud but his eyes watch my mouth reading every word. Nodding his head he looks away a tick in his jaw as he takes my response.

"We all have something to fight for. To earn back." He says, not asking or telling.

It's a statement that rings true for us all. I've lost so much yet so have they. I've killed for them and for myself. From the way people look at us standing in the center of the floor I can gather that they've done the same. We have so much to answer for but they're asking me to stand next to them while we figure it all out. So many questions continue to plow into me but a flash of blue hair from my right grabs my attention. Dainty painted fingernails hold out a red solo cup and a wide smile.

"I owe you one hell of a drink, little sheep." She says, her tone light.

My gaze rolls over her, taking in the way she cocks her hip, the way her tattoos spread over her pale skin. Oakley is one hell of a beast and I stood my own against her. Taking the cup from her hand I return her smile with a raspy laugh.

"Can't say it was fun but..." I trail off.

We all let out a laugh and slowly start to shake off the previous bullshit from downstairs. The heat of everyone's eyes on me still has me on edge but the warmth of the liquor helps settle my stomach. There's a commotion coming from the kitchen that has me, Oak, and West walking towards the open doorway. I spot Haven and the two other men around a keg placed in the middle of a bare living room ignoring the bodies pressing in closer to them.

I don't miss the way her eyes land on me and then travel over to West where his hand is placed at my back. It takes effort not to flash her a wink staking my claim on my Stone boys, instead I tip my chin at her in respect. From the corner of my eye West is meeting her glare with a smooth playboy smirk that has his lips tipped in a crooked grin. He knows how to make their legs weak but she doesn't flinch from the pressure of his stare.

"Don't you have somewhere to be?" G barks.

Shoving my way through a group of jock fuckers, I finally break through the crowd to see G closing in on the same redheaded woman from downstairs only this time the man at her side is nowhere to be seen. She sucks the front of her teeth making a show of not being bothered with his proximity. A brave one.

"I'll let my brother handle that." She coo's, patting G on the chest.

He trembles under her touch, a feral animal banging against a cage, his expression threatening. Caging her in against the counter top they continue to go back and forth but their voices lower leaving us out of the conversation. West ushers everyone from the kitchen ordering them to find somewhere else to fuck off. Looking around the dimly lit room my gaze falls on a streak of purple hair, my breath catching in my lungs. Reaching out, my nails dig into flesh, my knees buckling from the onslaught of memories. The taste of acid and betrayal is strong on my tongue.

Wincing, West jerks his arm from my hold, "What the fuck, Kens." He questions.

He follows my line of sight and tisk, "Later." He urges.

Shaking my head I ignore him, my feet already in motion, I cross the room before she looks over from the girl she's talking to. Ally wears a pleated leather skirt that's barely covering her ass paired with spiderweb stockings and black biker boots. Her hair looks longer but the purple has begun to fade showing that she hasn't colored it in a while. A small part of me recognizes the subtle changes in her appearance but the larger much angrier side shoves it away. Her purple polish nails hold a red solo cup in her hand with a smile painted over her face in mid conversation.

In one swift move I've snatched the drink from her hand tossing it back letting the warmth skate down my throat. When her eyes meet mine I swing my fist swings out landing a punch to the side of her face. White noise fills my ears when her wide shocked eyes meet mine but what I see looking back at me has me stumbling back.

"Kenna?" She asks as if she can't believe I'm here.

"Everyone out." I garble behind rage.

No one moves. No one breathes. Somehow the music has been shut off and all eyes are on our small group.

"Everyone OUT!" I scream.

All stares shift to G and West watching and waiting to see what they do but when G moves from his place at the counter to stand at my side they all scatter like roaches. The redhead takes the opening and walks out the kitchen but not before blowing G a kiss over her shoulder and flashing me a sneering look. West steps up beside G, his gaze roaming the space around us and then his gaze meets mine. For a split second we both see the same thing. Gio holds more power than we anticipated. Three men step up behind G waiting for an order to fall from the punker's lips but the most notable change is the placement G chose. G no longer stands behind us instead he's chosen to step beside us.

A shift in the air has everyone on edge yet I ignore it all to turn back to Ally who has her hand on her red cheek.

"Kenna." She breathes.

Stepping forward she steps back, hitting the wall behind her.

"Addington." I spit.

The last name I use is a reminder of her disloyal choices. Everyone has something to answer for and hers is being a rat.

West grabs my shoulder, "Not here." He says.

Looking over my shoulder at the sets of eyes on me I sigh.

"She's coming with us." I hook my thumb over my shoulder.

Oakley and Haven huddle around the island countertop pouring more drinks when someone's phone starts to ring. G waves off his guys letting them know things are all clear leaving us with the core crew remaining.

"Slade?" Oakley says into her phone.

It must be the way she says his name that has Havoc and the new guy circling around her with questioning stares. Haven moves back to let them get closer to their woman but she doesn't fully step out of the circle they've formed. Whatever the person on the other line says in response has her dropping her cup onto the counter spilling the clear liquid.

"Sav?" New guy says his tone low and gruff.

West pulls me behind him looking for a possible threat from all angles. Oakley looks at Havoc and the new guy with a haunted look before hanging up and grabbing Haven. Spinning towards West she looks past him at me for a long moment. My lungs scream at me from holding my breath with the tense air around us.

"You've got this?" She asks, but instead of asking West she's aiming the question at me.

Licking my lips I nod my head once giving her the out she's needing.

Moving around her men she drags a shocked Haven behind her as she rushes for the door. "We have our own little issue back home and we need to go now."

Whatever's going on with West and Haven has him jumping into action following them out the front door. His large hand grabs Haven yanking not only her to a stop but Oakley as well. Havoc whips around heading for West who now has Haven pressed against his chest.

"I don't know what the fuck is going on but she's not going anywhere." He snaps.

Havoc and Oakley look at each other before coming towards us. Haven places her palm on his wide chest looking up at him with a soft look.

"I'll be fine but if it's bad we need to go now." Her words are soft and low only meant for him.

He covers her hand with his own fierce look crossing his face. "I don't think so, kitten."

Sighing, Haven looks to me for, fuck if I know, but I just shrug and laugh. Oakley waves off her guys ordering them to go gather the bikes and car. Walking closer she looks over West and the way he vibrates with uncontrollable possessive energy. Pulling out a pocket knife the blue haired devil flicks it open and points it at West. Moving closer she pushes the side of the blade into his cheek.

"I'll only give you one warning. Fuck with Haven and you'll find yourself in pieces across all fifty states." Her threat settles between all of us but I don't move to defend West.

I'm enjoying the way her knife digs into his skin. Oakley is doing what she thinks is right for her family blood or not. Who am I to stop her from doing what the brothers do for me? Raising an eyebrow I watch in amusement when he flinches from the pinch of pain. Haven looks between the two completely confused when Oakley breaks out a smile.

"Haven it's your choice but I'm leaving now." She says softer in tone.

The way she's giving Haven the power to make her own choices has a lump forming in my throat that's almost impossible to swallow around. Haven's bright eyes stare into West's making me feel like I'm intruding on a personal moment.

"I've got to go, Playboy." She says under her breath.

Releasing her hand West steps back letting her go completely. His expression changes, dropping down his easy going mask letting the tense moment pass with a laugh. Oakley grabs Haven's hand and tugs her towards the now waiting car. Haven looks back over her shoulder with sad eyes but West doesn't give anything away. Placing my hand on his forearm I squeeze.

"Let's get out of here."

Oakley climbs on the back of a bike after shutting Haven in the passenger seat of a blue skyline race car. Turning away I spot G and Ally on the porch of the vacant house going back and forth but I don't have enough energy to give a shit what it's about. With a new target in sight I storm towards them with West on my heels. No one acknowledges the scene that just played out instead we all head to the blacked out SUV parked on the curb. Literally on the damn curb like fucking animals.

G walks us to the car but then steps out of the way to close the door behind Ally.

"I have a mess to clean up." His eyes meet West in the driver seat.

Nodding, "Meet us back at the house." West states.

With that we drive off with Ally in the back and Oakley's crew in our rearview mirror. West ignores my stare on the side of his face the entire way to the mansion. The closer we come to the house the more my hands start to tremble. The closer I come to Ryker the more my heart pounds behind my ribcage.

Chapter Thirty-Three

RYKER

Cole looks out the window at the passing scenery while we go back and forth about our next move. I'm too busy shoving down my irritation at him for handing the keys to Kenna for her to walk out the house when he turns to look at me.

"She's not going to go quietly." He says.

His words linger in the space between us, the truth in them undeniable.

My eyes don't leave the road, "Pride will be the death of us all." I remark.

We don't have to say the words because we both know the outcome of what's bound to happen.

"Kenna will want her dead." His words are lower this time.

Being the youngest must make this harder for him. I was born into a completely different family than him. By the time our parents had him they'd learned how to be parents from me and West. Our mother was a cold callous woman but she loved hard in her own way. Or so we thought but there's more to her than we knew but we find ourselves catching on quickly.

"Are you going to tell us what you found?" I push.

It's not the first time I've tried to push him to tell us what he really found that day but it's like pulling fucking teeth. Cole may be my brother but I don't do secrets well. The only thing that's kept me from shoving him too hard on it is knowing that he's only hiding it for us. We move as a unit and when we step out of place it's only ever to cover the others. If Cole feels the need to hide this I can only assume it has something to do with two things. Either Kenna and her family or our father.

He looks out the windshield, taking his eyes off me, "I can't do that yet."

It's all he gives me and I choose not to ask for more. Taking the curve the tires slide on the asphalt when the ground changes. Pulling off the road down a long driveway we both straighten the closer we come to the foundation hall. It's not far from the school campus and we rarely meet here but today's a surprise visit. We heard from a little bird that there was a secret meeting being called today with a special guest so we decided to do a surprise popup.

Shutting off the headlights blanketing us in darkness I let my eyes adjust to the night before I press the gas sending us down the long winding driveway. Slowing when I pass a large open metal gate with two massive statues placed on either side we both lean forward to see better. The winding driveway curves into a large u-turn area near the grand entrance showcasing just how opulent the entire estate is. Pulling to a stop and cutting the engine we sit in silence for a few seconds our minds in different places.

"Fuck it." I say, opening the SUV door and stepping out.

Cole follows my lead and together we make our way up the massive stairs to tall double doors that house large metal knockers shaped like snakes. The details of each small piece standing out against the obsidian paint. Gold scales line the coiled snakes shining when the porch light hits it at the perfect angle. Pushing the overly heavy doors open I don't bother to close them. Instead I continue into the foyer passing under a crystal chandelier hanging above a tacky fur rug that is too expensive to be fake. Rolling my eyes at the artwork lining the walls we continue to move through the building until we hear voices coming from a conference room towards the left wing.

"What did you expect when you came back Marcus? That things would be handed over to you with no effort on your part?" A voice says.

Marcus? I rattle my brain in search of the name but come up short. Cole places his hand on my shoulder pausing my forward movement. Looking over my shoulder I quirk a brow in question. Holding his finger to his lips he signals me to listen.

"I'm sick of the fucking brothers strutting around like they own the place. We have a foundation for a reason. The Stone name isn't the only one of power and it's time they learned that. It's not my fault you allowed them to forget their place, old man." A younger voice says.

My head tips to the side waiting for a response to follow.

"I assure you my boys won't be a problem but speak out of turn again about my family's name no less and I'll be sure they find you strung up by your throat." A sugary voice spits.

Ahh mother. Always so charming. Grabbing the doorknob I shove the door open revealing a full foundation meeting minus the heirs themselves.

"It appears that we missed the call for a meeting." Cole says, coming to stand beside me.

Five sets of eyes fall on us but only three seemed surprised. Our mother hides her shock well behind a perfectly manicured appearance but I can see past her bullshit.

"Mother." I nod.

Micah Morales glares from across the long wooden table that seats far too many fucking people. A younger version of him sits in the chair beside him with a sneer of his own plastered across his face.

"Ryker, Cole, this doesn't concern you. I'm the head of the family." Our mother speaks.

Holding my hand up to stop her I walk further into the room moving to stand behind the empty chair at the head of the table. Ironic how that place has been left empty. Tapping the wood at the top of the chair I look over the faces seated before us and try to read the room. The twins look far too relaxed with our presence bringing me even more questions. Micah and son look at each other before his mini me looks up at me with disdain.

"I believe you're not needed here." He says, venom dripping from his tongue.

"And you are?" I edge.

Cole takes a seat next to our mother and to an outsider it would look like he's trying to hold up a front but I take it for what it is. A threat.

"Marcus Morales." Is his response.

Marcus. The name from earlier.

"Ryker–"

I wave off my mothers next words. "You're done here. You are no longer the head of the Stone family and you will be removed from council immediately." Pulling out the chair I sit with my hands folding on the table in front of me. The twins quirk a lip but the grin is gone almost as instant as it appeared.

"Marcus, was it?" I ask. "You seem to be a little lost so let me catch you up. The Stone family hold the head seat at the table." I widen my arms in a show of where I'm seated and why it was left empty. "I assume you realized your father took up a spot to the side, correct?" I push.

His face reddens and a laugh falls from my mouth in response.

"Let me guess he promised you something he couldn't take for himself?" I turn to look at his father. "What a pity you'd send your own flesh and blood into the wolf's den without proper knowledge." I taunt.

Cole twist in his seat to face me, "Now brother, you know it's not fun to play with your food. Let's tell them why we're really here." He opens the door for our next piece to fall into place.

"Ahh that's right. How silly of me to forget. Dearest mother, we've come here today to denounce you from the Stone family business effective immediately." Leaning back into the thick cushion of the wingback chair I wait for it.

All eyes fall to the beauty that is my mother. In a way she reminds me of an older Oakley ready to rip someone's throat out with her teeth. In this moment that someone is me and I relish the thought of her trying.

"May we ask the details of this new declaration?" One of the twins asks.

"Hmmm." I smile sweetly, "Well it seems that we've had a bit of a family situation that would make Mrs. Stone unfit to sit on the foundation." I state.

"And what would be the cause for this?" The other twin questions.

This time it's Cole that speaks up in his raspy distorted voice, a reminder of something darker. "If you'll take a look at the files I've emailed each of you, you'll find more than a decade of crimes against the foundation and this town that predates the marriage of our mother and father. One event in most recent accounts is the property exchange of Kenna Kingston into the hands of Hank Harlow. A known associate of our families. Now, if you'll excuse us, we have another pressing matter to attend to." Cole finishes, looking down at his phone and then up at me.

Taking that look for what it is I push the chair back to stand, "We'll be seeing you." I speak to everyone but the look I pass my mother gives her everything she needs to know we're coming back for her. "Oh, Marcus?" I call.

His tall lean frame straightens under my stare.

"I'd take note of how to stay out of our way if I were you. The last thing we want is to have another foundation member disappear." The threat lingers around us.

Before we make it to the door his voice breaks through the silence, "The contract calls for a union between two of the families. Since the Kingston girl is no longer on the list I'd suggest you find a replacement soon or the Stone family will no longer hold that seat." His words are shakey yet true.

Rolling my shoulders I ignore the reminder and continue through the doorway leading us back to the car. Once we close the doors to the SUV making sure no listening ears can hear Cole shifts in the seat his eyes meet mine.

"G sent us a message. We need to get back to the house before Kenna kills Ally."

Cole looks worried but all I feel is a thrill to see my little Killer at work. All the pent up resentment towards Ally is sending Kenna over the edge and I plan on watching her set fire to the entire world in response. Only I hope to redirect that rage to someone who actually deserves to die.

"Don't worry brother, I won't let her hurt your girl too bad." I laugh as the words leave my mouth because as true as I wish they were I know I'd never stop her from spilling blood.

Chapter Thirty-Four

KENNA

Ally's bitching from behind me about the way West drags her along the smooth tile floor by the back of her neck. Satisfaction courses through my veins when she lets out a low squeak of pain.

"Be happy she hasn't asked me to rip your tongue out." He laughs.

"It crossed my mind." I spit from ahead of them.

An intake of air has a smile spreading across my face knowing he'd do as I'd ask even if he doesn't agree. I hear the footsteps pause and then a scuffle before we're moving again. The open shutters on the windows cast a warm glow through the icy home. A chill passes through me the further I go into the Stone's home.

"I hope you have a plan, Princess." West says catching up to me.

Ally fully in tow at his other side she looks between us. Her cheeks are flushed red from the struggle she continues to put on but I ignore her attempts instead choosing to let West deal with her.

"I wouldn't call it a plan if I'm winging it." I reply drily.

My thoughts are all over the place but I try to grasp at anything to make sense when an idea strikes me. Spinning on my heels I take a turn down the hallway passing through the living room and around the corner where the kitchen begins.

"Shit." West says no longer next to me.

Grunting and arguing spark up behind me forcing a sigh to fall from my lips. Reaching the garage door I search for what I need. Pulling a memory from a movie I once watched with the boys I make the perfect combination of wickedness for our guest. My stomach churns with the thought of having to see his face again but I push through. By the time West makes it to the doorway I'm hauling what I need barely able to hold all of it alone. Ally's eyes widen in panic when she takes note of what I'm carrying but West jumps into action releasing her to help me.

"You're coming with me." I stare at her from the corner of my eye when I step past her.

She tries to back away, "Kenna please."

Pleas drip from her in waves washing over me but the numbness blocks out her cries. A door opens somewhere towards the front of the house and several voices bounce off the walls.

"West." Cole calls out.

His words sound distorted even now after all the time he's had to heal and it makes me wonder if he'll ever heal. I don't ask the question, instead I look towards the open doorway leading to the kitchen when Ryker crosses the threshold.

"Killer." He breathes when his dark chocolate eyes land on mine.

His shirt hugs his body in a way that has my mouth watering fighting against everything I've tried to shove away. His gaze falls to the stuff in my arms, looking between me and West, he connects the dots quicker than I thought he might. At first I prepare to hold my ground but before I can speak he smirks.

"Come to play, Killer?" He rasps.

Stalking over to me, wearing a shit eating grin across his beautiful face, everyone around us melts away. I hold his stare until he reaches me. The only space between us is what I hold in my hand.

"Cole." He calls out without dropping my gaze.

Suddenly the weight in my arms disappears leaving me empty with no wall or barrier giving us space. Closing the gap his hand cups the back of my neck squeezing tight. Sucking in a deep breath my chest rises faster taking up the rest of the space between us. His intoxicating scent floods my senses casting over the ledge into a free fall of sensations and fear. Sudden panic crawls up my spine when his head lowers to hover over my mouth. Swallowing, my tongue slips out, swiping across my dry lips. I watch the way his eyes drop to my lips darkening with a hunger I haven't seen in months.

"Fuck." His voice is raw and real.

Our worlds slowly collide bringing us into the darkness we've been bathing in for so long. Our breath mixes dancing together creating a heady taste in the air around us. Somewhere in the middle of everything the room is now empty leaving us plunged in privacy and insanity.

Rubbing his thumb in circles at the base of my neck he applies just enough pressure to send a jolt of pain through my bones. It's unlike anything I've ever felt when his mouth closes the gap taking mine in a deep kiss. His tongue sweeps out, shoving its way between my lips consuming every inch it can. My legs lock with the intrusion but this feels different. The way he tastes, menthol and Ryker, his flavor coating my mouth.

"Let go, Killer." He says against my mouth. "Burn with me." He begs.

The guttural sound that escapes the back of his throat sends me spiraling through the eye of the storm we built. Pulling back his dark eyes skate over me laying me bare down to my blackened soul. Biting my lip I let my eyes fall closed under the heat of his gaze. One second. Two. Another. My eyes open. Whatever was holding him back shatters like glass releasing him to the monster beneath his skin, the one I fell in love with. Using his hand he shoves me to my knees. A sharp pain shoots up my legs into my hips when I slam into the tile flooring.

"You still crave the feeling of my monsters, baby?" He grits between clenched teeth.

My mouth falls open with heavy breathing, my head nodding on instinct. I watch as he visibly shutters when my teeth sink into my bottom lip. His large hands move to slide his pants down letting his dick bounce free. My stare shifts from his mesmerizing face to the massive part of him now in my face.

"Open that filthy fucking mouth of yours, Killer." He orders.

Tipping my head back and opening my mouth wide my tongue hangs out waiting for it to be filled. Unable to hold himself back any longer he grabs both sides of my face and plunges in deep immediately gagging me. Our eyes clash, with each thrust, he continues to plunge deeper. Humming in the back of my throat from his salty taste I swallow around him watching the way his eyes roll back from the feeling.

"Goddamn." He groans.

My body ignites beneath his praise; the way it rolls over me has my thighs clenching. It doesn't escape the notice of the monster standing above me but he ignores the way I crave his touch instead stealing every part of me. Digging his nails into the side of my face his hold is bruising, tears spilling from my eyes, he fucks my mouth in brutal thrust.

"Fuck, your pretty little mouth missed me didn't it." He moans. "Shit." He mutters.

Thrust. Swallow. Thrust. Suck. Thrust. Swallow.

His head falls back his eyes now closed and I revel in the way his face falls into the deep throws of heaven when he fucks my mouth harder. Losing balance my hands grab onto his hips giving us both more leverage and that sends him spiraling closer. Moaning around his cock in the back of my throat I can taste the salty pre-come leaking from the head of his dick.

"That's it, Killer." He praises.

One more thrust and his hips meet my lips, shoving all the way to the back of my throat, choking me completely. Unable to breath he holds me there, my name falls from his lips as he coats my throat with his come. Trembling from his release his eyes meet mine brighter than they were before. Pulling out he steps back watching the way I drink down everything he gave me. Wiping away a drop from my chin he presses it into my mouth groaning when my tongue curls around his thumb sucking the liquid from his skin.

Leaning down he lifts me under the arms hauling me to my feet. Brushing away the hair pressed to my sweaty face he claims my mouth with his in a dominant kiss that steals the air from my lungs. Flames and smoke. Fire and Ice. We collide.

Spinning us around I end up pressed against a cabinet with his thick fingers peeling my thong to the side.

"Are you soaked for me?" He rasps.

My nod is jerky and my chest shutters with my next breath when he slips between my legs pressing one finger in at a time. Crowing me into the cabinet he leaves just enough room for his hand but then his mouth is on me. Nipping and biting my neck, my ear, my jaw leaving me raw and on fire.

"I won't fuck you until you're begging me for it but I'll let you come like a good girl for fucking me so goddamn good with that sinful mouth of yours." His growls in my ear.

Plunging two fingers knuckle deep inside my dripping cunt he fucks me faster and faster. My legs shake but he holds me up with his knee. Using his free hand he forces my pants down my legs to my ankles never removing his fingers from their place deep inside me. Pulling his fingers out he shoves them in my mouth forcing my back flat against the cabinet bending me backwards completely. My core aches for release and a cry forms in the back of my throat. The tangy taste of my own flavor spills onto my tongue while he holds me there by my mouth.

"Don't move." He orders.

Running his free hand down my side a sudden pressure at my clit has me tensing.

"Easy, Killer."

He rubs between my legs pressing into my clit and sliding between my lower lips coating his dick with my wetness. He doesn't try to press inside me instead he fucking sides between my legs against my core slowly building a low burn in the pit of my stomach. I try to suck in air but the pain of the orgasm climbing mixed with the panic in the back of my head makes me dizzy. I want to beg him to stop but my body screams for me.

"Rye." I moan.

His hand leaves my mouth moving to my throat cutting off my next breath.

"Beg for it." He growls.

His punishing thrust slams into my clit over and over. My knees shutter under the pressure between my legs. Squeezing my eyes shut the voice in the back of my head screams a hollow sound but with each touch of my skin from him I let that voice fall away. The overwhelming need to be consumed by him rattles my bones.

"Please. Please." I chant into the empty room.

Another brutal thrust between my legs.

"Please what?" He pushes.

My head thrashes against the hardwood underneath me, unable to speak. Applying pressure to my throat he pulls me forward slightly forcing my gaze to his. His brown eyes are damn near black with greed.

"Consume me." I beg. "Consume me with everything you are until there's nothing left of me, but you." I cry out.

Shaking, my body anticipates his next move waiting to be filled by him yet instead of slamming into me he slowly glides in one inch at a time. Tears flow down my cheeks with the all consuming flood of emotions combining with pure pleasure. Wiping away a tear that's falling down my face he watches the way my face contorts with each slow drive forward. For a moment time stands still, the oxygen in the room thinning. Our movements slow leaving us barely moving only to take in the way we feel around each other. Leaning down his teeth, biting into my bottom lip hard enough to break skin, a drop of blood dripping into his mouth.

"Bleed for me, baby." He grunts.

And then he fucks me hard and relentless until my legs give out and we're both broken on the floor.

Chapter Thirty-Five

KENNA

"Honey I'm home." A voice rings through the silence cutting through it like glass.

Ryker and West turn towards the open doorway while Cole helps me make the adjustment needed to my rigged powerhouse. Ally plants her ass in a chair across the room from us with her knees to her chest picking at her nails. Periodically shooting her a glare I watch her from my place at the table holding my masterpiece.

"Are you sure about this, Kens?" Cole questions.

Twisting my lips to the side I tip my head to the side letting my gaze travel over his hardened face. His boyish looks long gone, fading into harsh lines and troubled days.

"I'm tired of this." Looking down my voice lowers, "I have to do something that makes sense to me." I beg him to understand without saying the words.

Placing his hand over mine he waits for me to lift my head.

"We're not killing her." He says his declaration is calm but fierce.

"We're not killing her." I confirm the corner of my mouth twitching when I try to hide my smile.

G makes his way through the door when we finally finish putting the parts together, making a super machine ready for what I have planned. Cole and West grab the heavy parts while I carry the only piece that I care to touch. Ryker stands at my back, leaning into my hair at the back of my neck, inhaling and sending a chill down my spine.

"Come on, Killer." He draws in a lazy tone.

Is it ironic that we've become the killers? That somehow we house a hostage starved and broken in another room? Part of me wishes I'd died during my time with Hank to escape the very thing I'm becoming but the heat from Rykers hand at my lower back shoves that sinister thought away. Jerking my head towards Ally, G heads over to drag her along, looking at me with a questioning stare.

"A plus one." I remark on my way out the room.

Following my boys through the house they lead me to a dark portion that feels degrees colder. The chill sinks into my bones, raising goosebumps across my flesh. West steps past Cole to open a large door letting out a rancid smell that has bile churning in my stomach.

"Holy fuck." West gags.

Ryker rubs my lower back letting out a low laugh. "Smells like the pussy West used to fuck."

The joke does its job and eases the tension around us. Cole flicks the light on to the bare square room walking further into the space allowing us all to enter. G and Ally are the last ones through the door pulling it shut behind them.

"My fucking eyes are watering." I snap.

"Welcome to the party, Princess." The way that name rolls off his tongue makes me lash out at smack him in the back of the head.

West rubs at the spot turning to flash me a wink, "Don't act like one then." He laughs, bouncing away from my next hit.

Cole and West move to set the modified generator in the corner of the room near a plug in that's needed for it to work. The cold metal in my other hand feels heavier now that I've come face to face with Hank Harlow. Looking over at the man tied to a small wooden chair in the middle of the room, I take my time taking note of every little detail. The way his eyes are hollow the stark resemblance to what my were is chilling. The way his clothes are soaked with urine and shit sours the air around us and the floor around him. Even now, beaten and bruised, he still leans forward when I step closer, his eyes sparkling with excitement.

"Killer." Ryker warns.

He's on edge with me being close to the man who stole so much from me. From both of us.

"Princessa." He rasps.

The sound of his voice sounds like nails on a chalkboard scraping across my skin. A shiver courses through me bringing with it a wave of memories. My skin feels stretched over my bones, my soul beating against the filthy feeling coating my body. Slamming my eyes closed I try to drag in a deep breath but the only thing I can taste is the way his mouth felt on mine. Shuttering from the onslaught of emotions that bombard me the room fades away taking me back to that room.

Ryker reaches out for me anchoring me in the present but the haze over my mind feels like a weighted blanket curled around me. Trapping me inside my own head.

"It's just me and you, baby." He murmurs. "He'll never touch you again. You're making sure of that." he says.

Swallowing past the lump in my throat my hands shake at my sides.

"Lilies and fire, Killer. You burn, I burn, We burn." He whispers, pressing a kiss into the side of my head.

Feeling the presence of the brothers surrounding me in the room even Ally being here comforts me. I'm not alone. They didn't leave me. He lied. He stole a piece of me. I am wanted. Every broken and fractured part of my soul is held together by the forged bonds we made. Opening my eyes they connect with shallow blue irises.

"You don't get to steal time from me anymore." I say, my voice steady.

Pulling against the ropes that bind him he tries to reach for me, but he's bound completely.

"Reach for her again and I'll remove your hands from your body." Ryker says calmly. The threat lies underneath his calm demeanor.

Rubbing my lips together, I try to push away the haze and numb feeling that starts to climb up from my fingertips. My lungs rattle under the pressure of facing the man before me. West and Cole move around to the edge of my vision leaning against the wall to my left. They moved into my line of sight in a show of support if I needed it and that warmth floods my veins.

"She doesn't belong to you anymore. Go on, ask her yourself. Princessa, who owns you now?" Hank coo's.

His blue eyes shine under the hanging light in the center of the ceiling. The way his words rush out in anticipation disgust me. That distant inner voice at the back of my mind claws her way forward trying to plant small seeds of doubt but the feeling of Rykers mouth on mine flash in black and white in my head. My skin heats from the stare on the side of my face, but I can't take my eyes off Hank.

"I've always belonged to you." My words are soft but sure. I've never been more sure of anything in my life. I've never owned my own body. It's always been his.

Stepping forward my gaze falls to the floor trying to step around the mess he's made while coming closer to the monster that's owned my worst nightmares. Stealing back that control isn't something that will happen with his death. No, I'll live with the faded feel of his touch. The feeling of hunger gnawing at my insides reminding me of my time with him. The brand that I've hidden from the man at my back, a scar I'll bear for the rest of my life. His death doesn't take away the mark he's leaving on my soul but I'll take back a part of my darkness in the process.

Opening the thick metal I watch his eyes widen and the flood of urine that releases when he sees what's in my hand.

"You'll only feel a fraction of the pain you've caused me." I spit. "I've thought of what I might do to you when given the chance." I look around the room to the array of faces covered in different shades of pride. "I'm not giving you a second thought."

Leaning down I come within inches from him, his stale breath knocking the air from my chest, I spit in his face. "I can't wait to see how you crumble at my feet."

Striking out fast to keep him from moving I close the metal around his neck and slide the lock into place. Stepping back with a wide manic grin, I allow myself a full minute to admire the way Hank panics and screams.

"Shut the fuck up." My eyes roll at his wails.

Nodding my head at Cole who stands next to the generator against the wall he flips the switch. My eyes follow the cord hooked to the machine across the floor, through a puddle of yellow piss, up the back of the chair, and into the collar now clasped tight around his throat. High voltage courses through his body forcing convulsions from him. I watch every tear fall. I take in every drop of piss rolling down his bare legs. My gaze soaks in the way his head shakes back and forth so fast it's like he's in an exorcism. Ryker wraps his arms around me from the back, dropping his lips to my ear.

"I fucking love every dark corner of your soul." He groans against my skin.

Planting a kiss at the edge of my ear he holds me while we all watch the devil in the room fry to death. Ally covers her eyes but I can see her peeking through her fingers making a laugh fall from my lips.

"You can't hide the crazy, Ally baby." I call out.

Suddenly the room erupts into laughter, the empty walls echoing our dark hearts. Hanks cries fall away leaving nothing but the sound of a low buzz from the collar around his now fried throat. Looking away from him I lose interest in the mess I've made instead latching onto something else to focus on. The power surges the machine pulling too much energy so West lunges forward yanking the cord out of the wall taking away the electricity that was coursing through Hank's body. Once the power is fully gone the body slumps forward pulling on the binding until the weight tips the chair sending him into the floor face first in his own fluids.

"Well fuck." I giggle.

Somewhere in my manic brain I'm disgusted by the entire picture but the darkest part of my soul sears the image into my brain as a reminder of what I'm capable of doing to those who wrong me. Shaking off the cold feeling I spin in Rykers arms planting a kiss under his chin.

"Let's go, Rye." I whisper.

The way his name drips from my tongue makes my heart ache with pride. I'll heal one dead body at a time. Speaking of, I look over my shoulder at Ally where G is propped against a wall with his phone in his face. He's been all over the place lately and I don't let the scene at the Basement slip my mind with that thought.

"Is there something we need to know about redheads?" I push.

G looks up from the screen, his brows dipped in confusion. Shaking my head I keep probing.

"Don't give me that look." I say.

He shrugs, flicking that damn lip ring, "Just a bitch from the bar." He says.

Ryker tugs me towards the door trying to distract me while tossing orders back at West and G to clean up the mess. Cole walks behind us with Ally in tow following like a good little rat. I know I should let her off the hook but every cell in my body tells me she's still hiding something. It's gotten darker outside by the time we reach the front room where the windows are drawn closed and the lights are lower. When we step into the living room a shadow is sitting in the single chair surrounded by two couches. Ally pauses behind me, but Cole and Ryker come to stand at my sides providing a show of strength at my sides.

"I should have know it'd be a fucking Kingston." Her voice is laced with malice.

Ryker puts his arm across my chest trying to push me backwards but I stand my ground against the snake in a ruby red dress and high heels.

"I'm no more Kingston than I am Stone." I state knowing it's going to piss her off.

Standing, she straightens her dress before striding towards us the sound of her heels and my breathing the only noise.

"You stupid stupid girl." She clicks her tongue. "I've done well with getting rid of Kingston women that get in my way yet here you are fighting against all odds with my sons' help no less." Her words are filled with venom.

Realization slams into me like a semi truck. I stumble back a step or two at the confession she lets slip by. Ryker and

Cole close the gap between us blocking me from view completely.

"Foolish boys." She spits. "We have a legacy to preserve yet here you are sleeping with the product. How do you think we managed to gather such power in this town?" She raises a brow.

Leaning around Ryker my eyes connect with her cold ones. "My mother was born and raised here. The Kingston name holds more than just wealth." I toss out.

Waiving a finger she laughs, "Oh no darling. Your mother was a pawn in a pretty dress with a beautiful face. I was contracted to marry your father but she swept in like a fucking viper stealing the name I was promised. Instead your fathers family chose her and when he took HER name, erasing his completely I knew it was about more than just power. He loved her."

My ribs ache from the heavy breath I drag through clenched teeth. My hand reaches out for Ryker grabbing his arm to hold myself up.

"You killed her." It's not a question.

She lets out a humm, "She isn't the only one." She admits.

She looks at me sheepishly, a soft smile crossing her features, almost comforting in a wicked way. "Any minute now and you'll finally be an orphan but don't worry dear. I have plans for you." She claps with a tinkling laugh.

By the time it dawns on me G is rushing down the hall with his phone to his ear. When his eyes meet mine I'm thrown into action. Spinning away from the Stone family I break out into a run towards the exit of the mansion leaving Ryker facing down his mother. It's not until I'm yanking at a locked door handle that I realize the keys aren't with me. A click has me spinning on my heels with panicked eyes.

"Cole." I choke out.

Without a word he ushers me to the passenger side

opening the door to help me inside. Shutting the door my nails start to dig into my fingertips pulling at the skin waiting for him to start up the car. Jumping in Cole starts the engine and jerks it into drive rolling down the driveway at an ungodly speed.

"Breathe, Princess." He says.

Chapter Thirty-Six

RYKER

Kenna and Cole rush from the house headed to the only remaining parent she has left while I face down with mine. Chagrin forward my hands stretch out moving to grab my own mother when a glint of metal shines in the light of the den.

"Don't," she says.

Pausing, I can feel G tense behind me looking towards the open door looking for someone. I can hear footsteps coming from the back of the house knowing West can't be far behind. Ally is frozen in fear to my right where she's visibly shaking in place. Looking over my shoulder at G I signal for him to pull her out of the room when the gun is shifted towards him.

Licking her red lips, "I've been meaning to take out the trash." She says. "My sons have given you too much power and in doing so the dogs you feed start to look at the boy as a master."

"Observant are we?" I pry, trying to take the focus off my best friend.

"If I'm not, you three would ruin everything our family

has built. Allowing a foot soldier to have more control than you is exactly the reason I have to come in and clean up your messes." She waves her hand around the gun swaying with it.

West sneaks in behind Ally pulling her into his chest as our mothers eyes fall on him.

"If it isn't the whore himself." She sneers.

West blows her a kiss, distracting her while he pushes Ally to the side, out of her line of sight.

"I learned from the best." He quips with a dry laugh.

Swinging the gun to his face my entire world slows with the sound of the trigger being pulled. My body leaves my mind behind taking action on its own lunging for my mother. We both slam into the tile floor. Her head smacks against the floor knocking her out instantly. Rolling off her limp body my ears ring from the sudden shot fired. West.

"G!" I yell.

"Already on the phone. Hold on man, hold pressure. Look at me Wes." Gio urges, using his name for my middle brother.

Crawling on my knees to West where G is pressing his hands into his upper shoulder, crimson liquid pours from a bullet wound. Faded brown eyes look at mine with horror.

"Ally." He croaks.

Looking away from him I see Ally laying across the floor to our left spread out on her stomach.

"It's okay, everything's okay." I reassure her with my hand on her back. Rolling her over my face falls at the blood pooled beneath her.

"She took the bullet for me." West says his voice is weaker.

Fuck. Fuck fuck fuck. Ripping open her shirt my gaze falls to the single shot to her chest in the center of her ribcage. Balling up the fabric I scream at G to put a rush on it. The color starts to seep from both of their faces.

"Wake up Ally." I pry tapping her face with my other hand.

A moan slips from her mouth.

"That's it girl come on." Another slap.

"She saved me, Rye." West's eyes meet mine.

How the hell did we get here?

Chapter Thirty-Seven

KENNA

Cop cars swarm the parking lot of the prison, the flashing blue lights blinding in the setting sun. My door is open before Cole has a chance to put that bitch in park. My feet hit the ground as soon as my seatbelt is removed. Running towards one of the cops my voice is shaky.

"What's going on here?" I rush out.

The male cop turns to face me with an annoyed look crossing his face until he sees the man walking up behind me. The man has a thick black mustache over his top lip with deep sea blue eyes that look over both of us before choosing his next words.

"We were called out for a riot but we're on the tail end of things." He rubs at the long baton on his hip.

He watches me like I'm a fucking threat which sets me on edge and pisses me off at the same time.

"Why aren't your men inside yet?" I snap.

Moving closer I stop barely a foot away. The fire in my eyes may not be enough to get answers from him but I'll kill the fucker if he doesn't speak faster.

Running a hand down his face he looks to Cole as if to say

control your woman. Pressing my chest into his I tip my head back with a feral look blanketing my face.

"I asked the question so look at me. Why are you lazy fuckers just standing here?" I spit.

Looking over his shoulder at the large group of probably twenty men he says, "By the time we got the call and made it here it was over. Now we're just waiting for all the inmates to be put back in their cells before we can comb the open areas."

He doesn't seem worried about the prison inmates at all.

"Who's hurt?" I probe.

Looking around the parking lot there are several EMT vans yet none have their lights on sending a shiver through me.

"Anyone inside that building that needs a bus, isn't breathing." He finally says.

"How many?" Cole is the next one to speak his tone filled with irritation.

The dickbag cop straightens his stance under the watchful eye of a Stone brother.

"Ten." He sighs. "Look, I'll report back what I can but for now that's all I know. I have to get back to my men so we can move forward."

With that he walks away. Dropping to my knees the asphalt digs into my skin. A scream bubbles out of me releasing from my throat when my head falls back. Somewhere in a dark corner of my heart I can feel that my fathers gone. She wouldn't have planned this if she didn't know she could pull it off. She had someone on the inside stage this to get to him all because of me. Her obsession with my family has cost me both parents. The organ in my chest pinches at the utter loss I feel in my soul.

"Come on, Kens." Cole whispers against my hair.

His thick arm curls around my waist dragging me into his

chest. Walking backward towards the car several cops turn to watch the show. Low whispers and comments spark up turning into a low buzz that I try to tune out. Lifting me into the truck Cole rushes around the other side sliding into his seat. Turning to face me his fingers pinch my chin forcing my eyes to meet his.

"I can see where your thoughts are but we don't know anything for sure, Princess." He rubs his lips together looking out towards the parking lot. "We don't know anything." He says more to himself.

Putting the car in reverse he whips the SUV around flooring it out of the parking lot. Halfway to the house a call comes through to the truck speaker, the name on the screen is Gio. Leaning forward to press the button on the call a voice burst through the speakers.

"G?" I call out.

"West has been shot." A frantic voice says on the other line. Cole jerks the wheel to the side before gaining control.

"What the fuck do you mean?" I screech.

Oh god what's happening. A panic attack creeps up starting at my fingertips making my skin tingle.

"Ally took the brunt of the bullet for him but he's been hit." G's voice breaks off when the sound of an EMT bus echoes on the call.

Cole opens his mouth to speak when a cry falls from mine right as a large black truck plows into the side of the SUV. Glass shatters. My seatbelt jerks my neck back digging into my skin. Our tires slam into something jolting us to the side, sending us into a roll. Everything blurs together spinning uncontrollably. Coming to a stop my vision darkens clouding my eyesight completely. Pain laces down my right side, the feeling of something wet rolls down my face.

The last thing I remember is Cole calling my name and thinking not again. I don't know if we'll survive this again.

EPILOGUE

You came here to read more? You thought I'd leave a trail of blood for you to follow?

Hehehe nothing is that easy! Sorry but this time there is nothing but darkness until next time. So I guess this means you have to follow along to follow the trail that the Stone and Kingston families are on.

- Till next time! Happy hunting ;)

WHERE TO FIND ME

C.M Nyx Reader Group: https://www.facebook.com/groups/2456518418o6224

Website: https://covenandcopublishing.squarespace.com/

TikTok: https://www.tiktok.com/@c.m.nyx_author?lang=en

ACKNOWLEDGMENTS

This book took me through the wringer. Literally.

If it wasn't for my amazing Alpha girls I may not have finished this one. So, this is for the girls. For the Pain and Panic to my manic Hades.

Red, Shea, Panic, Pain, and my Dark Phoenix. You ladies make my world go round and I know I blow your minds with my words so does this make us even?

After that ending I guess not but here's to many more books and a fuck ton more laughs!

I love you all. Thank you for being you.

9 798330 504770